AT FAULT

To order additional copies of this book, contact:

Xlibris Corporation

1-888-7-XLIBRIS

www.Xlibris.com

Orders@Xlibris.com

AT FAUL

Warmest Regar

Angus Mac

6/15/0

Angus MacDona

C
LI
IS

A
a
r
i

ALSO BY ANGUS MACDONALD
Middle Ground—M. I. T. Press

AT FAULT

AT FAULT

Warmest Regards,
Angus MacDonald
6/15/01

Angus MacDonald

To order additional copies of this book, contact:
Xlibris Corporation
1-888-7-XLIBRIS
www.Xlibris.com
Orders@Xlibris.com

For my mother and father
Anna Theresa and Angus Harold

PART ONE
Third Week in May, 2002

2092-MACD

TUESDAY

CHAPTER 1

9:00 A.M. EST

All his life, Max Gebhardt had yearned for a Florida vacation. As a long-time aviation buff, he wanted to make the trip in a wide body jet. Now, as he leaned on the railing of his balcony and breathed in the spring air redolent of jasmine, he marveled that both wishes had been granted. *And I owe it all to my son Jack.*

During this, his first time aloft, he walked the length of the jet, as if it were his kingdom to survey. *Three hundred and five people. Wow!*

On the way to the hotel in the limousine provided by his son, he leaned out the window taking pictures of palm trees with his new Polaroid, a retirement gift from the owner of the bagel factory where he had worked since he was a young man. Neither Max nor his wife Winnie was prepared for the opulence of their hotel: a new forty-five story building with a large pool, tropical garden, tennis courts, and a lavishly decorated lobby smelling of orange blossoms. "EVERY ROOM A RESORT" the leaflet had crowed and as if to verify the boast, Winnie gaped at the decor while Max, an elfin man given to generous enthusiasms, darted from room to room in their "suit". He stopped at the glass doors leading to the balcony and watched a jet in the climb-out phase of its take off from the Miami International Airport—dangerously low over the tall buildings, he thought.

So this was Jack's world, Max reflected the next morning, standing on the balcony. Getting to know his son had been late in coming, but to a man of his modest expectations, that it had come at all was an occasion for rejoicing. When the boy was nine, Max left his wife for Winnie, a neighbor's daughter ten years his junior, and his son was slow to forgive him. He saw little of his father until years later, when he left his wife and suffered the wrath of his young son. Now he took a kindlier view of his old man and gave Max and Winnie the trip to Florida on their thirtieth anniversary as a token of forgiveness.

Max stood still, staring. A nude body moved past the window adjoining the balcony. Oh boy! he's at it again, he thought, remembering the previous evening when he and Winnie had held hands on the balcony and peered directly into the lighted bedroom. "Jesus, Max, look at the two of them! Look where he's kissing her!" Winnie had laughed.

Now, after a night's sleep, Max's desire rose. He returned to Winnie in bed and kissed her on the forehead. She smiled and left for the bathroom. When she came out, she snuggled next to him. "Now, Max," she said. "Don't get no fancy ideas."

Max lolled in a plastic bean bag chair in the living room waiting for Winnie to return from the lobby with the morning newspaper. *What a life! Nine o'clock and not even dressed!*

There was a shrill whine, like a large vacuum cleaner beyond the glass doors leading to the balcony. *What's that?* Max leaned forward, straining to find the source of the noise. "Oh my God! Winnie, Winnie! he'll kill us all!" he screamed and sat bolt upright at the sight of a huge jetliner, flying too low and coming too fast straight for the building. Instinctively he threw his left arm across his face. His last thought as he gaped at the bulbous silver nose hurtling toward him was not of Winnie, nor of impending death, but of why the captain, peering in horror through the cockpit window, had not shielded his face as well.

* * *

A half hour earlier Captain William "Billy" Hanley, resplendent in his captain's uniform stepped aboard Flight 181 for Chicago at Miami's International Airport.

He was aware of the expectations of his charges, and during the walk to the cockpit of the Starflight 610, managed a look that was both forthcoming and professionally distant. He was aware, too, of the clichés that surrounded his profession and grinned as he removed his coat and eased himself into his seat. If they only knew why their captain is in such a hurry to get to Chicago, he mused.

"What's the latest poop on the weather?" First Officer Scott Roberts asked, looking up from the keyboard of the plane's inertial guidance computer.

"Gorgeous, Scott. My wife says spring has finally come to the windy city."

" 'Bout time after all the winter crud."

"Can't wait to get to my lil ole place and Miracid the hemlocks I planted last Fall."

"Sure sign of old age. More worried about fertilizing the trees than the ladies."

"You know it! Look at the gray hair."

"Gray? Looks white to me," laughed the Flight Engineer Sid Cohen seated behind Roberts.

Roberts returned to the navigational system and punched in the latitude and longitude of the departure gate. Hanley poured over the sheaf of printed computer readouts received from Operations. The computer, he had found, never made a mistake but before each trip he felt compelled to put pencil to paper for a rough check of the critical aircraft speeds which Roberts would soon be calling out to him: V1, the runway speed at which takeoff is mandated even after an engine failure; VR, when the nose is rotated skyward in preparation for lift-off; and V2, the safe takeoff speed. Satisfied, he glanced at his watch.

"On time this morning, fellas," he said. "Eight forty-five on the button. Let's get this fucker out of here."

"Shoulder harness," Roberts began, reading from the printed checklist.

"On," Hanley answered.

"Start pressure . . ."

They began the taxi check on the way to the end of the runway.

"Door warning lights."

"Out."

"Wing flaps."

"Fifteen degrees. Indicator fifteen. Green light."

"Yaw damper and instruments."

"Checked left and right."

"Weight and balance finals."

"We're at five hundred thirty-seven thousand pounds. Stabilizer set looks good at twenty-seven decimal five. Vee speeds are one thirty-nine, one forty-five, one fifty-three."

"Engineer's taxi check."

"Complete," said Cohen.

"Flight one eighty-one heavy," the tower operator radioed. "Taxi into position and hold. Be ready for an immediate."

Hanley keyed on the intercom. "Ladies and gentlemen, we have just been cleared on the runway for take-off. Flight attendants please be seated!"

"Transponder," Roberts said.

"On."

"One eighty-one heavy cleared for takeoff. No delay on departure if you will. Traffic's two and a half miles out for the runway."

"One eighty-one heavy underway," Hanley said into his headset and pushed the three throttles slowly and deliberately forward.

"Eighty knots," Roberts called out, meaning that Hanley now had rudder control as the plane picked up speed.

"Vee one!"

The plane continued to accelerate.

"Vee R . . ." Hanley eased back on the control column and the craft rotated about its wheels to an angle of ten degrees.

"Vee two!"

The wheels left the ground.

Bang!! The cockpit shook. A powerful explosion came from the right side of the plane.

"What the fuck was that?" Roberts yelled.

"Shit!" Hanley exclaimed. "Those fucking blades again!" He slammed his left foot hard against the rudder peddle to compensate for the sharp yaw of the plane to the right. *Mind the store . . . keep her going straight . . . wings level . . . stable flight . . . gotta get altitude!*

"It's number three engine!" Cohen shouted, his eyes fixed on the engine pressure ratios. "Loss of power!"

"Increasing number one and two to full emergency power," Hanley said calmly, pressing the first two throttle levers beneath his right hand forward to their stops.

Roberts keyed on his mike. "Miami Tower, flight one eighty-one reporting an engine problem. Standby. Over."

"Roger, one eighty-one heavy, we copy you."

Easy there, easy . . . Hanley exerted slight fore and aft pressures on the controls, concentrating on holding the proper nose-up angle displayed on the instrument flight director in front of him. "Fan blade failure," he said to Roberts. "No sweat. Had one on takeoff from O'Hare last year. Just gotta get up and away from the ground where bad things can happen."

But now the entire first stage fan section at the inlet of the number three engine had exploded with the force of a howitzer shell. Sections of the wing not visible from the cockpit were ripped apart, destroying hydraulic lines and electrical cables. These losses in turn caused the leading edge slats on the right wing to retract. Normally these high lift devices, extended to coax more lift out of the wing at the relatively low speeds of takeoff, retract in unison. If they do not, a slat disagreement light flashes in the cockpit. But the wiring in this system, too, was destroyed along with the stall warning device, and Hanley had no way of knowing that the right wing was about to stall because of a retracted slat. As they approached four hundred feet altitude, the left wing suddenly rose and the plane went into an uncontrolled roll to the right.

"Jesus Christ, we're headed in!" Hanley shouted, his eyes fixed on the sky blue upper half of the plane's horizon indicator now rapidly rotating toward an indication of inverted flight. *Keep the blue side up!* He eased the controls forward, pointing the nose downward to increase speed and restore lift to the stalled wing. *Little more . . . That's it.* The plane swooped down like a swallow and leveled out at two hundred feet altitude, headed east toward Biscayne Bay.

"Whew!" Hanley sighed, and turned to Roberts. "Engine shutdown check list."

"Number three fuel lever," Roberts said.

"Off," Cohen said.

"Fire protection."

"Actuated."

With the plane now in level flight, Hanley looked up from the instrument panel and saw the top stories of the high-rise hotel directly ahead. "Shit! Shit! Shit!" he exclaimed! *Watch that stall. Gotta keep up airspeed, gotta tough it out. Come on baby! We can make it.*

Roberts looked out the window. "Back, Billy, back!" he shouted. "Get her up!"

Hanley stared ahead, the controls clenched in his hands. *Come on baby!*

"For christsakes, Billy, back!"

"Losing power in number two!" Cohen reported, his eyes fixed on the engine instrument console.

"Billy, we're going in, *Billy!*" Roberts screamed.

"I know . . ." Hanley said. *This is the way I am going to go, this is the way I am going to die.* At that instant he saw a man lolling nude in the white bean bag beyond the glass doors and watched him throw his left arm across his face.

*   *   *

The nose of the widebody jet penetrated the building just above Max's balcony. There were no vertical beams across the width of the suite and the forward section of the fuselage continued to plunge deep into the structure instantly crushing Max into a bloody smear of flesh and mangled bones. Only the steel floor beams impeded the jet's progress, slicing off the upper and lower portions of the aluminum shell with the ease of a carpenter's plane. The main impact of the crash was transmitted to the building when the wing beams met the vertical load-carrying beams spaced every thirty feet across the face. The outer columns were torn from their joints; the wing continued to gouge a short distance into the interior. Forty-eight thousand gallons of fuel spewed from the ruptured tanks into the building, flooding down stairwells and through air conditioning ducts. The two eight thousand pound wing-mounted engines tore loose and continued on their way. Failed number three shot through the building and out the other side for a block where it ricocheted off the asphalt of a vacant parking lot, smashed through a residence and came to rest sizzling at the bottom of a nearby swimming pool. Number one penetrated the brick and steel enclosure of an elevator shaft in the hotel. There it sliced through four wrist-thick steel cables, rebounded off the rear steel wall, and plunged down the shaft, coming to rest on the top of the elevator car that had fallen four hundred feet to the basement.

At the moment of impact, the entire building shuddered and shed its windows in an explosion of shards which glistened like raindrops in the sun. An instant later, the cement foundation piles rooted in the moist sand of the Florida subsoil failed under the immense toppling force of the five hundred thousand pound plane hitting the building at two hundred fifty miles per hour. In a literal sense, the building lost its footing and reeled under the impact to an angle twenty degrees off vertical with the fuselage and tail section stuck like a dart five floors below the top.

All but a handful of the seventy-five passengers in First Class and Business sections died instantly along with the cockpit crew. The few survivors lying bloodied and broken in the midst of the torn and shredded metal of the forward part of the fuselage were incinerated in a ball of fire that enveloped the upper floors when a spark ignited the fuel-vapor mixture. Further back in Economy, seats with their occupants strapped in were torn from their floor fastenings by the powerful g forces, and became deadly missiles, caroming around the cabin through a lethal rain of carry-on luggage from overhead bins. Miraculously, over half the two-hundred and thirty passengers survived. Moments later, though, tongues of flame and smoke from the inferno below roiled through the cabin toward the tail, drawn by the draft created in the upwardly canted fuselage with its broken windows. As the fire intensified, feral screams of agony now drowned out the muted moans of the dazed and dying. "Get me out of here!" Sam Stockman in the rear of the plane cried out as he struggled to free himself from his seat thrown against a window. "Help! Help!" he shouted to the outside, and waved his arm out the opening.

"God, dear God, please—somebody do something to help!" Sue Deacon lay bleeding on the grass across the road from the hotel and wailed when she saw the man's pitiful gesture. "They're being burned alive in there." Waiting for help herself after being cut by flying glass while jogging, she could see the smoke and fire shooting from the windows, see the man's futile gesture, hear the heart rending screams. *I can't stand it! Those noises, strange shrieking noises, noises I've never heard, noises I'll never hear again.* She saw people jumping to the ground from the tilted entrance to the hotel; saw a Niagara of burning fuel pouring from the upper windows like molten steel into the swimming pool beneath the tilted building; saw guests clinging to their balconies; saw hundreds of others in empty window frames desperately trying to escape the flames and smoke; saw an elderly man on the fifteenth floor dressed in his white jockey shorts jump for the thatched roof of the outdoor bar now directly under his window. *He made it, he made it!*

All the while the weight of the building off vertical was putting an extra load on the footings on the side opposite the crash. The plaster coatings on all structural beams required by the Building Code for fire protection were cracked during the initial impact, and the beams were now weakened by the fire.

"My God, the building's falling!" Sue screamed. "Help those people in there! They'll all be killed."

She watched as slowly at first, then with increasing speed as the center of gravity moved further off vertical, the building toppled over on its side, the plane stuck dagger-like in its steel structure. At the base the severed water main which had served the hotel's sixteen hundred occupants spouted a glistening fountain fifty feet into the air, creating huge billows of white steam among the black smoke as it sprayed onto the burning building.

CHAPTER 2

8:00 A.M. CST

Alan Fisk cautiously opened his front door and peeked out at the flagstone walk and driveway beyond. Satisfied, he sauntered nude into the fresh spring air, bound for the pool and an early morning swim before his nine o'clock meeting at company headquarters in the Sears Tower Building in Chicago.

Despite the frustration of months of working for someone else after the sale of his company to Hi Tech, a diversified aerospace company, he strolled with a carefree gait, his mind filled with a sense of well-being. He was among the fortunate few, he reminded himself, in a world where privacy was becoming increasingly rare, who could go outdoors in the raw. With no servants, no children living at home and shielded by thick trees in the suburbs north of Chicago, he was free as an animal in an isolated forest.

Fisk looked back at the house. With native-stone walls and a tile roof reminiscent of Burgundy, it was not pretentious by Lake Forest standards; the Gothic splendor of the Swift and Armour mansions across the road were more in keeping with the aura of the town. Indeed, the informality of the dwelling had sold him on the place; that and its location on a piece of property known for the beauty of its wooded landscape. A great home, Fisk now thought, for the kid who grew up on the second floor of a tenement house in St. Louis.

At the end of the walk, he picked his way across the crushed bluestone driveway, cursing the sharp stones underfoot. The sun beamed through tall oak trees, dappling the dew-laden grass with gold, and he sought out the sunlit patches, delighting in the sudden feeling of warmth on the soles of his feet.

Further on he stopped at a small fern garden containing two outdoor sculptures: the one, his first work titled "QUEST", was a lustrous six foot tall rocket with the clean, pure proportions of an early single-stage vehicle. Cast in stainless steel and burnished with the finest jeweler's rouge, it rose from a base of billowing exhaust sculpted of aluminum anodized to enhance the subtle shadings and color of roiling gases.

The other, titled "ARTIFACTS", was representative of his recent work. A fanciful rendition of one of his company's jet engine blades, it was cast in titanium and mounted on a large black obsidian spear point he had sculpted with the primitive tools of ancient flint knappers. I'm getting close to expressing what I'm after, Fisk thought, remembering a critic's recent evaluation of the piece . . . "a striking and original vision of the richness of technology, the density and complexity of man's thoughts across the ages embedded in seemingly simple objects."

He ran his hand along the blade, delighting in the feel of its graceful twist. *All those people's minds living on in metal . . .* Suddenly he felt panicky. *Christ, look at my sweaty palms! Why, why, when I was feeling so happy? . . . The dream last night! Again?* His heart pounded as he remembered the horror of his recurrent nightmare: a man's savaged face being sucked through a plane's window broken by the catastrophic failure of one of his blades high over Albuquerque twenty years ago. First the head, then the body, propelled by the pressurized cabin air racing to escape through the small opening. Would he ever forget his vision of the man's fall to the desert forty thousand feet below?

Come alive, he told himself angrily. Lighten up. But was it that simple? He had sold his company to stop the nightmares that had tormented him for the past twenty years. But now, working for his new boss, he felt more vulnerable to guilt than ever. And after what he had heard the other day . . .

* * *

"I thought you were going for a swim, and I was coming to join you. I don't see my first patient till ten."

He watched his wife Martha approach from the pool through the rays of light. At fifty three, two years younger than her husband, she had the body of a woman many years her junior. He reached out and patted her bare fanny. "You came along at just the right time," he said.

"I can see that," she said, laughing. "You're some sight standing there."

He pulled her close.

"Not now," she said, and turning with a suddenness that sent her auburn hair swirling, she took him by the hand and led him to the pool. "Let's cool off." They both jumped in.

Fisk erupted from the surface like a Trident missile. "Ke-rist it's cold!" he shouted, and after two laps, swam for the ladder. He passed her with her arms outstretched, floating.

He stood in the sunlight, toweling off by the poolside cabana. *Just what I needed!* He patted his stomach with the palms of his hands as if it were a drum.

"Tell me," Martha said, sitting on the edge of the pool, feet dangling in the water.

"Tell you what?" Fisk said, sitting next to her.

"What's been on your mind."

. . . "On my mind?"

"Something's troubling you. The last few days you seem— depressed."

"It's the office."

"Cutler bullying you again?"

"I can handle that. No. Something else that could be serious. I heard about it from Otto." He was referring to Otto Gitner, his first boss and mentor. "He called me from Paris. Says he sat next to Buzz Beauchamp on the flight over. Remember my number one competitor, Beauchamp, that horse's ass from Sedalia,

Missouri who was such a prick while I was building up Cast Profiles?"

"I've heard you call him worse."

"Inherited his company from his father, the little shit. Anyway, Otto says he got plastered on the plane, bragged how he had the Chairman of the Senate Armed Services Committee in his pocket all the time we were competitors."

"You mean a payoff?"

Fisk smiled at her wide-eyed astonishment. She was still capable of naiveté. "Payoff, bribe, baksheesh, take your pick. He was slipping the senator shares in his company every time an Air Force contract for jet engine blades was awarded to his plant in Sedalia—the senator's home town. Remember my telling you Cutler was finalizing the purchase of Beauchamp's company while he was negotiating to buy mine?"

"You bet. Did it behind your back."

"Exactly. And then Cutler springs Sedalia on me after our deal is buttoned up. Beauchamp leaves to 'pursue other interests' and I'm saddled with his shit house of an operation for the past year."

Fisk felt the twinge of the panic he had experienced in the fern garden at the thought of what all this might mean to him. "Now listen to this," he said, his voice rising. "Beauchamp told Otto that Cutler paid the senator a finders fee of a million dollars for his part in suggesting the deal."

"A million dollars!! To a Senator? Do you believe it?"

"After the way Cutler acted in the negotiations with me, sure. I'm beginning to believe he'd do anything to benefit his company. He's not the man I thought he was. The minute I realized what he'd done, I should have had it out with him. All that sweet talk about continuing to run my own show, but less responsibility if I sold to him. All the while he knew I would be running Beauchamp's company along with mine—and killing myself cleaning up the mess Beauchamp left behind."

Fisk paused, feeling sheepish. "He gulled me; I'm not proud

of it. And I tell you, these new machinations have me on edge."

She shook her head. "I don't blame you."

Fisk could tell she wasn't finished by the way she wiggled her toes in the water.

"You had the dream again, didn't you?"

"Yes. The first time since I joined Hi Tech."

"I could tell by the way you were thrashing around last night. You're very worried aren't you?"

"Sure am. And not just about Cutler's honesty. All the talk about Beauchamp has made me face up to the effect his former company may be having on mine now that I'm combining them to increase efficiency. Just last week a shipment of metal arrived from Sedalia with the wrong documentation tags, and the wrong alloy found its way into a production melt for commercial jet engine blades. Our people picked up the error during final inspection before shipment, but it's the kind of mistake that easily could have been missed. And this is less responsibility? I haven't produced anything new since ARTIFACTS."

Martha looked at him with a concern that matched his own. "You're tearing yourself apart. You know where I stand. Give up the business. You could lead an exciting, productive life as a sculptor. Your gallery has been after you to do a one-man show. This is the time in life to do what you want to do. Make a decision. At least confront Cutler over what you've heard."

"Not yet. I want to get my facts straight. You don't discuss anything with Cass without the facts. Otto Gitner's back and we're having a drink at Berghoff. Maybe I can get a feel for how much to believe."

"What if Otto's right about what Beauchamp said?"

"And if I come up with hard evidence?"

"Yes."

"I'd have to resign. But right now I have more work to do. I want to give it one last try. I owe it to my people."

"Just remember," she said, "there's only one thing I want and that's a happy husband. Do whatever makes you happy."

"Right now?"

"Right now."

"I want to give you a back rub."

"Thought you'd never ask."

"Do you want the deluxe model or the super duper?" Fisk said, taking her in his arms and holding her close. "I love you."

"Today," Martha said. "I want the works."

She sat by the pool watching Fisk, his backside beginning to sag a bit, make his way up the hill toward the house. One last try, she thought, reflecting on their talk. Isn't that what I love about him? He knows he should get out, but he loves his company, loves his work. A man who really cares, who knows what responsibility means—responsibility is a long, long word.

She lit a cigarette, letting the smoke curl from her nostrils. How could she convince him to be more responsible to himself? If he could only see how alive, how passionate he was when he expressed his feelings about his art . . . like that time in Florida, she remembered, during the liftoff of Apollo 11 the year they were married . . .

Seated among hundreds of spectators in the V.I.P. grandstand at the Cape Kennedy launch complex, their eyes and thoughts were fixed on the launch site four miles away across a scrub-filled landscape. From her husband's description on the flight down, she had expected to see a monster-size machine, solid and business-like, "taller than a football field set on end with five first stage engines about to burn over three tons of fuel per second". Instead, at that distance it struck her as an elegant turreted tower, a sort of white apparition, incapable of fury, shimmering in the sun. "It looks so small, so innocent," she said.

"Just wait," Fisk answered, without turning to address her.

She loved the look of concentration on his face and knew that in his mind's eye he was picturing the dense flow of electronic information throughout Apollo that he often spoke of with such passion; knew that the human element fascinated him . . . not only the activities of the three-man crew, but the way the craft was examining itself for readiness, probing everywhere with thousands of instruments and systems designed by engineers. *He loves to think that way. He's in heaven!*

"One minute to liftoff and counting," the loudspeakers blared.

Fisk took her hand. "Don't be frightened by the sound, sweetheart. It's pretty brutal once it reaches us. The acoustic energy can kill birds that fly too close, but the engineers have it figured that four miles is safe for humans."

Kill birds and not injure me? "I hope they're right."

. . .

"Ten seconds to liftoff and counting . . . nine . . . eight . . ."

Orange flames erupted from the base of Apollo, a trickle at first becoming a roiling inferno wrapped in billowing clouds of steam from the cooling water spray under the pad.

"We have ignition, repeat ignition . . . seven . . . six . . . five . . . four . . ."

My God, something's wrong! It's so quiet. Is it just going to sit there and blow up?

". . . three . . . two . . . one . . . T-zero . . . Lift-off, we have a lift-off!"

Fisk jumped to his feet. "Go, baby, go!" he shouted as Apollo rose slowly up the side of the launch tower. "Look at her go!"

The silence at the grandstand was shattered by the sound waves. With the gradual throttling up of the engines, the intensity of the roaring increased. *Uh, oh!* Martha felt the sound pounding her all over as if she were being whacked by a big stick. *I can't stand this any longer.* She turned to her husband, fear in her eyes. His smile reassured her; a moment later the intensity began to subside. *How can they be so precise in their calculations?* The exhaust plumes became an incandescent white as the rocket picked up speed and began to slant from vertical, seeking its programmed trajectory. *Hey, I'm beginning to like this!* Fisk, tears streaming down his face, squeezed her hand so hard it hurt. "The incredible density," he said, "the packing of human thought we're witnessing out there—the genius of thousands of men and women living on in metal. That's what I'm trying to express in my sculpture. I think it's the most human thing I've ever seen."

By the time she got back to the house, he was already dressed and on his way down the driveway. My businessman-artist, she thought. He needs the show now more than ever. And the gallery won't wait forever.

　　　She lit another cigarette and took a long drag . . . *So . . . We'll work around him, put one together on the sly. We'll surprise him. On his birthday.*

CHAPTER 3

9:15 A.M. EST

Dusty McGinty felt the insistent vibrations of his Sky Page beeper against his stomach. Once, twice, three times. Emergency! Urgent! Keenly attuned to potential disaster, he had set the beeper to the silent vibratory mode before climbing into the dentist chair for his semi-annual cleaning. Bad enough to suffer through the hygienist's spirited probing of his gum line. What if an unexpected beep from beneath his protective apron made her jump?

Dusty pointed his finger urgently in the direction of his lap. The hygienist removed her instrument. "You have to pee?"

"No."

She removed the saliva suction tube. He threw aside the apron and bolted from the chair, his ruddy complexion flushed with emotion. "Sorry. It's an emergency." He removed the beeper from his belt and noted the calling number in the window. "Damn! 'Bad News' Lieberman." He reached for his cell phone.

Hal Lieberman, director of the National Transportation Safety Board's bureau of field operations, had no doubt just received a call from the FAA's communications center in Washington where first word of a major air crash is received. As this week's posted investigator-in-charge of any NTSB crash investigation, Dusty knew that it was Liberman's duty to notify him as soon as possible. He dialed Liberman at his office in the Department of Transportation building on Independence Avenue.

"How bad is it, Hal?"

"Terrible. Really major. Worse than American at O'Hare.

Worse than TWA 800. A widebody with three hundred and five passengers at Miami International."

Worse than O'Hare? Dusty's stomach lurched. He had been investigator-in-charge at the crash in May 1979 that had killed all two hundred and seventy-one on board and two on the ground, the largest number of fatalities in U.S. aviation history at the time. Could anything be worse than the carnage he had witnessed that evening? "Any survivors?"

"Not a chance. Ten minutes ago flight one eighty one heavy flew smack into a hi-rise hotel full of guests north of the Orange Bowl off I-95. The whole damned building went over with the Starflight 610 stuck in it. The reports coming in say that the casualties are worse on the ground."

A hotel full of guests! He felt his mouth go dry. Jesus! Five hundred, maybe a thousand people. "Who's at the scene?"

"Jose from our Miami field office."

"Tell him to begin taking eye-witness reports as soon as he can."

"The controller in the tower said he observed what appeared to be a massive failure of the number three engine during climb out."

"Then it's essential that Jose secure the runway and the area under the flight path where the failure occurred. Start a search if he can. We've got to get to those engine parts ahead of the souvenir hunters."

"He's already been in touch with the sheriff and the Florida Air National Guard. And the mayor's on his way. Says it's his jurisdiction and he's taking charge."

"Oh Christ! Not that again." Dusty ran his fingers restlessly through his flamboyant red hair. "An old fart on the loose hell bent on stirring up shit. If you get a chance before I do, just tell him to go fuck himself."

"Go easy on him, Dusty. There's a big Hispanic vote down there and that won't be lost on our President."

"Fuck him too!"

"Where are you?"

"The dentist in Georgetown. I can be across the bridge and home in fifteen minutes. We leaving from National?"

"The FAA Gulfstream in hanger 6," Hal said, the usual arrangement. As one of the smallest agencies in Washington, the NTSB practice was to use the FAA plane if available, otherwise commercial.

"I'll grab a bag, be there at ten. How about the rest of the Go Team?" Dusty was referring to the air safety investigators from the NTSB who are on twenty four hour call. Their job demands the combined skills of detective, engineer and trail scout; they "go" whenever a serious accident occurs—they're the "tin kickers" in the trade who pick through the wreckage and try to figure out what went wrong.

"The calls are going out now."

"We need a good man on engines. Who's posted this week?"

"Pete DiBella."

"The best. And the board member on duty?"

"Mary Joy Lemay. I just got off the phone with her. She's on the Coast and won't get to Florida until tomorrow morning."

"Ah, Mary Joy, friend of the President. Just what we need. We've never been together on an investigation."

"Try it you'll like it," Lieberman said. "She knows her stuff. She's one tough cookie, and fair." His voice trailed off . . . "Pete's calling in. We tracked him down at his son's graduation at the University of Maryland."

"Then I'll get off the line if you'll switch me to your secretary. I want her to call home and ask Betty to pack for me."

Dusty jumped into his car at curbside, and with a screeching getaway that turned heads, started for home. One hand on the wheel, he surfed the radio and tuned in on WMIA's morning newscaster:

"At approximately nine a.m. a fully loaded Cross Country

Airlines Starflight 610 jumbo jet apparently lost an engine on takeoff from Miami International Airport and crashed into the new Surfside hotel off I-95. Early reports say that the plane toppled the forty five story building resulting in an all-alarms fire that is now in progress. Little hope is held for the passengers. More casualties are expected on the ground. Emergency equipment from all over Dade County is headed for the site. Listeners should stay off I-95 north and south unless it is absolutely necessary. Rubbernecking is causing bumper to bumper traffic, seriously restricting emergency access. Stay tuned for further news. We hope to have continuous coverage from the scene within the hour."

Dusty could see the headlines: "**WORST CRASH IN AIRLINE HISTORY—WIDEBODY JET TOPPLES HOTEL IN MIAMI—ONE THOUSAND FEARED DEAD**". The media would jump on this one big time: reporters jockeying for information at every turn. The boisterous coverage he remembered at O'Hare would be pale in comparison. That was nineteen years ago, and times were different now, weren't they? The crash of United at Pittsburgh, ValuJet in the Everglades, and TWA off Long Island—each had set a new level of media frenzy. By noon, hundreds of reporters, photographers, and TV cameramen would be on site; dozens of mobile broadcast trucks rolling in with satellite dishes atop ready to beam news of the tragedy around the world. And unlike the recent crashes, he was again the investigator in charge, the Al Dickinson of the TWA tragedy who daily on TV took the heat from reporters, victims groups, media-conscious politicians, and an FBI wedded to the theory of terrorism.

Dusty's shoulders sagged at the thought of the enormity of the stakes he faced. Jesus, the President would be calling! Congressmen, Senators, out there clamoring for action; heads of the airline, airplane builder, suppliers—any party potentially at fault—dashing for the exit marked "innocent". As the central figure in a maelstrom of conflicting interests, he would have to see that all the facts were carried forward in search of the truth. And the truth, he knew, would be unbearably painful to someone, some company—an outcome to be foiled by them at all costs.

No mistakes this time, Dusty cautioned himself, remembering his early foul up during the O'Hare investigation. Soon after their arrival at O'Hare, the Go Team had found that during the wide body's takeoff climb, its left engine and wing attachment structure had separated from the wing and fallen to the runway. A quick inspection pointed to failure at a point where the structure is bolted to the wing by an elaborate set of bulkheads and fittings. A member of the structures team found the critical thrust bolt broken into two parts both lying in the grass adjacent to the runway. And in preparation for the first press briefing, the NTSB board member on duty asked Dusty if the broken bolt could have caused the crash. Yes, he volunteered. It looked like a fatigue failure. To Dusty's horror, the evening headlines read "I found it!" accompanied by the picture of a man racing down the runway holding the bolt. But it was soon apparent that the broken bolt was a result, not a cause. The final NTSB report cited a maintenance-induced crack in the aft bulkhead flange as the probable culprit.

Dusty pressed down on the accelerator. Hot damn! he thought. CCA 181. Maybe my last hurrah. The most important week in my life.

CHAPTER 4

8:30 A.M. CST

Cass Cutler anticipated the day's events with pleasure: a swing by the office for a brief nine o'clock meeting, then on to an early lunch and afternoon of fishing at his club near Elgin with George Trueslow, heir to the Trueslow Chemical fortune and the second largest shareholder of Hi Tech. At night, there was a black-tie affair at the Drake where he was to be recipient of the B'Nai B'Rith's Businessman of the Year Award. The feeling of engagement, a mode of existence in which he fancied everything smoothly related to everything else, pleased him. Double and treble benefit. Business did not intrude on leisure. They were mutually reinforcing.

From the balcony, he returned to his bedroom where his wife lay sleeping, quietly slipped into his jogging outfit then left the house and walked to a small shed hidden in a grove of greening shadblow trees—the home of Billy the Goat, his jogging companion for the past five years. Billy had arrived at the house on Cass's sixtieth birthday in a mysterious gift-wrapped crate sent by a childhood friend. "From one old goat to another," the enclosed card read.

When Cass finished jogging, he fed Billy, walked to the nearby pool, swam fifty laps, then toweled himself dry. With bulging biceps, worn face, and a prominent scar running through his right eyebrow, an observer might have taken him for an aging boxer. Presently he moved to a pillow under the eve of the pool house and sat cross-legged, torso erect, in the yoga position. Strong . . . strong . . . he repeated to himself, in rhythm with his breathing.

Strong . . . strong . . . He rode his sense of well-being like a surfer enjoying a wave, until a thought intruded. "Maybe Felix is right." He went over his conversation with Felix Reston, the company's investment banker and a director, shortly before the last board meeting. Reston, a firm believer in raising important issues in private, had broached the subject of his possible successor. "The time's coming when the board should know your intentions. You're no spring chicken, you know."

"I'm strong," Cutler had snapped, and abruptly walked away.

Strong . . . strong . . . he continued but it was no use. Reston's remark was still on his mind. The board would allow him to continue as long as he had his health, wouldn't they? Into his seventies. Maybe even . . . Well, look at Strom Thurmond. But what if the board pressed him for an answer? Would he propose Woody Bentley, his executive vice president and director of Hi Tech? Over his dead body he told himself, remembering an article in Business Week featuring the "outside man"—Cass—and the "inside man"—Bentley—of Hi Tech. Its emphasis on Cutler's contacts with Washington and heads of foreign countries gave the impression that while the boss man was traveling the high road, hard-working Bentley was responsible for the flow of profits. One more caper like that and I'll have his ass, Cutler thought. I know damned well he planted that article.

What about Alan Fisk, who had accomplished everything asked of him, and more, in the twelve months since the acquisition. The board, impressed, had been willing to make him executive vice president and director equal in rank with Bentley. But was he strong enough? Such a goddamned boy scout at times, mouthing all that shit about business ethics. Maybe in time he could toughen him to the realities of running a big company like Hi Tech. After all, didn't he see Fisk as potential CEO material the day they first met at Lake Forest's Onwenctia Club. And his first impressions were usually on the mark, weren't they?

"Who was that fellow you introduced me to at the club?" he asked George Trueslow that night.

"Alan Fisk? I'm surprised you've never met him. Owns a company in Waukegan called Cast Profiles. Blades for jet engines, I think."

"Inherited the business?"

"No. Made it on his own. Bought the business some years ago from the company he worked for, run by a man named Gitner, Otto Gitner, a Kraut who came here after the war. Started a company making dental appliances, and later diversified into jet engine blades. Sold the company recently for a bundle. Today he's one of the richest men in Chicago."

Cutler thought, jet engine blades! And determined to get to know Fisk better.

Shortly before he met Fisk at the country club, Cass Cutler had testified at a Senate appropriations hearing in Washington. After the meeting, Josh Rushmore, the Chairman of the Senate Armed Services Committee, a lanky, pink-faced man with a full head of snow white hair and deceptively avuncular manner, invited him to his private office. Uh, oh. Trouble, Cutler thought.

"We need your hep," Rushmore said. "The country needs it. The good state of Missouri needs it. And 1200 hard working, Godfearin' employees in my home town of Sedalia need it."

Cutler gave him The Look as it was known to his employees, a slow back and forth scan of the other's face, like a radar sweeping the horizon. To be euchred was the worst thing that could happen to a man. Letting yourself be had was the mark of a ninny.

Rushmore came quickly to the point. Sedalia's major employer, a manufacturer of turbine and compressor blades used in jet engines, was facing bankruptcy. Cutler was the man to come to the rescue and acquire the company. All they needed was more capital and a broader base of research and development; the mere availability of Hi Tech's resources would bring about transformation in the company's fortunes.

Rushmore had studiously skirted the issue of management. Cutler continued to scan the old man's face.

"Cut that crap with the googly eyes," the Senator exploded. "Save that shit to intimidate your hirelings. Are you going to hep me or not?"

Cutler shrugged. "You know I want to."

Hi Tech's near monopoly in solid rocket boosters for strategic missiles was particularly vulnerable to competition, and Cutler was well aware of the Senator's reputation for axing anyone who crossed him. But the company he was being asked to buy was a dog! Rumor had it that they would have gone bankrupt were it not for their patron saint in Washington.

The Senator peered over his glasses at Cutler, his face now crimson red. "Then do it, boy! You just do it, hear me!"

"I'll call you," Cutler said, fighting to control his anger.

The dossier Cutler received a few days later from his treasurer confirmed his suspicions. The president of the company, Buzz Beauchamp, spent little time managing the business. Nor was there a capable second in command. Cass saw, too, the block of stock registered in the name of an offshore corporation in the Netherlands Antilles. Perhaps the Senator had a more personal stake than the professed welfare of his townspeople.

"Hep me," Cutler muttered, mocking the Senator's words. "Hep me." The venal bastard. He's at it again.

As the deadline for his answer approached, he had all but decided to say no. His success was built on paying good prices for companies with superior management. Why change and find you'd been euchred? Still, he had trouble making up his mind. Was he missing an opportunity? With the right man running the company, he might ingratiate himself with the Senator and at the same time earn a fat profit.

Cutler dialed his treasurer at home. "I want every scrap of

information you can lay your hands on about Cast Profiles in Waukegan and its management. Bust your ass! I want it Monday afternoon."

Now, with the dossier in hand everything he read convinced him that he had the makings of a triple play. The marketing section of the report listed Cast Profiles as a direct competitor of the ailing Sedalia company. Penciling in the total of their respective market shares, Cutler saw that if he acquired both companies and combined them into a single division under Fisk, Hi Tech would be the dominant factor in the field.

As for Fisk, at fifty-five, he was the right age to play a role in top management, perhaps vying with Bentley, who was getting uppity anyway. And anybody who could take a peanut-sized investment and make a bundle for himself and his investors in ten years had to have his head screwed on right. Having always worked for a large company, Cutler was especially interested in reading about Fisk's acquisition of twenty percent of the stock of Cast Profiles for two hundred thousand dollars, most of it borrowed, and the entrepreneurial spirit it suggested. He was quick to note, too, their similar social backgrounds: midwest, blue collar. Most of all, he envied him his engineering education.

Satisfied, he put aside the papers and called his secretary. "Get me Alan Fisk."

The acquisition couldn't have worked out better, Cutler reflected dressing at the pool house. Rushmore's throwing more business our way, and Fisk and his division are a great success. Bentley's even showing me a little respect. Turning to the mirror, he pulled gently at the wattle of skin that hung from his chin. I may not be a spring chicken, he laughed, but the old brain is still working.

The phone rang. "Cass Cutler speaking."

"It's George Trueslow, Cass. I'm afraid our fishing is off for this afternoon. You hear the news?"

"What news?"

"Hi Tech stock. It's already off ten points."

"Ten points . . . ?"

"My broker's on the other phone. I'm out ten million; he says it's still falling. The tape's carrying news of a terrible crash in Miami; a plane flew into a hotel. Hi Tech's being linked to it somehow."

Gotta get Burke on the phone, Cutler thought. "Any more details?"

"Lots dead. The whole building went over."

"Appreciate the call, George. I have to get on this right away," Cutler said, and hung up.

He sat back in his chair and took four deep breaths. Strong . . . strong . . .

CHAPTER 5

9:00 A.M. CST

Tom Burke, Hi Tech's lawyer, was pacing the office when Fisk arrived. "Sorry for barging in," Burke said. "But we have to talk about the crash."

"Crash?"

"You haven't heard? At Miami International. Flight one eighty one, a widebody headed for Chicago. About a half hour ago. Two eye witnesses at the airport reported seeing an explosion in the right engine of the Starflight 610."

"Anybody killed?"

"All three hundred five passengers."

"Three hundred five . . . dead? . . ." *Oh my God! . . . My blades are on those engines. Could they have . . . ?* Hot pain shot down Fisk's neck muscles and into his shoulders. *Did they . . . fail? He had seen what happens when a failed blade escapes the engine's steel containment ring, hadn't he? Blades did kill people. Blades did bring down planes, big planes. Jesus!* He massaged the back of his neck.

"Crashed into a hotel near the airport on takeoff. The whole friggin building went over with the plane stuck in its side. It's on all the stations. They're saying it's the worst crash in history."

"Then more must have been killed in the hotel."

"More . . . Maybe everybody. The burning fuel ran through the building and finished it off."

Fisk turned and sprinted to the board room. With the

push of a button he exposed the large-screen television mounted in the wall.

"Just tell me one thing," Burke pleaded. "Are we on that plane?"

"My Waukegan plant is the sole supplier of the Starflight engine fan blades"

"Jesus Christ!"

Fisk dialed Channel Two, his hands damp with perspiration. An on site report of the crash was in progress. A reporter was interviewing a dazed old man sitting nude except for his white jockey shorts under a palm tree near the yellow tape cordoning off the crash site. "We're talking to one of the survivors," the reporter said into the mike. "Can you tell us, sir, how you got out alive?"

The man continued to stare hollow-eyed at the raging inferno in the distance. "Jumped . . ." he mumbled. "Jumped . . . My Emma wouldn't jump . . ." He began sobbing.

Fisk switched to Channel Four. ". . . We're witnessing a biblical scene," the reporter was saying. "Everything larger than life. The whole building on its side, barely visible through the flames. Oh, it's horrible, horrible! The fire, the smoke, the sounds; those who escaped the building lying injured on the grass waiting for the ambulances to get through. A few Med Vac helicopters and six fire trucks are on the scene so far, and dozens more on the way; you can hear their sirens everywhere. Please, please, folks, let 'em through! Stay off the roads, especially I-95, Route 1, and 64th Street. The fire marshal is telling us there's no way any of the three hundred and five aboard the plane or the guests trapped in the hotel could still be alive. We're hearing that the count might eventually approach a thousand dead. So give the injured a chance, folks. Stay off the road!"

A thousand dead . . . ? Fisk's shoulders felt like they were being seared with a hot poker.

Burke turned to Fisk. "Alan, this means trouble," he said.

"You're telling me?"

"Worse than you think. The plane was loaded with orthopedic surgeons returning from a convention in Miami Beach."

Fisk jumped to his feet. "High priced cargo you're saying. All their families ready to sue. God dammit Tom, I can't believe you!" His voice rose. "They're not cargo. They're people. Real people. You've never been to a crash site, have you? Never seen a man lying dead charred black like an overcooked steak. Or the legless half of a woman with her baby still clutched in her arms. Well I have! Look at the screen, Tom, and that's just the beginning. And I may have caused it . . . I may have caused it."

Burke looked at him in amazement. "Be careful what you say. When the litigators start computing the worth of their probable future earnings . . ."

"Fuck the litigators! I don't want to hear about it!"

"Together with the losses on the ground the liability could be several billion! Whether we're at fault or not, Hi Tech will be joined in the suits. They'll try the case here where most of the passengers lived—and we're the deep pocket in this jurisdiction."

Fisk stood glowering at him. "Tom, I'm warning you!"

"Christ! I'd better get to the insurance department. Cass called from home. He's due any minute."

Fisk, lost in his own fear-filled thoughts, didn't see him exit.

He remained at the television, desperate for information that would confirm or deny the early reports of engine failure. His hands were shaking. Get hold of yourself, friend, he admonished himself, realizing how he had overreacted to Burke's legitimate business concerns. You can't forget Albuquerque, can you? Anticipating the worst again. It could have been a disk failure. A recent NTSB study had documented such events, hadn't it, cases where rapidly rotating titanium disks that hold the blades fail and escape the engine's steel containment ring at high velocity, causing extensive damage to the plane.

Fisk felt relieved. Yes, the disk! Oh, God. I hope so, he thought, and chided himself for caring more about himself than the victims.

He tried to reach his friend Dusty McGinty at the NTSB but was told he was on his way to the crash site and could not be contacted.

Martha, he thought. Gotta call Martha before she leaves the house.

"Glad I caught you," he said.

"Alan, your voice is quivering! Something has happened."

"A wide body crashed in Miami an hour ago."

"Yes, I heard about it." She paused. "So awful . . . You're involved, aren't you. I hear it in your voice."

"The blades on the engine. Witnesses say the engine exploded on takeoff."

"But that doesn't mean . . ."

"I know, I know. But I can't help thinking the worst."

"Is there reason to believe . . ."

"Listen to me! I have to know whether I killed all those people."

"All . . . !"

"They're estimating a thousand dead."

"A thousand? How could. . . ?"

"Three hundred five on the plane; the rest on the ground. Nothing like this has ever happened before. The plane crashed into a hotel packed with people."

"Oh, darling, I hear you. This must bring back the past."

"What do you mean, the past?"

"What happened in Albuquerque."

"Don't bother me with that!" he snapped. "I'm rushing."

"Don't bother you!" she cried. "You don't have to cut me off like that! This morning I heard how worried you are about

Sedalia's sloppy practices; your fear that something like the Albuquerque tragedy could happen again. And now you tell me it may have. One thousand dead this time. You must be devastated."

He hesitated. I always get angry when she's right, he thought. "I'm sorry. I am devastated," he said. "Terrified, actually. One foul-up like Sedalia's shipment of the wrong alloy last week can bring down a plane, a big plane. We caught that mistake, but I'm scared stiff at the thought of others that could've gone undetected in that hellhole of confusion Cutler stuck me with."

"Then let's talk a minute; you need to calm down. I started to ask: Is there reason to believe your blades are to blame? What little I know about jet engines suggests they're a complicated piece of machinery."

Always on target, he thought. "Complicated? You betcha."

"Then there are other parts that could have failed, right?"

"Yes, but . . ."

"Alan! Ease off on yourself. Of course you're devastated if there's the least chance your blades caused the crash. That doesn't mean you have to let the past overwhelm you." He heard a gentle laugh. "It's not good for your health."

God, how I love that woman! he thought. She knows me better than I know myself. Yet she never oversteps, never turns analyst and makes me feel like I'm her patient.

"No it isn't good for my health," he said. "But if I don't get off this phone, the present's going to overwhelm me."

"You sure you're okay?"

"Much better, thanks to you."

"Do you want me to cancel my patients?"

"No. I'll be tied up all day."

"Then call me as soon as you can. Promise?"

"I promise."

"I'm so sorry, Alan"

"So am I. For all those people."

She sighed. "And for yourself."

*　　*　　*

Cass Cutler's voice came through on the office intercom. "Tom Burke tells me you were mouthing off to him about causing the Miami crash. Are you out of your mind? A thousand people dead, and saying you—Hi Tech—may have caused it. For christsakes, Alan, explain yourself!"

Fisk felt exposed. "You're right, I overreacted with Tom," he said. "His news of the crash caught me off balance. Our blades are on the engines."

"He told me."

"The thought that they might have failed and killed all those people tears me apart, Cass."

Cutler, after a pause: "I know how you feel . . ."

Now there's a switch. The caring father routine. He's pissed but thinking how to handle me.

". . . but this is different from running your own business."

"You really believe that? You think my problems at Cast Profiles weren't as agonizing?"

"Hear me out. When you're running a big public company . . ."

Here it comes. Toughen up to the realities of the big time.

". . . there are others to consider: shareholders, employees, suppliers, the community."

"And the victims, Cass, the victims!"

"Of course, the victims. Okay. But we have to be careful how we handle ourselves from this point on," Cutler said. "Burke tells me we may be under-insured by several billion dollars. Rumors are flying on the Exchange that we're involved and our stock's now off eleven points. I've told Burke to set up a damage containment team with Bill Sperling in Corporate Affairs as Chair. Nobody but the V.P. speaks to the outside world. Any calls from the media, stockbrokers, lawyers, whoever, are to be referred to him."

Hundreds of people dead and that's all you can think of?

"The game is played in the press, . . ."

What do you take me for? Fisk thought.

". . . everybody involved jockeying for position. Give it some thought."

"Come off it Cass! You're pissed. Admit it. You're sounding patronizing."

"Okay, I am pissed at you involving the company in your guilt. Let's move on. Why the blades? Why not an oil seal, a bearing, or a disk. Yeah, what about the disk?"

He's smart. Always on top of every detail. "Could be."

"There you go! It's the disk! Now you're thinking positively. There's a history of problems, isn't there?"

"Extensive. The trouble usually starts with an anomaly in the metal or a stress crack in the disk that wasn't detected during inspection."

"Whose disks are on these engines?"

"General Tech."

"Sam Barker, that turd," Cutler exclaimed. "What does he know about business? Three star general; who gives a damn? Just because he managed a big chunk of the Pentagon's budget before he retired doesn't mean he can run a multibillion dollar public company. Hell, I felt him out at an industry get together last year after he was brought in as CEO. We got to talking about interest rates and he kept referring to basic points. I asked him what he meant by "basic points", and he said. 'You know, one hundredth of a point in the yield of a bond.' Christsakes! He doesn't even know the word is 'basis point'. The piranhas on Wall Street will eat him alive."

Fisk heard the sound of Cutler's new Market Watch computer being activated.

"Wait a minute! Let me check the market . . . GTH 47 1/8! Ah, ha, his stock's off too. I'd love to see him get hit with this."

I bet you would, Fisk thought. He knew that something had happened between them in the past, and wondered what might have stung Cutler enough to make him repeat such a petty slip. "Could happen," he said.

"So what are your plans?"

"I'll get my men cracking on the NTSB investigation as soon as we hang up. We have to find out who's at fault, wherever that leads—and fast. We owe it to the victims."

Fisk thought he detected a note of concern in Cutler's silence. *What I was afraid of. Okay, as long as it doesn't lead home.*

"Gotta go," Cutler said abruptly. "The Stock Exchange is calling. I'll see you in my office later."

Cutler strode to the window in his corner office overlooking Lake Michigan. *Insolent son of a bitch! Of course he's upset by the crash. We all are. I tried to go easy on him, give him a little advice, and what does he do? Keeps sticking it to me. Thinks I don't see what he's getting at. "We have to find out who's at fault, wherever that leads." Wherever! About as subtle as a kick in the ass. Doesn't give a shit about Hi Tech and its people. Thinks he's superior—like he's the only one with feelings. Well I've got a message for him. I've got feelings, too. I just don't go around making a thing about it.*

He returned to his desk. *Maybe I should fire him . . . Hey, great idea, Cass. And have the finger pointed straight at Hi Tech from the beginning. No, there's a better way. This is a job for Joe Bledsoe,* he thought, referring to his pal from high school, now Hi Tech's largest independent rep handling foreign and domestic sales out of his office in Miami. Through his long friendship with Cutler, he enjoyed a back channel to the boss, often handling sensitive affairs Cutler wished to keep from the company's watchdogs.

Yes, with so much at stake, Joe was the man to look out for Hi Tech's interests as the investigation proceeded. He could trust Joe. Joe had never let him down.

Cutler picked up the phone. "Get me Joe Bledsoe in Florida."

"But the stock exchange is waiting," his secretary said.

"Transfer the call to Bill Sperling in Corporate affairs. I want Bledsoe now. Call him on his beeper if you have to."

His secretary reached Bledsoe quickly.

"Hello, Joe? You aware of the CCA crash out of Miami International?"

"Impossible not to, Chief. It's on all stations. Why, are Hi Tech's products involved?"

"Yeah, the blades on the engines."

"They're saying it's an engine failure."

"That's why I want you to get over there as soon as you can. Nose around. As our rep, talk to the NTSB guys when they arrive. See who's the investigator in charge so we can get a line on him. Find out all you can and call me."

"You really think the blades let go?

"A possibility."

"Good God, Chief, I hope not! From what I hear about casualties, Hi Tech could be on the hook for billions; the company is at stake."

"Exactly! So our job is to keep the investigators away from our doorstep; to point the investigation in the direction of the engine disks which also have a history of problems. Planting a replay of the United crash at Sioux City in eighty nine would help; caused by a fan disk failure you know."

"I remember. A terrible crash. Really caught the public's attention."

"And keep a sharp eye on Alan Fisk as the investigation progresses."

"Fisk? Last I heard he was on the fast track at headquarters. Sorta the crown prince."

"He has the makings, don't get me wrong. But the crash has unhinged him. He's never gotten over the death of a passenger years ago when one of his blades failed. Says we have to get at the truth wherever it leads. The little shit."

"I see what you mean. A loose cannon."

"That's why I'm asking for your help. And Joe, this may become very sensitive. Handle yourself accordingly. But do what you have to do. Whether the blades did it or not, we have to be in the clear."

CHAPTER 6

10:15 A.M. EST

Sam Barker returned to his office overlooking Central Park from a meeting in the board room with the staff of General Tech's Forged Disk Division. With the belligerent toothy look of a badger on the warpath, he strode to his desk and switched on his Market Watch computer. Damn! he thought, looking at GT's last trade on the New York Stock Exchange. Off another five points. And news! He double clicked on the asterisk beside the quote: * GTH 45 1/4 - 5 1/8. A window popped up on the screen.

NEWS SCREEN

ID LXQSNP Src:DJ TM 10:15am 28 May NYC Page 1 of 1
us:GTH   General Tech   45 1/4   DN5 1/8
General Tech, Inc. A Potential Party In Investigation Of CCA 181 Crash In Miami.

MIAMI (Dow Jones)—Sources close to the NTSB investigation said that an air traffic controller has confirmed other witnesses' accounts of an apparent massive failure of the PT number 3 engine during climb out. Past investigations of jet engine related fatalities usually focus on the rotating parts, especially the compressor blades and disks which have a well documented history of failure. PT has confirmed earlier reports that the blades were outsourced

from the Cast Profiles Division of Hi Tech: the
disks from the Forged Disk Division of General
Tech.

(END)   DOW JONES NEWS   10:15 EDT   05 28 02

Barker sat staring at the screen. The day not half over and we're
off fifteen percent. Shit! Couldn't have happened at a worse time
with our two hundred million stock offering in the works. The
directors didn't bring me on board to see this happen on my watch.

He reached for the computer and punched in Hi Tech's symbol: * HTH 76 1/2 -13 1/4 . . . Off thirteen! The market's trash-
ing them too. Interesting. Cass Cutler's company. A sardonic
smile lighted Barker's face. Looks like we'll find ourselves in the
ring together again. This time, with higher stakes.

He buzzed his secretary. "Please see if Ms. Donovan is free."

His Vice President for Special Projects appeared in the doorway. A tall woman of fifty four with a luxuriant head of jet black
hair, glade-green eyes, and a beautifully proportioned figure, she
walked with a cane. She had been Barker's Intelligence Officer in
Vietnam, injured on a "dirty tricks" mission behind enemy lines.
Barker smiled as she approached. Thirty years together, he mused,
and I still get a kick out of watching her enter a room. Some
woman. He rose and joined her at a nearby coffee table.

"What a morning, Rosie. You've kept up with the news since
we talked?"

"Yes, General. Made it the order of the day."

"The crash is more serious for General Tech than I thought."

"I take it your meeting with the division was disappointing."

"They're our disks all right. On every Starflight. And I heard
more about the mechanics of disk failures than I ever wanted to
know. Showed me an NTSB special report called 'Turbine Rotor Disk Failures, 1976 to 1995.' Pretty grim. Our stock is off
again."

"You've heard the latest estimate of fatalities?"

"No."

"Seems they've recovered the hotel's registration list. There were sixteen hundred twenty one guests. Only three hundred or so escaped the building, many seriously injured. "

Barker's mouth dropped open. "So you're saying sixteen hundred dead counting the passengers?"

"At least. And many of the injured are in critical shape."

For a moment Barker lost his solid military bearing. His shoulders sagged and his head drooped to one side. Sixteen hundred people! He had seen hundreds of innocent men, women, and children die in the villages of 'Nam in a dirty war, but that was different, wasn't it? Or was it? And on his watch again. He shuddered at the thought.

Barker saw Rosie studying his reaction and squared his shoulders.

"There is some good news," Rosie said. "The IIC of the investigation is an old friend of mine. Remember Dusty McGinty?"

"Yes, I remember. He saved your life in 'Nam."

"Right."

"You were close for awhile."

"Let's say we were good friends, Sir."

Just good friends? he thought. Spending a week together on leave in Saigon after she left the hospital?

"Still see him?"

"Not since 'Nam."

Barker saw he was making her uncomfortable. "Tell me," he said. "What do you know about Cass Cutler, head of Hi Tech?"

"Just by reputation. Never met the man. Smart, successful, built a great company. But I hear he has an ego as big as all get out. Whatever he's engaged in, likes to think of himself as king of the mountain. His competitors hate him."

"Figures. I've heard that too. Strange fellow."

"You know him?"

"Met him twice. Casually. The first time was in Wyoming;

the yearly industry get together at the A Bar A Ranch. The Conquistadors Del Sol. Ever hear of them?"

"Are you kidding? Aerospace's version of Tail Hook where the boys gather for fun and frolic. If they get around to letting women in, you'd better watch yourself, General."

"Now, now, Rosie," he said smiling. "After all these years? You should know better.

"Anyhow, I was the new kid on the block, and Cutler homed in on me like a sidewinder missile. Pops a question, then gives you a searching look like you're on trial. Obviously was trying to size me up. Probably pretty good at it. Along the way, though, he overplayed his hand; couldn't resist a few digs about the military's business acumen. Knew damn well I had just left the army. He sought me out at the bar when most had left, and we had a couple of brandies. Then right out of the blue he gave me that look again, and said: 'What about a little arm wrestling?' I had been warned about the ploy when he first meets you; always wins. I said: 'Okay'. I was the all time shot put champion at the Point, you know. We put our elbows on the table and locked hands. His face got beet red straining to force me down. I kept us vertical for awhile. Didn't want to embarrass him. Then I slowly muscled his hand flat on the table. He threw down the rest of his drink and left me sitting there."

"You saw him again?"

"At a White House conference. I walked over to him, shook his hand, and asked him how he was. 'Strong', he said, and turned to talk to a Senator."

"Amazing how deeply some men react to a put-down."

"Put-down? He brought it on himself."

"All the more so."

Barker paused. I'm running off at the mouth, he cautioned himself. Bad as Cutler. Carrying a grudge too.

"Rosie," he said brightly. "One of the many things I admire about you is that you listen, and that's important."

"I've never found you engaging in talk talk," she said. You have something in mind."

"I suppose you're right. Dow Jones has just put the spotlight on General Tech and Hi Tech in the crash investigation. Probably why both stocks are at a new low. Their blades or our disks. So I think Cutler and I will be squaring off again."

"He plays rough I've heard."

"That's just it. I'm going to need your help. We'll play the game his way. Keep an eye on him and his people. I wouldn't put anything past him. Until the investigation is concluded, I want you to spend full time doing what you need to do to protect our interests. Consider your mission a black op reporting directly to me. Sorta like old times. "

Rosie sat up. "Yes Sir!"

Yes, sorta like old times, Rosie mused, as she reached for the Rolodex on her desk. She could use a little excitement, couldn't she? The last three years at General Tech hadn't been exactly soul-stirring; none of the adventure of their years in the military. Now the same focused look, the same measured tone: do what you need to do to protect our interests. No instructions, no questions. Deniability for the boss. Just do it. And they got along just fine. A frightening life at times, but never boring. Better than a life with a husband and a house full of kids, she laughed.

She called Mindy Seltzer, administrative head of the Disk Division. "I need a search of the literature for reports of engine blade failures that have resulted in a fatality," she said. "NTSB reports, newspaper clippings, anything you can dig up. And I need it ASAP."

Then she dialed Craig Cook, a former intelligence officer on her staff in Vietnam, now with the CIA in Miami.

"Craig, I need your help," she said. "The name of a local who could handle a delicate op down there."

"Serious stuff?"

"Well, it is and it isn't. Nobody gets hurt."

"Then your man is Victor Gonzales. Rough but straight. We've used him for borderline stuff. If he can't help you, he'll know who can. Want his number?"

"Yes."

"I'll have my secretary call."

"Thanks, Craig. Hope I can return the favor."

CHAPTER 7

10:45 A.M. EST

Dusty was sweating under the load of the two bags as he approached the FAA operations lounge at Washington National Airport. The smaller, a blue canvas flight bag, largely untouched between trips, contained the basic tools of the investigator: screw driver, pliers, wrenches, a camera, tape recorder, lots of extra tape and film, compass, identification badges, tags for wreckage, a tape measure, and all sorts of forms, grease pencils, and magic markers. The other was stocked with basic articles of clothing, toilet kit, and standard crash site outfit: rugged leather boots, blue coveralls, and matching baseball cap emblazoned with the NTSB emblem. And today, an extra supply of shirts hastily added by his wife.

The FAA hanger manager was on the phone when Dusty entered. "Perfect timing," he said, cupping his hand to the mouthpiece. "Your Miami field rep wants to speak to you."

Dusty dropped his bags near an empty chair then walked to the manager's desk, waving to the five members of the Go Team already gathered in the room. "You're on conference Jose," he said, switching to the speaker phone on the desk so the others could hear.

"No problem. I need an idea of your ETA."

"Twelve noon plus or minus. The Go Team's here except for Pete DiBella and we're expecting him any minute. Can you fill us in a little?"

"You'd better prepare yourself for what you're going to see. There's never been anything like it! Four times as many casualties on the ground as in the plane. And a major fire."

"I heard on the car radio on the way here."

"But we're getting things under control. Except for that shithead Cadiz who calls himself mayor, the cooperation's been great. Especially the National Guard. Between them and the state police we had the crash site completely cordoned off a half hour after the crash."

"What about the runway?"

"Still closed. I have twenty guardsmen walking the last third and on into the rough for another mile."

"Find anything?"

"Nothing but a pissed-off water moccasin. It ain't going to be easy."

Dusty shuddered. Born in the mountains of West Virginia, he hated snakes.

"What about metal detectors?"

"We're using the one the guards brought along and we're scrounging around for more."

"Well, keep at it. We've got to find those parts."

From the tower operator's report of a "massive" engine failure during climb out, Dusty knew the ground below would be littered with parts flung shrapnel-like from the core of the engine rotating at ten thousand rpm. Close examination of these parts—bearings, shafts, blades, and the disks to which the blades are attached—would provide vital clues to the initial point of failure.

"We have the number three engine secured. Off site; three blocks away in a guy's swimming pool."

Eight thousand pounds! Three blocks away? Dusty flinched at his sharp sensation of the forces involved.

"When the main wing spar met the building's steel columns number three engine just kept going. Lucky it did because you'd have had a helluva time getting to it in that wreckage. And it's the suspect engine. Number two's no problem. We'll be able to get it out of the tail with a crane tomorrow."

"And number one?"

"Must be somewhere in the ruins."

"Any indications?"

"Indications?? Of what?"

"Actual engine failure. You have number three in hand."

"Yeah, at the bottom of a pool. For Christ sakes Dusty! Lay off. I'm busy out of my fuckin mind setting up a command post and securing three separate sites, and you guys get here and you ask me a dumb ass question like that an hour after the crash. You expect me to dive in and have a look?"

"Sorry."

"This place is a madhouse. Three dozen ambulances from all over, nine med-vac helicopters, more fire fighting equipment than you'll ever want to see in one place and still coming. I-95's bumper to bumper out as far as you can see. With all that jet fuel loose we're lucky the foam trucks were able to get here. Dumb luck too that there was an Amhoist truck mounted crane at work nearby. Now that the fire's under control, she's being maneuvered into place to hoist rescue workers to retrieve the dead and injured from the top rooms. We thought she could reach the aft door of the fuselage, too, but she just misses. The National Guard called in a Skyhawk twin rotor helicopter for a hover retrieval of the passengers."

Horrified at the thought, Dusty pictured the plane's near vertical fuselage and the scene inside: passengers burned beyond recognition fastened in their seats; loose bodies in a smoldering heap at the bottom end. "Any chance of survivors?"

"No way. And it's hard to imagine many survived in the building except the few who escaped before it went over. I've heard there were over sixteen hundred guests. Would have been more except for off-season."

"But the tail section's intact you say."

"Don't you worry," Jose snapped. "The flight recorders are safe. It'll be one hell of a job, but we'll have them out of the tail and ready for Washington by later today."

"Pete DiBella's here," Dusty said abruptly, feeling put down. "I've got to go. Where have you set up the command center?"

"The Sheraton River House next to the airport."

"See you there."

*   *   *

A man dressed as a maintenance worker knocked on the door of the conference room of the Sheraton River House which Jose had leased earlier in the day as the Safety Board's command center. When no one answered he glanced up and down the hall, donned a pair of gloves, then opened the door and slipped inside, locking the door behind him. At the conference table, he replaced its stock ashtrays with the two he had brought along in a carry bag. They were of a more elaborate design, glass bowls resting in a carved wooden base. Then, removing a screwdriver from his leather tool belt, he hurried on to the single phone on a table in one corner of the room and removed its back plate. In less than a minute he had crimped into place a transistorized transmitter no larger than a matchbook. He replaced the plate, called the local weather station to make sure the phone was working, then left and took the service elevator to a third floor room directly over the command center. A neatly dressed young man in a seersucker jacket, oxford blue shirt and red striped tie answered the door and handed him an envelope. Behind him sat another man in shirtsleeves wearing headphones plugged into a tape recorder. "The call came through loud and clear," he said to the visitor. "Glad to hear this heat wave's about to break."

All seven men were aboard the FAA Gulfstream when the hanger manager ran onto the tarmac waving his arms. The copilot opened the door.

"Got a message for Dusty!" he shouted above the scream of the engines. "Jose's calling again. Wants to get word to him before he leaves."

Dusty appeared in the doorway. "Yo."

"Says to tell you he just heard from the search team. Found what he thinks is a first-stage compressor fan blade in the swamp grass bordering the drainage ditch at the end of the runway. It was fractured near the root dovetail as best he could tell from word from the field. Any of this make sense?"

Root dovetail? The point of maximum stress, Dusty speculated. Blade failure? Could have caused the crash. "I read you. Anything else?"

"Part of the engine cowling with half its fan blade containment ring."

"That all?"

"He thought you might like to know before you leave."

"You betcha. Thanks."

The plane taxied out. Dusty returned to his window seat next to Pete DiBella. "Don't get up," he said, squeezing his way past Pete who sat with a lap full of manuals and reports fat with information on the make and model of the engines known to have been powering the crashed plane.

"What do you think?" Dusty asked after relaying Jose's message.

"Gotta be an uncontained engine failure. I had a hunch that was it from what Lieberman told me over the phone. Now all we've got to do is dope out the failure mode. And why this one ended in fatalities."

Dusty knew that uncontained engine failures were a frequent cause of aircraft accidents—two hundred and two non-containment "events" in a seven year period, according to a recent NTSB Special Study.

"Remember Colts Neck?" he asked, referring to an L-1011 climbing out of Newark over Colts Neck, New Jersey.

Pete glanced at him . "Remember it? You kidding? How can I forget? We had a twofer that day. Two majors within hours of each other. You went off to Colts Neck and I left for Miami International with your backup duty officer."

"You're right. I am losing my marbles. The day of the Air Florida accident."

"The report's here in the stack," Pete said, opening to a page and pointing to the abstract. "It's virtually the same as Colts Neck except it involved failure in the turbine section, not the loss of the compressor fan disk and its blades."

*   *   *

"About 1848 e.d.t., September 22, 1981, Air Florida Airlines, Flight 2198, a McDonnell-Douglas, Inc., D-10-30CF sustained an uncontained failure of its right underwing engine (No.3) during the takeoff roll at the Miami International Airport, Miami, Florida. The engine failure occurred at about 90 knots indicated airspeed; the pilot rejected takeoff and stopped the aircraft safely.

"The aircraft was damaged by the release of high energy engine debris. The resultant damage caused an uncommanded retraction of the right wing outboard leading edge slat. Components of the No. 3 engine control system and fire protection system, the electrical system, and the Nos. 1 and 3 hydraulic systems were also damaged by engine debris.

"The National Transportation Safety Board determines that the probable cause of this accident was the failure of quality control inspections to detect the presence of foreign material in the low pressure turbine cavity during the reassembly of the low pressure turbine module after installation of the stage one low pressure turbine rotor disk."

"How do you like that for bureaucratic gobbledygook?" Pete said. ". . . the presence of 'foreign material.' Shit! We traced it to five pieces of M-50 alloy steel like the kind used in tools. Some dumb ass mechanic left his wrench in there."

Dusty was busy thinking about the current disaster. "So far we've found a broken fan blade and half the blade containment ring. Maybe we're looking at blade failure," he said.

"Or a disk or bearing failure. How about a bird strike or screwdriver?" Pete said. "Who knows? We'll have to find out, won't we?"

He continued to thumb through the report while Dusty, pen in hand, began outlining his on-site organization chart, a format he had invented to keep track of the makeup of the working groups as the representatives of the "parties"—Cross Country Airlines, Ambassador Aircraft, Power Technology, ALPA and FAA—began to arrive at the crash scene. With so much at stake additional parties would no doubt show up, certainly the blade and disk suppliers, and perhaps other engine component manufacturers. He reached into his go bag, snipped off a piece of scotch tape and taped a slice of paper to the right hand side of his chart to allow for additions.

ON SITE ORGANIZATION CHART

PARTY → WORKING GROUP ↓	AIRLINE CROSS COUNTRY AIRLINES	AIRFRAME AMBASSADOR AIRCRAFT	ENGINES POWER TECHNOLOGY	ALPA	FAA
STRUCTURES MUNSON					
POWER PLANTS DIBELLA					
OPERATIONS ABERNATHY					
SYSTEMS MINSKY					
SURVIVAL FACTORS YOUNTS					
HUMAN PERFORMANCE WOOD					

IIC— McGINTY
BOARD MEMBER - LEMAY
PUBLIC AFFAIRS - SINGLETON

Dusty studied his handiwork. I'll be ready for them, he thought. Let 'em come.

*   *   *

The Sheraton River House was a good choice as the command center, Dusty thought, as his plane approached Miami. Close to the airport and crash site, and with enough accommodations for the scores of men whose names would soon fill the blank spaces

in his chart, it also contained an auditorium ideal for daily brief-
ings of the press and the eventual public hearing.

Dusty knew that after the working groups were formed, forty
or so men would leave the center for the crash site with a com-
mon aim: to find out what happened. He also knew that as the
investigation began to focus on all the things that didn't happen,
one or more parties would feel the finger of blame pointing at
them and start building defenses. And they would do anything
to prevent penetration of these defenses, he reminded himself,
remembering all the badgering, all the attempted bribes, all the
political pressure he had experienced over the years. Now, with
so much at stake, he would be hounded unmercifully from all
sides.

Dusty smiled. There you go again! Bragging through com-
plaining. Center stage. Isn't that where you like to be? Lighten
up. It isn't often you get to be at the center of something
really big.

Dusty directed the pilot to fly low over the crash site as they
neared Miami International. Through binoculars, he viewed the
cordoned off area near I-95. In the middle of it all lay the toppled
building, oblong in a pall of sooty smoke. A tangle of cables and
pipes hung from its base like the roots of a storm felled tree. The
structural steel framework, denuded of its floor to ceiling glass
panes, remained surprisingly intact except for the severely dis-
torted area around the fire blackened fuselage and tail section of
the plane that was still stuck deep in its innards. Rescue workers,
fitted in their protective clothing and breathing apparatus, were
lowering bodies from the top rooms to the ground one by one
on a stretcher rig under the crane's hook while others entered
outer rooms of the building through the empty window frames
and removed the dead and injured with hook and ladder equip-

ment and smaller cranes. The Skyhawk helicopter hovered over the plane, a rescuer being lowered by cable to the rear cabin door.

As he continued to watch, part of Dusty's brain tried to relate what he was seeing to the abstract equations in the monographs that occasionally came across his desk on the effect of aircraft "impacting" tall buildings. The Germans, especially, were concerned about their nuclear power plants located in many instances near NATO airbases. But now, as he continued to survey the scene, he was sickened by the sight. "Goddamit!" he exclaimed. "It had to happen one day. All those fucking hi-rises around airports."

Pete reached for his arm. "You're going to make yourself sick. Let's get down to work."

"I will. I just need some time. I know what we're going to see."

"You think I don't?" Pete said.

"Yeah. Let's get down to work."

They were briefly silent.

"Who manufactured those blades, do you know?" Dusty asked.

"Cast Profiles in Waukegan."

"Damn! That's Alan Fisk's company." Poor guy, I hope it's not the blades. He'd shoulder all the blame again.

"A friend of yours, isn't he?"

"A good friend, ever since my first investigation as IIC—a blade failure over Albuquerque. Remember that one?"

"Yeah."

"I don't think Alan's ever gotten the pictures of the man out of his mind. The original straight shooter. All through the investigation he was too concerned about the victim, too concerned about getting at the truth, to spend time pointing fingers like the rest of the bunch. And when it was determined that his blade, not engine overspeed, was at fault, he was quick to accept blame although it almost busted his company. He's my kind of man."

"You ever see him anymore?"

"Not for awhile."

"They're now part of Hi Tech, you know. Merged about a year ago."

"Wait a minute. Hi Tech? That's Cass Cutler's company!"

"Right."

"Shit! Alan's one of the most honest men I've ever met. And now I may have to investigate him again in a possible blade failure case. He'll be trying to play it straight, and if my past experience with Cutler is any indication, he'll do anything, I mean anything, to have Hi Tech come out of it clean."

Wait a minute, Dusty reflected. I haven't seen Alan for a couple of years. I've gotta call him. Feel him out, see where he stands with Cutler. You never know. Funny things happen to guys.

The wind direction had shifted since morning, requiring the plane to approach Miami International from the west over Big Cypress National Preserve. Dusty looked out the window at the dozens of National Guardsmen searching the marshland beyond, filled with ponds, lagoons and drainage ditches. Fuckin snakes! he thought. I'm stay'n outta there.

CHAPTER 8

11:30 A.M. CST

Come on, guys, Fisk thought. He was sitting at his desk, waiting for news from his team in Waukegan. Gimmie a break. The whole morning shot on the phone and still not a word about the Starflight's blades inspection documentation. He shifted restlessly in his chair and reached for the phone. "Get me Mike Belmonte," he said, referring to his number two man whom he had carefully groomed to take over one day.

"What the hell's going on up there, Mike? I need that information. Need it bad."

"We've been scrambling all morning. Haven't been able to connect with the right people at Power Technology to get the order number for that particular Starflight's blades . Without it, we can't check our inspection records for possible defects. If you think things are in a frenzy around Hi Tech, think of what's happening over there."

Fisk was angry at himself for not anticipating the problem. Of course they're busy at Power Technology. Anxious like the rest of us. "Then what do we do?" he asked. "Can't wait all day."

"Stay on top. Minutes ago I found out that our acquisition in Sedalia has supplied replacement blades for Starflights over the years. Waukegan thought we were the sole supplier. Apparently they slipped in. On price, probably."

"Sedalia!" Fisk said, his pulse racing. "We've never heard that."

"We're finding there's a lot they never told us before the acquisition."

Fisk paused, incredulous. "You're sure of your ground? No rumors."

"Certain."

So they could have been Sedalia's blades, not ours! He was speechless, stilled by a tidal wave of relief.

"You still there?" Mike asked.

"Yes."

"Thinking, I'll bet. How nice if it turned out they were on that plane."

Fisk didn't appreciate being reminded. "Have you tried getting through to CCA's maintenance department? They'll know in a minute whether they were Sedalia's."

"They don't answer the phone."

"Keep trying. Make it the order of the day. Maybe you'll know something before I leave for Florida."

"When's that?"

"The evening flight. Think it's possible?"

"I doubt it. But I've got an idea. I have a friend in their overhaul center. He's down the line but I think he may have access to the information."

"Go to it! I'll call you from O'Hare."

Fisk put down the receiver and exhaled deeply. Could it be true? he asked himself. Oh, God, I hope so. But even though they may not be my blades, Hi Tech owns Sedalia, so there's going to be trouble either way.

He glanced at his watch. Time for the midday news. He hurried to the board room and turned to Channel Four.

"We have a late breaking story for you, folks," anchorman Don Raucher said, standing on a grassy knoll with the crash scene in the distance. "The renowned crash litigator, Jack Schnell, has set up offices in Chicago and Miami and is already at work signing up relatives of the deceased in a class action suit . . ."

Fisk slapped the sides of his chair in disgust. Schnell! The louse who handled the Albuquerque suit. Didn't mean shit to him that I took responsibility. Did everything he could to make me out a money grubbing, hardhearted, businessman.

". . . The death toll stands at seven hundred eighty-three, and climbing. Authorities are estimating a count of fifteen hundred dead, and hundreds more injured—the worst crash in airline history . . ."

He'll have a field day.

". . . And now for another Channel Four on site exclusive . . ."

Fisk stared at the sight of a telephoto close-up of the plane's fuselage, blackened and splotched with a layer of white foam, now canted at an angle of thirty degrees to the flattened building. The camera focused on a jagged hole where the jammed rear door had been cut away. Two rescue workers were struggling with a black body bag as a stretcher rig being lowered by cable from a large helicopter descended toward the opening. Removing the bodies with a Skyhawk, Fisk thought. Ingenious.

Raucher reappeared on the screen. "We are fortunate to have with us the first man to enter the fuselage by helicopter after the fire was extinguished." He turned and extended his hand to a short, balding, man, his face still marked with the heart shaped outline of a tight fitting oxygen mask. "Mel Trimble from Miami Station House 39 rescue squad. Tell us, Mel, what did it feel like up there?"

"Just awful, Don. You know, like climbing into a tomb. Pitch black except for little rays of light where the fuselage buckled open. Spooky, you know. When I turned my lamp on, I saw the first two bodies strapped in their seats near the door. Looked like they was charred barbecue, they did."

Fisk's stomach turned at the thought.

"Hot it was, too. When I returned I advised the captain to schedule short rounds for the men, half hour at most in that hellhole. The smell gets you too, even through the mask. Horrible. Have you ever smelt burned people, Don?"

Fisk gasped. For christsakes, Mel. Cut it.

"Watch it, Mel. There are relatives out there," Raucher said quickly.

"Sorry, Don, but that's the way it is. Horrible, just horrible!"

Change the subject, Don, Fisk prayed.

"The steep angle of the fuselage, did that give you trouble?"

"The worst. We were always struggling uphill, oxygen packs and all. Had to rig up a rope and pulley from the rear bulkhead to haul the bodies to the opening . . ."

Raucher cupped his hand over his earphone and listened intently. "Sorry to cut this short, folks, but the NTSB Go Team has just arrived at Miami International."

Fisk studied the eight members of the Team surrounded by state troopers making their way through the crowded terminal. That looks like Dusty McGinty . . . I'll be damned. It is Dusty! Past security they faced a tumultuous mob of reporters and photographers. The crowd surged; bulbs flashed; shoulder mounted cameras whirred. Surrounded by troopers like prize athletes heading to the locker room after a game, the team moved briskly toward the exit and a waiting van.

"Was it an engine failure?" a reporter called out."

Mat Kalitinsky, the team's P.R. man, moved swiftly to the side of Dusty walking at the head of the group. "Too early to comment," Kalitinsky said. "Mr. McGinty here, the Investigator In Charge, will hold a press briefing tonight in the Sheraton auditorium."

Dusty, the IIC? He'll be busy out of his mind. No time to see me tonight.

"Give us background on the Go Team!" another reporter shouted, thrusting a microphone toward Kalitinsky. "People want to know about them, how they got to the job. How about you, Mr. McGinty?"

"Later," Kalitinsky said. "I'll have copy for you tomorrow."

Copy, Fisk thought. The usual poop. Dustin McGinty, former TWA pilot. born in . . . Bor ing. She'll never hear the real reason he's where he is—seeing his father die in a crash on approach to Kennedy that never should have happened. When he confided the story, I knew we were friends.

Fisk watched the Go Team enter the van, then returned to his office. There he sat staring at a miniature copy of "ARTIFACTS" on his desk. He felt shaky, unsettled. Charred barbecue! Another nightmare in the making. Would he ever forget the image? Was he responsible for all the pain and suffering? It had happened twice in the past, hadn't it? Albuquerque and yes, that night outside Pasadena . . .

Fisk was attending Cal Tech under the GI Bill after a hitch in the Navy. Driving to Pasadena with three roommates after a few beers at a bar in nearby Azusa, he was horsing around with the boys who were sprawled in the backseat of his prewar Ford. The road was narrow and dark, and as he rounded a curve, he drove over the centerline. Startled by a blaring horn and the glare of headlights, he turned to face an oncoming car. Fisk swerved to the right in time to avoid a head-on, but his rear fender struck the other car, spinning it out of control into the side of a stone culvert. The driver was thrown clear but as Fisk looked on terror-stricken, the man still alive and struggling to stand was engulfed in flames from gasoline flowing from the ruptured fuel tank.

"Oh my God!" Fisk shouted. "Please . . . please . . . no!" and bolted from the car to the edge of the pool of burning fuel, his hand outstretched in a futile gesture of help. Forced back by the blistering heat, he could only watch. The man collapsed to his knees, now barely visible among the roiling flames, with his head thrust back, mouth agape in a show of excruciating agony—screaming, screaming. Fisk again surged toward the flames, but again he was forced back. The man's screams quieted. His hair now gone and his clothes reduced to smoldering patches of fabric hanging from his tortured skin, his movements slowed and finally stopped. Rigid on all fours, his mouth was still agape even as his swollen lips began to bubble and crack.

Fisk, faint from the suffocating smell of gasoline and burning flesh, ran toward the car. "Do something!" he called out to his roommates still frozen in inaction. "Can't you help me? . . . Help me," he implored, his voice trailing off. For suddenly it became clear to him there was no one to help. The man was gone and he had killed him.

Fisk's secretary, Allison, announced that Dusty McGinty was on the line.

Dusty? Calling me? With all the pressure he's under. Uh, oh.

"Where've you been hiding out?" Dusty said. "I've sorta lost track of you."

"Not hiding, Dusty. Working my ass off. We've had some pretty major changes here."

"So I hear. You're now part of Hi Tech."

"Martha thought I was ready for a mid-course correction."

"The male menopause, you mean. But how in the hell did a nice guy like you get tied up with a shithead like Cass Cutler? He has the morals of a Saigon pimp."

He's telling me something. Does he know Cutler? Is there something between them?

"Take it easy on him. He does a lot of good things."

"So did Hitler."

"Whew!" Fisk said. "I'm not listening to the old pussycat I knew. What did he do to you?"

"Remind me to tell you sometime."

Allison entered the room and slipped Fisk a note. "Mr. Cutler has returned and wants to see you." He cupped his hand over the mouthpiece and whispered, "five minutes."

"Did you get my call this morning?" Fisk asked.

"No. I must have already started down."

"I recognized you leading the charge at the airport; heard you're the IIC."

"Saw the mob scene, eh? A little quieter at the moment, so I thought I'd call you."

Can't be that quiet. He's at the center of a fucking whirl-wind. So why did he call? What's he getting at?

"Is it as bad as it seems, Dusty?"

"Worse, lots worse. The ultimate nightmare. Far worse than Chicago. Makes TWA 800 look like kid stuff. And it's just my luck to be IIC on this one too." Dusty paused. "Alan, I hate to tell you this, but you'll find out soon enough. We've found one of your first-stage fan blades half a mile beyond the runway. Fractured near the root dovetail, they tell me. And one-half the fan containment ring further on."

A blade fractured . . . at the usual point of failure . . . Fisk's body shook with fear. *And the containment ring let loose? Musta been a hell of a force.*

Fisk was speechless. In his mind's eye he saw the fan disk with blades attached rotating at ten thousand rpm, the roots of the eighteen inch blades under maximum stress at take off power. Suddenly a blade with minute defects fails and . . . *Dusty, would he know whether they were Sedalia's blades or mine . . . no, of course not . . .*

"Alan?"

"I'm here, just a little shell shocked. Have you been able to retrieve the flight recorders?"

"Not yet. I'm going up myself as soon as the rescue squad finishes with the bodies."

"What about the disk? Is there any evidence that . . ."

"Whoa, man, you're way ahead of me. I didn't mean to scare you. Under the circumstances, I knew you'd want to be represented as one of the parties. I'm in the middle of organizing the teams now."

Under the circumstances. What's he really thinking? That the blades are at fault? Does he know more than he's letting on?

"Ed Schmidt, our Chief Engineer, will be on the next plane," he said. "You know him?"

"Good man."

"I'll be down as soon as I can—some time tonight."

"Great. I'd love to see you—hear how you're getting along with my friend Cutler."

Ah, so that's it. Where do I stand with the boss. He's wondering whether I've become a company man.

"I'll be late. After eleven."

"All the better. Call me in my room at the Sheraton River House when you arrive. I'll be finished with my first press briefing. By then I'll be ready for a drink."

"Where the hell have you been?" Cutler demanded as Fisk entered the office. "My secretary called five minutes ago."

Fisk bridled. What's the rush? "Five minutes and you're making a federal case of it? Come off it Cass, not today. I've got too much else on my mind."

Cutler grasped the arms of his chair in anger.

"I was on the phone with the IIC in Miami when your secretary buzzed," Fisk explained. "Dusty McGinty," he added. "The IIC."

Fisk noticed Cutler's stony, get-on-with-it silence. *So there is something between them.*

"The news isn't good," he said. "Early indications were that there was a massive engine failure. Now I've learned that a first-stage fan blade was found a half mile beyond the runway. And one-half the fan containment ring further on."

"You got that from McGinty?"

"A few minutes ago. I don't think it's out yet."

"He's a friend of yours?"

"We met years ago during his investigation of the Albuquerque incident. Yes, I consider him a friend." He's thinking that over. "Why, do you know him?"

Cutler dismissed the question with a flick of his wrist. "What about the disk?"

"No word."

"You didn't ask him?"

"He cut me short; had to go."

Should I tell him I'll see him tonight? No. Don't show your hand until you know what's up with the two of them.

"So where do we stand?" Cutler asked. "Our directors are hounding me for a report."

"I've spent the morning with my men at Waukegan trying to tie down the serial numbers of the blades so we can check our control samples for any defects before they left our plant. No luck so far. PT has to supply that information and we've not been able to get through. To further complicate our investigation, we've just learned that the culprit could be Sedalia's blades. They've made replacements for the airline's maintenance center in the past. The airline's not answering either."

Fisk was surprised at Cutler's sardonic smile.

"Sedalia, not your plant. Feel relieved?"

Fisk bristled at the slur. True, but why did he have to throw it up? "What are you trying to do, Cass? Knuckle me under? Is this a game of gotcha?"

Cutler glared at him. "Not a game. Whichever plant, Hi Tech's on the hook. And I want you to know I expect your loyalty to the company, its employees, and stockholders, no matter where those blades were manufactured. Now let's get on with it."

"Our chief engineer is on his way to Miami with his team to handle the field investigation."

"What about you?"

"Off to Miami this evening. I'm going to do everything I can to show the victims and their families that this company cares."

"You're what?"

"Flying to Miami to visit the area hospitals tomorrow."

Cutler's eyes assumed a threatening, hooded look. "This morning I told you that nobody, and nobody includes you, speaks to the outside world on this matter except Sperling in Corporate Affairs. That schlock lawyer Schnell and the media would cut you up in pieces and feed you to the sharks in Biscayne Bay."

Fisk throttled his anger, suddenly aware his hands were shaking. "I'm president of the division and I owe it to the victims whether Hi Tech's responsible or not."

"But I'm CEO of this company, and don't you forget it. We'll do as I say. Both of us. You too!"

Fisk felt his neck burn with rage. Goddamit! I've had enough. "I'm going and you can't stop me," he said levelly. "If all you care about is the company, that's your business. But listen to me carefully, Cass. That's not where I'm coming from. I want to see the victims get a fair shake."

"You won't go, and that's a direct order!"

"Bullshit. You know as well as I do you can't afford to fire me now. And you know and I know I won't quit. We also know this isn't all bad as far as you're concerned. For the foreseeable future I'll be busting my ass to give our employees and stockholders, as well as the victims, a fair shake whether or not it's Sedalia."

"Well, now," Cutler remarked with a smirk. "A boy scout with guts."

Fisk knew that Cutler was backing off and let the crack pass. When you lose, say little. When you win say nothing.

"Has Burke briefed you?" Cutler asked.

"Doesn't have to. I know the ins and outs of a crash investigation."

"Then you'll do me the favor of remembering to be careful about anything for the record, especially penciled notes, memos, anything. I want the files clean. Burke tells me that Schnell is preparing a class action suit and that we're being named as one of the parties. All these things are discoverable in a suit and I don't want any admission in the records that can be used against us."

"Even if it's the truth?"

"Especially if it's the truth. There's too much at stake. We have to be in the clear."

Their eyes met.

Then I have some serious thinking to do, Fisk thought.

"Keep me advised," Cutler said.

Fisk plopped into his office chair. *Shit! Money under the table to a senator, and now this. Maybe he would do anything when Hi Tech's fortunes are at stake. And if that's so . . .* He glanced at his watch. *One o'clock. Otto Gitner, I almost forgot. We're meeting for a drink at six. I can talk it out with him.*

CHAPTER 9

1:00 P.M. CST

Cutler paced his office after Fisk left. "Truth . . . !" he muttered. If I hear that word one more time I'm going to bust him in his yap. How can a well-educated, successful guy like that be so stupid about some things? Hell, maybe I've got myself one of those self destructive types. McGinty tells him it looks like engine failure, one of his blades was found on the ground, and he's so bound up in his own guilt he doesn't even think to ask about the disk.

He returned to his desk and punched the symbol HTH into his computer. I knew it! Off another six points since lunch. The market knows about the blade. Barker! I'll bet he's happy.

He stabbed at the computer's keys. Shit! General Tech up eleven and a half points. "Get me Bledsoe on his beeper," he told his secretary. "Where are you, Joe?" he asked when Bledsoe came on.

"At the crash site. I'm tracking McGinty nearby. Heard he's waiting for a helicopter to fly him to the tail of the Starflight to retrieve the black boxes."

"Good. Any other news? I'm leaving for the B'Nai B'Rith dinner in an hour. Unless it's an emergency, I'll be out of pocket until eleven."

"About time they recognized you. You deserve it, Chief."

"Yeah, yeah . . . the news, Joe, the news."

"Not good. They've found one of our blades ejected from the engine."

"Seems like everybody knows. That guy McGinty has let it get out."

"The one you had a run in with some years ago."

Did I tell Joe that?

"He's no friend of mine," Cutler hedged. "A buddy of Fisk's. Keep an eye on the two of them. Fisk is flying down tonight. He's set on visiting the area hospitals tomorrow. Wants to show the victims and their families he cares."

"And to hell with the company."

"You got it. So pick him up in the morning. Make the rounds with him, and call me. Any other news?"

"General Tech signed up as one of the parties."

"Spare me. That's news?"

"No, wait a minute. Their plane arrived with a woman on board. She's not part of their technical team. Rosie Donovan, Barker's Vice President for Special Projects. I've watched her poking around."

"You've heard of her?"

"Just what I learned from one of their engineers. Sounds like a tough cookie; was with Sam Barker in Vietnam—his Intelligence Officer. Stuck with him through the years."

"I see what you mean. Interesting. See what more you can find out and call me. Barker's up to something."

Barker . . . Cutler thought, alone in his office. Sounds like he's already started building the stockade. May have found something was wrong with the production run for that disk. I'd better call him. Feel him out; see where he stands.

"This is a pleasant surprise, Cass." Barker said. "How are ya big man? How's the arm? Staying healthy?"

Healthy! Had to dig me, didn't he? "Strong, Sam, strong. And you?"

"Oh, getting along. Busy with acquisitions the past year to counter all the military cut backs. Hits the bottom line pretty hard until you've been able to consolidate plants and make the layoffs. I see you've been doing a few acquisitions yourself."

Good try, Sam. Nice lead in . . . Oh, yes, Cast Profiles, the company whose blades just brought down that fully loaded passenger plane.

Fuck you.

"The medical equipment group we bought in ninety four is backlogged through two thousand," Cutler said. "Helps even out the downsizing. Actually, we're looking for a record first half."

Your turn.

"Good move on your part. We all need more winners like that."

Silence.

Cutler waited. He'd be damned if he'd be the first to speak of the crash.

"What's on your mind, Cass?" Barker said sharply.

What could he say? How's the world treating you old friend? He'd been euchred.

"This morning's crash. Our lawyer tells me Jack Schnell is preparing a class action suit naming the bunch of us as parties. Have you heard?"

"Seems fast, even for Schnell. No. Frankly I've been tied up all day in negotiations for another acquisition—a real sockeroo of a deal. I talked with our men in the Disk Division after the crash and they told me the records for the disk on that engine show it left our plant in perfect shape. So I'm letting them handle it. Schnell can do what he wants to do. He always does."

Lying bastard! You're as concerned as I am. They couldn't have checked the records any faster than we have.

"'Course, I guess you're in a little different situation, Cass. That blade they found. I heard about it a half hour ago. You worried?"

God damned McGinty! "It doesn't mean a thing this early."

"Yes, I guess so. Anyhow, I appreciate the call. Let's keep in touch."

*   *   *

Cutler slammed the receiver down. Idiot! What did I accomplish by that? Not a Goddamned thing except to let him humble me again. He sat back and pulled at the flesh that hung from his chin. It's not like me to wade into something without thinking through all the angles . . .

CHAPTER 10

2:00 P.M. EST

Dusty watched the Skyhawk land in a grassy area near the crash site. One by one, twenty in all, the last body bags were unloaded onto stretchers by the rescue squad and taken to waiting ambulances. Mel Trimble stepped out of the helicopter and approached him. "That's the last of 'em," he said, removing his mask. "Disgusting job! You going up there?"

Dusty, uncomfortable in his heavy clothing, leather gloves, and breathing apparatus, saw sweat pouring off Trimble's face. What am I in for? he thought. "Yes," he said. "What's it like?"

"You'll wish you drew some other duty. Cabin's still a stink hole; lots of sharp stuff waiting to stick you. Tough moving around, too. Sorta like going up and down a playground slide in hell." Mel looked him over. "You one of the Go Team?"

"Yeah. I'm after the black boxes."

"In the cabin?"

"No, the belly. The rear cargo bay."

"Won't be no picnic, but at least there won't be no charred barbecue."

Charred barbecue? Does he mean what I think he means?

"The passengers. Were they badly burned?"

"Beyond recognition, a lot of them thrown in a heap up front, sorta welded together. Had to pull 'em apart. At least they weren't spread all over the ground for the ghouls to see. A few at the bottom of the pile were even lying there real peaceful like; fuckin flames couldn't get at 'em . . ."

Dusty cringed. Sorry I asked. But true. The poor souls did have some privacy; no body parts hanging from tree limbs.

"One guy in a pin stripe suit looked right out of Macy's— except for the hole in the bottom of one of his fancy shoes. You get to see people's little secrets, you know." A sly grin flitted across his face.

Yes, I do know, and it's not funny, Dusty thought, remembering a gray headed victim of TWA 800 bobbing face down in the glare of a boat's searchlight off Long Island stripped of his clothing except for white boxer shorts emblazoned with the words: "LOVE ME." Poor man. You see things you were never meant to see.

"Gotta go," Dusty said as he heard the swish, swish of the Skyhawk's rotors. On board, National Guardsman Hank Jasper fitted him with a belted sling attached to a cable from the drum of a power winch. Dusty fingered the belt's quick disconnect attachment, then scrutinized the winch. So you'll be dangling hundreds of feet in the air at the end of that thing. So what? . . . So you're scared shitless, man, admit it!

"Takes some getting used to, I know," Hank said. "But the guys gettin the bodies picked it up in a hurry. We'll be hovering over the tail steady as we can. The thing to remember is that the air gets fluky from the heat rising from the ruins, and you may get banged around when you're about to enter. So watch the rough edges. First crew up there didn't waste any time tearing open all the doors."

I'm getting the picture!

"Take this pole hook with you. The trick is to stick it inside when your feet reach the floor. Grab on to something with it, anything that will help you pull forward a little. I'll be watching. When I see your feet touch and you leaning in, I'll quick give the cable some slack so you can disconnect. But do it in a hurry. If we get an up draft, you can be yanked back out."

Or fall out after disconnect if I lose my balance.

"I'll reel a basket down for the flight recorders when you signal. Heavy are they?"

"About fifty pounds in all."

"Roger."

The chopper took off and headed for the plane. Dusty sat on a bench, preoccupied with thoughts of the job ahead. Unique, wasn't it? Not the classic drill for retrieving the boxes from a land crash: Anyone who sees one first grabs it. With the plane sticking tail up out of the ruins, he was facing a one man high-wire act that belonged in a circus. But this time he knew exactly where the boxes were. The only problem was getting there.

Hank handed him the pole hook when they began hovering a hundred feet over the tail. "Signal me if you're in difficulty."

Dusty walked to the open door and looked down. He shook his head. Are you out of your fucking mind, he thought, and stepped off into space.

The rotors' violent down-wash sent him gyrating about as he descended. Halfway down the turbulence began to slacken, and he focused on the approaching cargo door. Damn! How'm I gonna do this? This baby's not like the cabin door above Trimble and his men've been entering through. The belly down here curves inward. Opposite the opening, he looked up. Just what I thought. The cable's against the fuselage and holding me off. He looked at his feet dangling in space. Too far out to pull myself in. Maybe I should signal Hank . . .

"Hell, no!" he whooped, feeling simultaneously daring and foolish, and put the end of the pole hook on the side of the fuselage and pushed hard. Like the weight at the end of a hundred foot pendulum, he swung ten feet out, then when the cable hit the upper fuselage on the return, he was flung forcefully through the opening narrowly missing the jagged edges.

Please, dear God, no up-drafts now!

He pulled the disconnect and crashed to the canted floor. Dazed, he tumbled down the slope and came to an abrupt stop against a jumble of smashed cargo containers that had surged forward in the bay at impact. He reached for the flashlight in his pocket and shined it around. Mel was right; fuckin stink hole; couple of poor dogs dead in their cages. At least no bodies.

Dusty knew from his study of the Starflight's systems manual that the cockpit voice recorder and the flight data recorder with a running record of important parameters such as airspeed and altitude were located next to the rear pressure bulkhead. Kneeling like a sprinter in a starting crouch, he began inching his way up the steep flooring toward the rear of the bay. There in an electronics rack on the starboard side he found the two recorders—steel boxes each about the size of a shoe box. They were fire-blackened, now truly the "black boxes" of the popular press, not their original international orange color. But will they tell us anything? he wondered in his moment of excitement. All you often heard was the split second professionalism of men in a desperate situation—keep the blue side up—and the horror of the last moments—I love you, Mom!

Dusty reached for his walkie talkie dangling from his belt and called Pete DiBella standing by at command headquarters. "I have them in hand," he said.

"Hats off! Any damage?"

"Good as new except for intense heat. Not enough to matter."

"The G-4 is waiting at the airport. How soon can you get down?"

"Maybe half-hour."

"I'll have a car waiting. Tom Beebe will be standing by at Washington National. I told him you want a transcript of the tapes as soon as possible, especially the CVR. With any luck, we may get a quick read on the cause of this one."

"Like the charter out of the Dominican Republic in 96," Dusty said, referring to the crash off the coast of a plane filled with German tourists. Information from the recorders recovered in seven thousand feet of water by a robot led to early determination of the probable cause.

"Hope so," Pete said. "We're due for one after TWA. Hurry on back."

CHAPTER 11

6:00 P.M. EST

Tom Beebe, a young black man in his mid-thirties with a perpetual air of nonchalance, felt an intoxicating surge of self-importance as the Safety Board's van pulled in front of the Department of Transportation's building on Independence Avenue. He knew the press would be waiting as he approached the entrance with his precious cargo in hand. The morning tabloids would feature his picture entering the building with the "black boxes" just recovered from the scene of the most calamitous plane crash in history. For days reporters would hound him for some hint of their content. His girlfriend would treat him with renewed respect.

At curbside Tom opened the rear door of the van and removed two sealed aluminum suitcases, one containing the cockpit voice recorder, the other the flight data recorder. By now the press had spotted his arrival and swarmed across the entrance plaza to intercept him. "No comment, no comment!" he repeated as the horde pressed around him, pleading for a glimpse of the instruments themselves, or at least some idea of their condition.

Once inside the building and through security he took the elevator to the eighth floor headquarters of the Safety Board and went directly to the Flight Recorder Laboratory, locking the door behind him. At the official playing of the tapes in a few days, representatives of the parties sworn to secrecy would be present. For the moment, Tom, as head of the lab, had been instructed by

Dusty to listen to the tapes alone, then call him at the command center with a transcript of the CVR as soon as possible.

He entered a small soundproof conference room equipped to listen to the recorders and removed the CVR, a steel box 5x12x7 inches and weighing 24 pounds from the suitcase. Thank God it looks in good condition! He placed it on the conference table and went to work, first unscrewing the side plate, then removing the crash-resistant alloy steel shell, and finally the thick inner shell of heat insulating material. Good, good so far. He picked up the cassette and examined it. I can't believe it! After all its been through, it's in perfect shape. With the cassette now mounted in one of the room's two playback machines, he switched first to the pilot to copilot mike, one of four channels monitored by the recorder. As the tape neared the end he listened intently. "Holy Toledo!!" he exclaimed and pushed the rewind button to replay the ending. He began taking notes of the ending he knew Dusty would want to hear immediately:

Copilot "Vee 1"
Copilot "Vee R"
Copilot "Vee 2"
(Loud bang less than one-fourth second duration)
Captain "Shit! Those fucking blades again."

Tom stared at the notes. Damn! he thought. The power to the recorder had failed an instant later.

It was six forty five P.M. Dusty sat at his conference table in the command center listening to the go team's reports in preparation for the first of his daily meetings with the press. Jose had just finished speaking. "The mayor was actually out on the runway?" Dusty asked.

"Most of the morning with a mob of reporters and photographers in tow. I hear they got pictures of a guardsman carrying the blade."

"That lousy publicity seeking son-of-a-bitch! Doesn't he know he's dealing with the federal government?"

"I turned him away at the crash site, then he took his gang to the airport."

"The runway was secured, wasn't it?"

"He bullied his way past the national guardsman in charge. Said it was the city's airport and as mayor it was his duty to see to it that the press has access so they could report accurately to its citizens."

"Bullshit! They all say that. I'll have his ass thrown in jail if he tries that again." Dusty turned to Rick Munson, head of the structures working group, "Will you take responsibility for forming a sub-group to oversee the runway search? Jose can't be in two places at once and the search is assuming top priority. Pete, do you want to explain?"

"Number one engine is still missing," Pete DiBella said. We're surprised. It must be in the building wreckage somewhere, but we still haven't found it. Number two is still in the tail. I had a look at it from the crane, and aside from some inlet damage, it isn't in bad shape. Tomorrow we'll have it in the hanger for a better check. Number three's a different story. The entire fan section's missing. Disk, blades, everything. And it's clear from what's left they were lost in flight."

"Then everything's pointing to a disk failure in number three," Rick said.

"Whoa, there. You're jumping to conclusions."

"Conclusions my ass. How many times have you seen a blade failure cause the whole damned fan section to exit the engine?"

"Not often. But that's not the point. We've got to find the disk and the rest of the blades, and then determine what did happen, don't we?"

Dusty saw trouble brewing. Pete had been Marine Air. Rick, Navy. They never did get along. "The first order of the day is to find the fan section disk and blades," he interjected. "All agreed?

It won't be easy. There's lots of water and wetlands around. We'll need a lotta footwork."

The phone in the corner rang.

"It's for you Dusty. Tom Beebe calling from Washington."

Tom read Dusty his notes taken from the ending of the tape.

Oh, for Christ's sake! Just what we needed, Dusty thought. "That's what it says?" he exclaimed. "That's all it says?"

"Except for the usual kidding around at the gate, everything was by the book up to that time. Taxi checklist was called out and routine. No flaps up warning horn sounded during takeoff roll. Nothing out of the way until what I just read you."

"And then it ended? Abruptly?"

"Yes."

Dusty cupped his hand over the mouthpiece and turned to the systems expert at the table. "Jay, which engine powers the alternator that supplies electricity to the CVR?"

"Number three according to the aircraft's manual."

"Tom," Dusty said, returning to the phone. "I want you to talk to Hal Lieberman first thing tomorrow. Have him send our guys the airline's complete maintenance records on the plane's engines. Also, details on any in flight engine failures on planes flown by the captain during the past year. And like I said before, don't let those tapes out of your sight."

The man in shirtsleeves in the room three floors directly above removed his headphones and handed them to his associate. "Wanna hear something interesting?" he said.

CHAPTER 12

6:00 P.M. CST

One of the richest men in Chicago, and you'd never know it, Fisk thought when he entered Berghoff Restaurant and saw Otto Gitner at a corner table trimming his frayed shirt cuffs with the scissors of a Swiss army knife. *He can't forget the early days, can he? I love the guy.*

The two men embraced in their usual vigorous bear hug, then sat down. "Terrible crash this morning," Otto said. "Just horrible. I heard the latest count on the way here: twelve hundred and seventy three people already confirmed dead."

The result of the crash on the lips of his friend and mentor made Fisk feel shaky and muddled, unable to reply. *What's happening to me? He was looking forward to their visit. Why this sudden feeling of helplessness, the need for solace?* He stared in silence at the familiar face across the table, the face of the man who had hired him fresh out of Cal Tech, the man who sold him the division he was running and made it possible to own his own company at thirty—the man who knew him better than he knew himself. Tears filled his eyes.

"The crash isn't it?" Otto asked, gently. "Are you involved?"

Fisk felt embarrassed, apologetic. "Yes."

"Do you want to talk to me about it?" Otto reached for his hand. "In confidence, of course."

"I have to get myself together . . ."

"Don't be embarrassed. Take your time. You've been dealing

with the crash all day. This is the first time you've had a chance to disconnect from all the excitement."

"There seems to have been an uncontained engine failure," Fisk said gratefully. "One of our fan blades was found off the end of the runway."

"That doesn't mean your products are at fault, does it?"

"Not yet. But what if they were, what if I messed up, Otto? All those people . . ."

The bartender called across the room. "The usual Mr. Gitner? Large stein of dark?"

"Yes."

"And bourbon on the rocks for you, Mr. Fisk?"

"A double." Fisk wiped his eyes. "The NTSB Go Team is on site since noon and my chief engineer is there by now representing us in the investigation. Dusty McGinty is the IIC—you remember Dusty."

"Good! Good! I know how much he respects you."

"I'm going to see him tonight in Miami."

"Then you're going to be there yourself?"

"To visit the area hospitals tomorrow."

"Just the hospitals? You're not going to the site to see for yourself?"

"My men can handle the field investigation. Besides, I don't think I can face it."

Otto sat back in his chair, his lip protruding in a way that usually signified a moment of deep thought. "That's the right thing to do. But what does Cutler think?"

"Good question. You've got the guy's number. He forbade me to go. He's scared shitless over the possible lawsuits."

"And?"

"I told him I'm going. That I owe it to the victims. And he backed down."

"Good for you. But you do have to be careful. Watch the media down there."

"I know."

"Listen to me! I mean really watch them. Use them, too, if you can. Add a little showmanship to that businessman's kit of yours."

Otto chuckled. Fisk had seen the reaction many times in the past whenever some memory suddenly tickled him. "What's so funny?" he asked.

"That union organizer . . . who came up to Wisconsin . . . when I started my company in the thirties." Otto seemed barely able to contain himself. "The blockhead stood there on the plant floor in front of my men telling them what a shit their boss was, and I let him run off at the mouth like that for half an hour."

Fisk began to laugh too, anticipating the outcome. He could visualize the young Otto standing there, his round face a study in innocence beneath the grease stained fedora he wore at the plant. Just one of the boys.

"I gave him enough rope, and then: Pow! I walked up to him and turned to face my men. 'Do I deserve this men?' I asked. 'Do I deserve this from some foreigner from Chicago coming up here to tell us how to run our business? 'No! No!' they all shouted. 'Send the bum back to Illinois where he belongs!'." Otto snickered at the success of his ploy. "The newspapers like that sort of story, you know," he confided. "A local reporter was there taking notes and next day it was all over the papers. The jerk took off and to this day they've never taken me on again."

"You're some piece of work," Fisk said. "Now that you've nudged me out of my funk, tell me about your talk with Beauchamp. Do you think we can really believe the little prick when he says Cutler paid Senator Rushmore a fee for promoting the sale of Beauchamp's company to Hi Tech?"

"Every word," Otto said. "I can tell when a lush in his cups is giving me a snow job."

Then I have a real problem, Fisk thought.

"I need hard evidence, Otto. Any hint of it in what he said?" Fisk could imagine Cutler's reaction if he came to him with hearsay. That old kraut? He's out of it; over the hill.

"He and Cutler apparently had an argument over who would pay the fee before they signed the sales contract. After Cutler gave in and agreed to pay, Beauchamp told me Cutler said: 'There is no finder's fee, get it! Nothing in writing. It didn't happen!' And since Cutler wouldn't acknowledge the arrangement in the contract, Beauchamp wrote a note in his private file confirming it for his own protection. I suppose you could say the note is evidence."

"Why do you think he was telling you all this?"

"I have the feeling Beauchamp thought the whole thing was a farce. You know the type."

Fisk thought for a moment. "Sounds as though he is telling the truth, and that puts me squarely in a bind. This morning before news of the crash, I told Martha about your call from Paris. After we talked it out, I decided I would have to resign if what you told me was true. Now, everything has changed. There's no way I can quit until responsibility for the crash is settled. You can understand that, can't you?"

"Of course."

"There's another sensitive complication."

"It'll stay with me."

"I've had doubts about Cutler's honesty, but they've grown since my meeting with him this afternoon. I think he's capable of attempting a cover-up if the blame heads in our direction."

"That's a serious charge. What do you base it on?"

"His offhand order to me as I was leaving that he wanted the files clean, nothing in the records that can be used against us."

"And you said?"

"Even if it's the truth?"

"And?"

"He answered: 'Especially if it's the truth'."

"He said that—those exact words?"

"Yes, and he added: 'There's too much at stake. We have to be in the clear'." Fisk could feel rage start up again. The volcano had been dormant, not extinguished.

"Wow . . . You know what I'd do, Alan. I'd forget about the finders fee business for now. You've got enough on your hands, especially after what you've just told me. Maybe look around in Beauchamp's company files in storage at some point. He may have left his personal records behind. He's that kind of guy. Hit or miss. Focus now on your relationship with Cutler. As you said, everything's changed since your talk with Martha this morning. Sounds to me like you and Cutler are headed for a king-size set-to if the investigation begins to point in the direction of your blades and he tries to make you hide evidence. When that happens, you'll need allies on the board. Have you thought of that?"

"Well, not really," Fisk said, thinking of the boring boardroom moments when he indulged himself contemplating the actions of his fellow directors. He had formed an opinion of where each man stood, hadn't he? Especially John Hancock, the largest stockholder, who was openly at odds with Cutler at board meetings. But allies? . . . Well, maybe . . .

"Yes and no," Fisk said. "Hancock intrigues me. He's the only one who openly crosses Cutler on issues. During my six months as a director, I've watched them have at it big time. Keeps to himself, too, as far as the other directors are concerned. Except for me. He often asks my opinion when we're alone; seems to like me."

"So you see him as an ally?"

"Possibly. He seems to have a visceral dislike of Cutler. I can't imagine his siding with him."

"It goes back to John's relationship with his father, Seth, founder of Hi Tech and a close friend of mine. The old geezer didn't believe in nepotism and refused him the position in the company he felt should be his. John joined Osborne and Jackson, the corporate law firm, and over the years, became senior partner. Meantime, Seth groomed Cutler as his eventual successor, and that was the beginning of the bad blood you see between Cutler and John. Cutler tried to cozy up to him when John joined the board after Seth died and left him his stock. But John never once had him to his house and snubbed him in other ways every chance he got. A social snub is something most of us never forget, right? And for a man of Cutler's ambition, it must have felt like a thousand painful cuts. It drove him wild."

Otto paused. "John never forgave his father; still thinks of running the company as his legacy, if you ask me."

"Come on, Otto. After all these years? He's too intelligent."

"Watch yourself is all I'm saying. You're dealing with something in human nature that deserves more respect. You referred to it yourself: visceral. That's what it is. Same for Cutler. Bad enough you cross a man like him. But there's more to it. He just doesn't like the guy. Okay? People who began with little often resent others they feel started life sucking the hind tit, especially someone who does his best to make you feel socially challenged."

"You sound like my wife," Fisk said, remembering his talks with Martha about Hancock's annoying air of prissy superiority. You quickly knew he was that John Hancock from the framed certificate on the wall of his office attesting to his membership in the Society of the Descendants of the Signers. And in case you didn't get it, there was always his personal signature, a meticulous copy of his ancestor's, to impress the hoi polloi."

"Don't seem so surprised," Otto said. "Listen to me. You have those feelings. I have, Cutler has. Come on. Fess up."

"Now Otto . . ." Fisk began.

"For Christsakes!" Otto erupted. "I can see you haven't learned a thing about human nature."

Fisk blinked at his outburst, then saw the smile on Otto's face and realized he had been had.

"Just a teeny weenie resentment at times?" Otto continued, measuring off a small gap between two fingers.

Fisk laughed. "Okay. Just a teeny weenie."

"What about the other directors?" Otto asked. "Where do they stand? Any potential allies?"

"One, maybe: Stuart Brattle, the university president. He likes to fit in, but usually votes his conscience. The two bankers and our outside lawyer are pitiful to watch in action. They make a show of being independent, but when push comes to shove, they're in Cutler's corner; the firms they head have too much moola to lose. The industrialist? He's a crony of Cutler's. That leaves Woody Bentley, my counterpart as executive vice president. I really don't know, Otto. He's young, ambitious, capable, and with his years with the company, feels he's Cutler's natural successor. I don't think that that's in the cards, though. Cutler senses he's bucking for the boss's job. The word's around that Bentley's recently been a little too open in promoting himself. Part of Cutler's reason for acquiring my company, I think, was to square me off against him and watch us fight it out from the catbird seat."

Otto reached for his scissors and snipped off another thread. "Brattle? . . . Umm . . . Maybe, if it doesn't threaten his directorship. Those guys like the money, you know. Helps their standing with other academics, too. Bentley? . . . Worth some thought. He'll be playing every angle. Who knows? But I think you're dead right about Hancock. He's the one. He might well stand with you in any blow-up. Get to know him better. And, oh, don't forget your friend George."

"George?"

"Trueslow, the man who introduced you to Cutler."

"George is not a director."

"But he's a large stockholder. Anyhow, keep him in mind. You may need all the help you can get."

Fisk wanted to follow the thought, but knew he was already late in leaving. Thanks, my friend," he said, squeezing Otto's hand across the table. "I can always count on you." He rose. "My plane leaves O'Hare at seven thirty."

Otto waved him back. "I've been wanting to ask you," he said. "Remember that little company in Evanston I kept for myself when I sold the dental end of my corporation?"

"Remember it well. Titanium Implants, Incorporated, wasn't it? Makes a line of surgical prostheses."

"That's it. I want you to meet the young man I've had running it for the past three years—when you don't have so much on your mind, of course. He's a crackerjack, done wonders with the business. You'd like him, I think, and be fascinated with the technology. He's taking the company into an entirely new area: lab-grown human body parts. Give it some thought."

"I will, Otto. Appreciate your thinking of me," he said, waving good-bye.

"Good luck. I hope you find your blades are in the clear."

Fisk managed a grin. "So do I. So do I."

Fisk called Mike Belmonte from O'Hare. "I'm about to be on my way. Any word from your friend at the airline's maintenance center?"

"Yes, I finally got through to him and . . ."

Fisk, always sensitive to the inflection of a person's first few words, shuddered at his downbeat tone. Uh, oh . . .

"They were Sedalia's blades, but . . ."

But what? He reached inside his jacket and massaged his sudden heartburn.

". . . shipped from their plant six months ago."

"Six months ago! On my watch, you're saying? After Hi Tech acquired them? He's sure?"

"Positive. Says he matched the engine serial number with an order number from Sedalia in December of last year. And that's not the worst of it. Bill Scott in Sedalia now tells me they can't find any record of final inspection of those blades."

Fisk felt a flush of blood redden his face. "They what?" he bellowed.

"I know, it's terrible," Mike said.

"Terrible? It's a disaster!"

"Musta slipped between the cracks," Mike added faintly as if thinking aloud. "They were shipped during the period we were centralizing quality control here in Waukegan."

"Then the inspection must have been done there. Have you looked?"

"Checked and double checked. No records either place. I'm sorry Alan."

Fisk groped for words to express his outrage. How could this have happened? he wanted to demand. Tell me how! But there were no words, only feelings of frustration. It was his idea to combine the Q.C. functions, wasn't it? Over the strenuous objections of John Scott the Sedalia manager who had insisted that he retain control of his product though shipment. And somehow, in pursuit of efficiency . . .

"I know what you're thinking," Mike said. "But you made the right move. We let you down handling the transition."

Careful now. You're the boss.

"It was my responsibility, Mike, mine alone. So let's get on with it. Have you talked with anyone at headquarters?"

"No."

"Ed Schmidt in Miami?"

"Not yet."

"Then don't. We have a few days before Q.C. becomes an issue. I have to think about how to handle it."

Fisk slammed down the receiver, his deceptive calm shattered by thoughts of the precariousness of his position. If he was to work with Dusty in search of the truth, he had to maintain his trust. He had been handed a bombshell; how long could he sit on it to see what else was out there? One day, two days? Eventually he would have to tell Dusty, perhaps even during his stay in Florida. Would Cutler sanction that? No way. So why tell Cutler before making his move with Dusty.

Fisk realized he was perspiring and trembling with anxiety. I need help, he told himself. I need Martha.

CHAPTER 13

7:30 P.M. CST

"I need you sweetheart," Fisk said. "Need you bad, real bad."

"Where are you?" Martha asked. "I'm longing to see you; hear your news."

"O'Hare," he said, close to tears at the sound of her voice.

"Then you won't be home?"

"Not until tomorrow night. I'm going to Miami."

"Do you have to go?"

"I'm afraid so."

"Then promise me you'll be careful until we have a chance to talk. I'm worried sick because I know what you're going through. My patients talked about nothing but the crash today. One woman fainted on the couch after she recalled a rescuer's description of the scene in the cabin. The victims reminded him of charred barbecue. Can you imagine?"

Charred barbecue! Fisk shuddered at the thought of the loathsome image. "I saw that. Heartbreaking," he said.

"And I'm sitting here watching the dead being carried from the ruins. Alan! The whole nation's in shock. You too. The crash is bound to affect you on a more profound level than you can imagine. Don't let it throw you."

"That's just it, Martha. It has. I feel lost."

"Is it that bad?"

"My neck's killing me. If I had a painkiller, I'd pop it."

"Don't you dare!"

"I just heard that the blades are definitely ours; shipped from

Sedalia and there's no documentation of their final inspection. None. Belmonte thinks there must have been a foul-up during the consolidation of our two plants."

"Oh, Alan! I'm coming down with you."

"No, you can't."

"Promise you'll call me. You're no good by yourself when you're in this state."

Fisk wasn't listening. "This is the sort of thing I was worried about this morning. And a broken blade was found on the ground." The words stuck in his throat. "Jesus, Martha!" he said. "I may have killed fifteen hundred people."

"It doesn't help saying you shouldn't feel that way. Of course you do. That's the way I think of you. You're a sensitive man. You're not Cutler."

Fisk paused, still shaken by his admission. "No, I'm not Cutler," he said. "He'll do anything to see that Hi Tech isn't blamed. Even went ape when I said I was going to visit the victims in the hospital. The guy can be intimidating. Gave me a direct order not to go. He's wary of me."

"He's wary of you for a reason. You're pretty intimidating yourself."

Me, intimidating? Fisk thought. She's getting at something. "I don't know how to take that."

"You stood up to him, didn't you?"

"I'm going if that's what you mean."

"Then take it in the best possible way."

Fisk shrugged. Trying to buoy me up, he thought. "Anyway, the two of us are headed for a run-in. I'll be seeing Dusty McGinty in Miami. You remember Dusty, don't you?"

"Of course. I've always liked him."

"He's the Investigator in Charge. At some point, tonight or tomorrow, I'll have to tell him the bad news before passing it by Cutler. I can't jeopardize the trust he has in me after Albuquerque."

"You haven't told Cutler?"

"I don't intend to before I return. He'd forbid me to discuss it with anyone outside the company."

"So you're asking my opinion; if that's the right move?"

"Yes."

"You have my vote. Just do it. Be your intimidating self."

Bless her, he thought. She's always there.

Fisk heard a loudspeaker blaring in the background. "They're calling my flight," he said.

"Then tell me quickly, what did Otto have to say about Cutler? Did you have the drink with him?"

"No doubt in his mind. Both Beauchamp and Cutler are guilty of payoffs to the Senator. There may be written evidence if I can find it."

"Where does this leave you?"

"With no choice, Martha, not now. I can't resign in the middle of the investigation. I need my base at Hi Tech to see this through."

"Then please quit once the investigation's over, whatever the outcome. This is no way for you to live. Get out, lead the life you yearn for."

The life of a sculptor, he mused. She's thinking of our talk this morning.

"You told me once there are wondrous things about this world of ours that you'd like people to see through your eyes; that in your heart you know you could do it if you ever really tried. Then commit yourself, Alan. This is the moment."

If I ever really tried! Have I?

"That may happen. But right now, I have to concentrate on the investigation. Otto agrees that Cutler and I may be headed for a dogfight. He suggested I start thinking about possible allies on the board."

"Really? That's interesting. What do you think?"

"He has a point. John Hancock is a natural ally. Hates Cutler, as you know. And from what I've seen of him in the boardroom, he's quality when it comes to doing the right thing."

"He likes you, too, doesn't he?"

"Seems to; feels comfortable with me. And, oh. Otto thinks our friend George Trueslow's a possibility because of all the shares he owns."

"George . . . ? Yes, I can see that. I've never understood how he puts up with Cutler. Every time I see them together, Cutler treats him like dirt. I could have pinched his head off last month at tennis when he drilled a ball just out of George's reach and made him stumble and fall with his bad leg. No apology. Just that shit eating grin of his and says: 'He doesn't want sympathy. Just wants to be treated like everyone else'. Bullshit! All you had to do was look at George's face."

"Yes, I remember that—embarrassing to everyone who was there. He seems to take pleasure in humiliating George."

The loudspeaker was blaring again. "Sorry, sweetheart, I have to run," Fisk said. "I'll call again in the morning."

"You're a fine man, Alan. I love you."

"And I love you."

CHAPTER 14

7:45 PM. CST

When the Starflight 610 took off from O'Hare, Fisk wondered whether he would ever again enjoy peace of mind. He craned back to observe the right engine, and peered into the air inlet duct, imagining with his engineer's eye the tragic series of events in Miami. Would he ever be able to forgive himself if his blades were at fault?

"Yes, I'll have a drink now," he said to the stewardess. "Bourbon—on the rocks. A double."

Presently he turned off the overhead light and sat staring out at the night sky, clear and filled with stars. Yes, he mused, there can be peace; more to this moment than thoughts of death if I can only let myself experience it.

He settled back in his seat . . . it was a time for drowsing . . . but he wanted to stay with that feeling of an elusive aura hovering behind his eyes. A kind of wonderment. Atlanta appeared off to the right and Macon far in the distance, sprawling splotches of radiance, he thought, putting forth gossamer roadways reaching across the landscape—like neurons, glowing nerve cells of a global brain, with Interstate 75 for an axon and a myriad of secondary roads as dendrites busily communicating with other cells spotting the darkness. A sort of earthly consciousness, wasn't it? And while he might never fathom the chemistry that produces a neuron, he was deeply moved by the knowledge that every brick, every pipe, every wire and piece of glass in the scene below had been put in place by human hands.

Fisk closed his eyes. Oh my, he mumbled, and fell asleep.

*   *   *

He hurried through the terminal to the main entrance and hailed the Sheraton courtesy bus for the five minute ride down N.W. 21st Street to the River House. Dusty was waiting for him, drink in hand, in the bar.

"Jumped the gun on you!" Dusty said, vaulting from his leather chair to greet him. "How the hell are you?"

Fisk looked at him anxiously. They were friends, sure, but wasn't his greeting a bit much? Or was he imagining things?

"Great—yes great, Dusty," Fisk said, extending his hand.

"Then let's sit down and order you up a drink."

"What are you having?"

"You have to ask?" Dusty said, swirling the ice cubes in his gin martini. "My crystal yum-yum, what else?"

"You never change. In that case, I'll have bourbon on the rocks."

Dusty ordered, then turned to Fisk with an angry look that had Fisk's heart racing. "Buncha assholes!" he said, downing the rest of his drink.

"Who?" Fisk asked, startled.

"The media. Always looking for something dramatic. I guess you missed my nine o'clock press briefing flying down. Fuckin ordeal. Mary Joy should have been running the show with me . . . you know, Lemay," he added after Fisk's questioning look. "The President's appointee on the Safety Board. She has the duty this week, but is on the West Coast until tomorrow. So-o-o," he said, motioning to the waitress for another drink, "I was red meat for the assholes until half an hour ago."

"Probably a mob scene like your airport arrival."

"Imagine twice the TWA crowd packed into the auditorium downstairs and spilling out into the street watching TV monitors. With every last one of them trying to get me to say the blades were a prime suspect."

Fisk's mouth dropped open. "The media know about the blade?"

"Don't get me started. That shithead mayor of Miami wormed his way into the early search with a couple of photographers in tow; took pictures of a guardsman carrying off the blade. You'll damned sure be seeing it in the papers."

Dusty's beeper sounded. "Just a minute," he said. "They've been hounding me all day; Vice President on down." He reached for his cell phone and dialed the number. "Dusty McGinty returning your call."

. . .

"Yes, Senator Bixby, I do know. From Illinois."

. . .

Dusty rolled his eyes at Fisk. "I understand you, Senator. Most of the passengers on that plane were your constituents, but . . ."

. . .

"We're doing all we can. The investigation is just getting . . ."

. . .

"No, we don't have a probable cause in sight. We had nothing to do with those photos. They're misleading at this stage. As I explained in my briefing, we go to great lengths to prevent that sort of thing. There is evidence of engine failure, but how and why is an open question."

. . .

"We want action, too, believe me, Senator. But responsible action. None of this 'Ah ha, it's this' one day— 'Ah ha, it's that' the next."

. . .

"You think I'm being flip? That's what you think?"

. . .

"Go ahead, call him if you want to. We've been independent of the Department of Transportation for twenty two years. Why don't you try the President?

. . .

"I appreciate your endearing confidence in me Sir. Thank you, thank you." And he hung up.

"See what I mean. Another asshole."

Vintage Dusty, Fisk was thinking. Polite and respectful, but up to a point. Don't try to push him around.

Dusty turned serious. "There are two late developments I didn't discuss at the press briefing," he said. "I'd like to pass them along to you in confidence, not as a friend, but as someone I think can help me. Can I assume you're still the man I worked with in the Albuquerque investigation?"

He's put me on the spot, Fisk thought. I'll have to tell him about the undocumented inspection. But not tonight. See what tomorrow brings.

Their eyes met in silent acknowledgment of the bond between them. "Yes, I am still that man," Fisk said. "I give you my word."

"You must speak to no one, repeat no one, about this."

"I understand."

Two men entered the half-empty room and sat at the table nearest them. "We'd better move," Dusty said. "I've seen that pair prowling the place all day—reporters or corporate gumshoes; could be either." Then, when they had taken another table in a secluded corner: "They do that, you know. Cruise the place, especially the bars at night looking for investigators blowing off a little steam. They'll try anything to get inside information when the stakes are this high." He sighed. "Years ago when that Eastern heavy crashed in the Everglades I had to order an electronic sweep of the command center twice a day after finding we were bugged. Which reminds me, I ought to arrange one first thing in the morning. And break out the burn baskets, too." Dusty drained the last of his drink. "You probably know that we recovered the flight recorders."

"Heard it from the cabby on the way to O'Hare. Seems to be all over."

"The news always spreads, but never what's on the tape. You're about to become one of a very small circle to know."

Dusty reached into his pocket for a folded piece of paper. "Not that you'll like what you're going to read."

Fisk felt panicky. I could tell something's wrong from the way he's acting, he thought.

"Just before the press briefing Tom Beebe, our head technician in Washington, called me with the transcript of the CVR."

Fisk struggled to stay calm. "In good condition I hope."

"Not a scratch. Here, I've written it down."

Fisk read the scribbled notes and brusquely handed them back. "That's all?"

"We both know that it probably doesn't mean a damned thing except the pilot had a knee-jerk reaction to an old emergency—happens all the time. But everybody's going to jump on it, especially the press if it gets out."

Jump on it is right! Fisk's brain was on fire. Especially if it gets out that we have no final inspection of those blades. "There had to be more than that said before the crash!" he said.

"No doubt, but the CVR lost its power. Number three engine supplied it. Which brings me to another thing you won't want to hear. The entire fan section of number three is missing—exited in flight, based on our examination of the witness marks left on its containment ring."

"The fan disk with the rest of the blades—missing? Jesus! How do you know?"

"The engine was found at the bottom of a guy's pool over a block from the hotel. One of our men qualified for scuba gave it a quick inspection and reported no evidence of bird strikes, or bearing or shaft failure. At the moment, it looks like either the blades or the disk failed. And we won't know which until we find that disk."

Fisk slumped in his chair, staring at the table between them. It's happened!, he thought. The worst has happened. The day has finally come. Strangely, he felt a certain relief.

"I know it's upsetting to you, but remember, the investigation is just beginning," Dusty said. "We still have a lot of work to do. First of all, to find that disk."

"I'll do everything I can to help. If my blades did it, I have to know."

"What are your plans tomorrow?"

"I'll be spending most of the day visiting hospitals."

"Bless you. But in case you want to visit the crash site, I've had the boys make up this pass for you. We're trying to hold security tight."

"Thanks, Dusty, but not the way I feel now. I don't think I could take being there. Ed Schmidt's handling that end."

"Take it with you just in case."

Fisk took the pass.

"Now look," Dusty said, "you've got to explain something to me. What's with this guy Bledsoe? I don't trust him. He has quick eyes."

"Joe? He's a leftover from Cass Cutler's early days with Hi Tech when the sales force were mainly independent reps. He still reps foreign and domestic sales out of his Miami office along with our direct salesmen. About Cass's age—knows his way around the overhaul shops and greases the way for our boys with a cigar here, a cigar there. Everybody likes him. Why do you ask?"

"He's been making a nuisance of himself trying to wiggle his way into the investigation. When I went to retrieve the recorders I saw him hanging around the Skyhawk's landing site. I asked Schmidt about him and he said he's not an employee of the company; to forget him."

Nosing around for Cutler, Fisk thought. That figures. Here's a chance to ease Dusty's mind on where I stand with the boss. "Ed was right. He has no place in the investigation. I hate to say it but Joe's probably doing a number for Cass. When I arrived at the desk tonight there was a message from Joe saying he'd be driving me tomorrow; obviously he's been told to keep an eye on me."

"Cutler! That horse's ass! It's just like him. I was told Bledsoe's known as his gofer."

What's this all about? Fisk wondered, remembering Dusty's angry reaction to Cutler over the phone. He never harbored grudges. "You really detest Cass, don't you?" he asked. "How did he get on your shit list?"

"The old fashioned way," Dusty said, waving to the waitress for another round. "He earned it. Tried to bribe me. Goddamn him! I can put up with a lot, but interfering with my investigation, no way. You really want to hear?"

"Yes."

"When I joined the NTSB after my father's death, my first assignment was to fly to Chicago to interview Cutler in connection with the crash of a Beech Baron, the pilot and two passengers killed. The performance of the altimeter manufactured by Hi Tech was in question. The official determination of the probable cause was a difficult call; it could have gone either way—Hi Tech's product, or pilot error. You have to remember," Dusty said. "I was new at the game. Cutler was middle management at the time, but for a guy like me in his thirties from Upland, Indiana, dealing at that level with a company like Hi Tech was intimidating, and Cutler played it for all it was worth. Shit! He knew damn well this investigation was small potatoes back at headquarters, not subject to a lot of scrutiny, and thought he could take advantage of the situation. He invited me for a drink at the Zebra Lounge over on State Street, kind of a hangout of his, I reckoned. First thing I knew we were joined at the table by a woman who had been sitting at the bar. She was close to Cutler's age, I thought, around fifty, one of those lonely women living by herself looking for a little romance. Built? You betcha! And bedroom eyes? Hell! You've never seen anything like them. I quick got to thinking that I'd been dealing on the wrong side of the age curve all my life, and wouldn't it be nice to try my luck with an older woman? Cutler, that prick, was one step ahead of me— says he has a meeting to go to and why don't the two of us go to dinner? She makes noises about going to the Pump Room in the Ambassador down the street, but I'm on per diem—forty dollars in those days—and I jockey us into a little Italian restaurant. Afterwards she invites me back to her apartment and changes into a see-through negligee. The sight of her coming out of the bedroom in that outfit almost brought a tear to my eye. I swear to you, Alan, she was the best fuck I've ever had. Made the thought of growing old a little easier."

Fisk laughed. "So what's your beef with Cass? Seems to me you should have made him a friend for life."

"Before I leave my hotel in the morning he calls and says 'she's a terrific lay, isn't she?'—kind of strange, I thought, for a man in his position. Then he says he has a real knockout all set up in an apartment in Washington and she's mine any time I want her. The bastard assumed I was on the take!"

"What did you say?"

"I was tempted at first to tell him to go fuck himself, and let it go at that. But he had gotten to me and I asked him what his fee for pimping was, because I'd like to pay for his services and he says 'Come on, Dusty, I was just doing you a favor,' and I said no, I insist, I want to pay you, and he hung up."

"I can't imagine Cass would be that blatant."

"I mailed him a check for fifty dollars made out to cash."

"You didn't! Did he cash it?"

Dusty grinned. "As a matter of fact, he did."

No doubt about it, Fisk mused on the way to his room. Cass is on one side of the street, and I'm on the other. And Bledsoe. I wouldn't put anything past him.

CHAPTER 15

11:45 P.M. EST

Fisk lay tossing in the darkness of his room, tormented by Dusty's remark about a visit to the crash site. Why should the idea of going to the site bug me like this? he wondered. All this backing and filling? Shit! Why can't I make up my mind . . . ? He threw back the covers and leapt from the bed. Because you're a goddamned wimp, that's why! Of course you've got to go. He reached for the plastic security pass on the night table.

Ten minutes and he was on his way, awakening the sleeping driver of an all-night cab in front of the hotel. When they arrived, Fisk asked the cabby to wait until he returned, then approached one of the National Guardsmen stationed along the yellow tape defining the perimeter. The man stared intently at the NTSB pass. "Cleared for all areas," he said, and waved him in.

Minutes later Fisk emerged from the far side of the dense grove of Australian pines shielding the property from the highway and stopped in awe at the sight of the fallen building a quarter of a mile away across a vacant tract, illuminated by dozens of diesel-powered searchlights. The plane's blackened fuselage and tail section pointed skyward from the gutted building like a surrealistic sculpture of failed technology, and he imagined the inferno that had condemned fifteen hundred souls to their personal hell. A light breeze was now wafting the suffocating smell of kerosene across the open space—kerosene and . . . Fisk sniffed anxiously at the air . . . the stench of . . . Oh my God! His knees began to buckle and he stood retching in the darkness, consumed by the vision of the man in Pasadena engulfed in flames, screaming, screaming, his lips beginning to bubble and crack. I can't make it, he thought. I can't! He experienced a desperate urge to run, but continued on, haltingly at first, then with a determined stride. I have to go.

From this far, the large equipment—fire trucks, special emergency vehicles, truck mounted cranes, generators—appeared to dominate the scene. Closer, he was struck by all the ladders, ladders everywhere, large and small, propped against the building for entry through the broken windows. He could make out extraction teams of firemen bearing victims in litters gingerly inching their way down towering truck ladders extended to the upper reaches of the building. Paramedics waited beside their Emergency Medical Service trucks ready to minister to any brought out alive. Closer still, he saw ambulances moving in and out of the entrance driveway, still on the go, removing the dead well past midnight. And everywhere TV trucks, satellite dishes and groups of reporters. A virtual daytime city.

As Fisk neared the uprooted base of the building, he saw a fire captain wearing a distinctive yellow helmet addressing four firemen near a truck ladder extended to the lobby entrance now seventy five feet in the air. Maybe this is the place to start, he thought, and listened.

The Captain, a short, older man with the look of a well fed burgher, acknowledged his presence with a quick glance at his pass. "As I was saying," he continued, "we know that one engine exited the building on the fly and ended up in a lady's swimming pool over three blocks away . . ."

"Exited the building?" one of the men exclaimed. "Through the whole damned building?"

"You're too young to remember, son," the captain said. "Same thing happened back in '45 when one of them Billy Mitchell bombers rammed into the Empire State Building in the fog."

"But through the whole building?" the man persisted.

"It has to do with momentum," the Captain said. "A second wing mounted engine is still in there. The experts say it penetrated the steel shaft of an elevator while it was in use, and cut its hoist cables. Big as my wrists they were, including the one that actuates the 'safeties' as they call them, sorta like brake shoes that clamp onto the guide rails and stop the elevator if it gets going too fast. We found the only other elevator in use stuck on one of the upper floors with three people roasted to a crisp. We're still looking for the one with cut cables. The Chief thinks it had time to fall to the basement in the seconds after the crash."

"With passengers?" another of the men asked.

"No way of knowing, Sweeny. That's for you and your men to find out. And if they survived the fall, they may be the lucky ones—fire didn't reach the basement. So take along a couple of back boards just in case."

Fisk reflected on the possibility of passengers in the elevator. Could they have survived? And what did they feel during the free fall? Stark terror? What would you have felt if it had happened to you? he asked himself and suddenly turned to Sweeny. "I'd like to join you in the search."

The Lieutenant studied his pass. "Not dressed like that you won't," he said. "Mike, get Mr. Fisk a spare outfit from the truck."

Dressed in beige heavy duty pants, coat and gloves with black boots and black helmet, Fisk followed the four fireman up the narrow truck ladder into the lobby entrance. To enter, they had to climb down a forty foot ladder onto the former left side wall of the room now serving as its "floor". Fisk felt disoriented by the confusing geometry. The right wall of the lobby was now the ceiling and the old floor the right wall, with the reception desk still attached and seeming to float magically overhead. An Alice in Wonderland upside down world, he thought, a setting made more weird by the whine of the portable exhaust fans and shadowy emergency lighting. Throughout the room the stench of burnt flesh and the overpowering odor of kerosene mixed with the unexpected smell of orange blossoms from a leaking fragrance atomizer fastened to the "ceiling".

The group proceeded to the center of the lobby where a stash of emergency equipment had been assembled earlier. Fisk felt he was walking through hell. He gingerly sidestepped the irregular spots free of oily soot he recognized as the stark outlines of bodies that had been recently removed .

"You still feel up to it?" Sweeney asked.

"Yes."

"Then you can be a big help to us. We can use another pair of hands." He pointed to two molded plastic back boards. "And you, Johnson, help Rutkowski with the Jaws. Get a move on, men."

Fisk marveled at how easily Rutkowski lifted the Hurst Jaws of Life rescue device. He knew firsthand of its heft and immense force, having once seen it used to pry open the crumpled doors in a three car pile up. Made of heavy alloy steel forgings in the shape of a three foot arrowhead split down the middle, it was hinged at its base where a powerful hydraulic actuator slowly, inexorably forced open the pointed "jaws" inserted in a crack between a door and its jamb. An ingenious artifact with possibilities as a sculpture, he thought.

Johnson carried the Jaws power unit, a skid-mounted gasoline powered hydraulic pump with thirty feet of pressure hose. The third man, a paramedic, carried a medical kit the size of a large suitcase. And Sweeny led the group bearing a high intensity flashlight and an ultra sensitive listening device. When they reached the "floor" of the basement on ladders put in place earlier by an advance team, he directed the flashlight around the topsy-turvey scene. "We're in luck, men," he said. "The elevator doors are in the floor over there like the Captain said."

Sweeny walked to the first elevator in the bank, knelt down, and placed the coin-like head of the listening device on the metal doors. "Somebody's alive!" he shouted.

Alive? Fisk thought, straining to hear the sounds. Somebody survived the fall?

"I hear moans. Distinct moans," Sweeney said. We've got to

get this sucker open and fast. Bring the Jaws Rutkowski. We'll see how this baby works here."

Fisk made a move to help, but Rutkowski waved him aside. He hauled the Jaws into place, pointed down into the slight crack between the doors. Johnson snapped the hydraulic hose onto the equipment and started the engine.

Fisk covered his ears at the deafening rat-tat-tat in the confines of the room. Slowly, slowly, the doors inched open until they were three feet apart. Gardenia, is that gardenia I smell? Fisk wondered. Sweeny shined his light into the crypt-like opening. Fisk saw two bodies sprawled on the bottom, one a black man, his eyes open, stark and pleading. *Those eyes* . . . Next to him a woman in a gaily colored cotton dress with gardenia corsage lying motionless with a newspaper clutched in her hand. Her eyes were closed, her face a pasty white. The man stirred and moaned.

"Turn that goddamned engine off!" Sweeny shouted. "The noise is scaring the shit out of him." He turned to the paramedic, "Give us a reading, Hal. Trauma or medical."

Hal lowered himself into the opening. "Respiration and pulse good," he said. "Trauma I think." Then bending over the woman, "Medical, maybe a coronary, Sweeny. Pulse and respiration practically zip."

But still alive! Fisk thought.

"Then let's get them onto back boards and to hell out of here where you can work on them," Sweeny said. "Give 'em a hand, Fisk."

"It's a miracle they're alive," Hal said. "How did they survive?"

"The guide rails were probably bent in the crash and slowed down the elevator's fall," Fisk ventured.

"Who the shit cares," Sweeny said. "They're alive! Get to it, men."

Rutkowski squeezed into the opening and helped Hal strap the bodies onto the boards. Gently they lifted the bodies out, and, with Fisk and Johnson helping, carried them up and down the system of ladders out onto the grass near a waiting emergency medical service truck. Three paramedics hurried to them.

"They're alive," Hal said.

"Alive you say? This woman has no vitals!" Sid the lead paramedic said. He was kneeling beside the woman with his ear close to her mouth monitoring her breathing and his finger on her throat artery for pulse. "She's in cardiac arrest!"

Cardiac arrest? Fisk was appalled by the thought. "Then she's dead?"

Sid ignored his question. "This other one's got a serious head injury, Gus," he said. "Otherwise he looks in good shape."

Gus pointed to the ambulance standing nearby. "Then get him to the hospital quick. I'll stay here." He turned to the remaining paramedic. "Gillie, start the breathing bag while I hook her up to the heart monitor." He ripped open the woman's dress down to the waist.

Gillie strapped a mask over her nose and mouth and began squeezing an attached rubber bag forcing air into her lungs, while Gus attached the three monitor leads from a portable life saving unit to her chest.

"She's in fib," Gus shouted, looking at the squiggle horizontal line on the monitor indicating ventricular fibrillation. "Get the endo tube ready!"

Endo . . . ? endotrachial tube? Fisk wondered, having once witnessed paramedics fight to save a heart attack victim in Chicago.

Gus positioned two defibrillation paddles from the life saving unit over her breastbone and under her left breast. "Giving her the maximum."

"She's showing a little rhythm now," Gus said, his eyes fixed on the monitor screen. "Come on lady, you can make it."

Gillie had his finger on her neck artery. "But no pulse, Gus. None."

"Damn! You ready with the endo?"

"Yes".

"Then do it."

Gillie removed the mask and carefully slid the plastic tube attached to a cylinder of oxygen into the woman's mouth and down her throat. He pushed a button on the cylinder giving her a shot of oxygen directly into her lungs.

Barely breathing himself, Fisk watched as Gus applied four compressions to her chest with the flats of his hands followed by another shot of oxygen. They repeated the procedure three times.

Between shots Gillie took her pulse. "Still no pulse Gus!"

"Quick, the IV."

Gillie turned to Fisk. "You," he said abruptly. "Hold this." He handed him the IV bag. "Hold it high." He slid the needle at the end of the bag's tubing into a vein on her left arm and started the saline solution flowing.

"Add a shot of epi, Gillie."

Gillie snapped a tube labeled epinephrine onto a disposable syringe and gave a shot of it into a special fitting along the tubing.

Gus's eyes were fixed on the monitor screen. "Now lido."

Gillie repeated the procedure with a tube of lidocane.

"Oh Christ! she's fibbing again," Gus exclaimed, and placed the paddles for a second defibrillation.

Gus stared at the screen. "Shit!" he exclaimed. "She's gone flat line."

Gone flat line . . . ? Fisk shuddered at the horror he heard in the words.

We're losing her Gillie. More epi," Gus shouted.

For the next half hour Fisk watched as they worked furiously, alternating a series of chest compressions and oxygen, with shots of epi, lido, and now, atrophine.

But she was gone.

And maybe—probably—he had killed her.

* * *

Fisk remained behind after they all left, standing in silence before the spot where the woman had lain, now cluttered with empty syringes, vials, and IV bags all marked "DISPOSABLE". This woman who was, and now suddenly, was not. Who was she? Why had she been in the hotel in her fancy outfit and gardenia corsage? Her honeymoon? An anniversary? She had lain there vulnerable and exposed in death as he at that moment felt himself to be in life.

He knelt on one knee. "Please . . . please dear God," he said, "Don't let it be the blades."

WEDNESDAY

CHAPTER 16

7:00 A.M. EST

Fisk read the morning paper's headline in horror: "**PILOT TO COCKPIT VOICE RECORDER : ' * ! THOSE * BLADES AGAIN !' ' '**" Beneath was a large photograph of a guardsman carrying the recovered fan blade.

Son of a bitch! he raged. Hands trembling, he scanned the page. Further down, he spotted an article that sent his pulse racing: "**Terror in The Sky Over Albuquerque**". Oh, my God! he mumbled. They're connecting the two. Here on the front page of the Times a graphic description of the man's fall to his death from forty thousand feet. Was this really happening to him—a living nightmare? He saw the man in his dreams; now he saw him awake. And on the second page continuation, a photograph accompanying the text. Jesus, it's me—for all the world to recognize! A subtle message, he thought: Make no mistake about it, folks. It happened then; it could have happened again. This is the guy to have your eye on. He clenched his fists, his fear returning to anger. I don't like the smell of this.

He was about to put aside the paper when an article on the third page caught his eye: "**Chicago Exec Flies To Miami On Mission Of Mercy**" the column heading read. And below, "**Era Of Corporate Responsibility?**" Short but favorable. Thank you—thank you. Somebody out there is on my side.

He called Dusty at the command center. "Can we talk?"

"The phone's secure," Dusty said. "I had our people in here

making a sweep before daybreak. This phone and an ashtray on the conference table were bugged."

"I'm pissed, Dusty. I saw the headline. This is a disaster for me and my company."

"You know it didn't come from us. The bastards must have tapped into Tom Beebe's call from Washington last night. Dealing with this crap is one of the shittiest parts of this job."

"And the piece about Albuquerque. Somebody's hanging me out to dry."

"I saw that. I don't blame you for being angry. You deserve better for the way you shouldered the responsibility."

"It took a lot of smarts for somebody to put that together."

"I don't know. Reporters are pretty swift."

"Any idea who's behind the leak?"

"Has to be somebody with a lot at stake. Illegally wiretapping a government agency is a big time felony."

"All this talk about the blades. What's happening in the search for the disk?" Fisk was aware of the hint of challenge in his voice, but unable to suppress it. "Any luck?"

"Not yet. At sun-up two hundred guardsmen continued looking. Another group will be joining them by noon. Rick Munson who's heading the search will be briefing me at the Command Center at six."

"Do you mind if I sit in."

"Well, . . ."

Fisk waited, alarmed at his reserve. Was he having second thoughts about their relationship? Had he made a mistake in showing interest in the disk? Dusty may have taken it as an excuse for dodging responsibility.

". . . okay."

"You hesitated. You sure?"

"Yes."

"See you there."

* * *

Fisk called Cutler with the headline news.

"You think I don't already know?" Cutler interrupted. "It's been all over television. This is serious business. Terrible business. When the market opens our stock is sure to be hit again. There's no excuse for a leak like that. And how did the Albuquerque investigation get front and center so fast?"

Wait'll he hears about the inspection foul-up.

"I just talked to McGinty. He told me they conducted a sweep of the command center this morning; found two bugs. Someone must have been listening in when the transcript of the CVR was called down from the Flight Recorder Laboratory."

"So he says, eh? Why did he wait until this morning to secure the place?"

"Come on Cass, give the guy a break. He's had his hands full."

"I don't buy that and neither should you. I'm going to have his ass over this. I never have trusted the guy."

"I'll know more before I leave tonight. I'm meeting him at six."

"Good. Then meet me in my office first thing in the morning. And oh, are you going to see anything of Bledsoe while you're there?"

And oh, Fisk felt like saying, why do you even ask?

"He's meeting me in the lobby in five minutes."

He reached Martha at home. "I just have a few minutes," he said, "but I have to talk to you. Have you read the morning paper?"

"I'm still in bed, Alan. It's an hour earlier here, remember?"

"You're going to see a headline that's a real shocker."

Fisk heard her gasp. "About the crash?"

"A transcript of the last words of the captain from the cockpit voice recorder. He implicates the blades."

"Can a pilot know that? I mean, if the engine just sort of 'explodes'."

God, she's quick! he thought. She picked that up.

"That's just the point. He can't. He probably had a knee-jerk reaction to an old emergency; happens all the time. What disturbs me is that somebody wants the investigation centered on me and my blades right from the start. Dusty told me a few minutes ago that his phone was bugged. He's convinced the call transmitting the CVR data from the Flight Recorder Laboratory in Washington was intercepted and leaked to the press."

"Does Dusty have any idea who did it?"

"No, but it takes somebody with a lot at stake to risk a felony conviction. Resourceful, too. There's a piece in the paper on the Albuquerque tragedy with my photograph front and center."

"Bastards! They're trying to discredit you. You okay?"

"Right now? Fighting mad," he snapped. "I'm determined to help find the missing disk."

"Wait a minute. Disk . . . ? What's that about?"

"Sorry. Last night Dusty told me the failed engine was found with its fan disk missing. That's both good and bad. Good that the disk is now suspect too. Bad that we won't be sure whether it was the disk or blades that failed until they find it."

"How big is the disk?"

"Two and a half feet."

"Surely they'll be able to find a piece that large."

"It's not that easy. There's a lot of water around. Two hundred guardsmen spent the day looking and came up empty-handed."

"What's Dusty doing about it?"

"He has more searchers joining in at noon."

"What if they don't find it?"

"They have to, Martha. I'm terrified at the thought of the investigation dragging on for years. TWA 800, remember? I couldn't stand living with the death of fifteen hundred people hanging over my head. Especially," he said, his voice dropping to a whisper, "after a visit to the crash scene last night."

"Tell me," she said.

"I can't. Later."

"Talk to me, Alan! Don't shut me out. Something terrible happened last night. I hear it in your voice."

For christsakes, leave me alone! he thought. You're holding me up. "I told you I'm rushing. A car's waiting for me downstairs."

"Then promise me you'll make the time when you get home. I'm worried about you, sweetheart. I don't like to see you with your thoughts bottled up when you're so upset. I want to help."

He felt his frustration and self-loathing rise in his throat, but he pushed it back. "I know you do, and I need your help. I'll be home late tonight. We can talk in the morning."

"I guess I'll have to wait," she sighed. "Meantime, Alan, do me a favor. Try to be a little easier on yourself."

"I will, Martha, I will." Fat chance.

Well I'll be damned, Barker thought, when he read the headline at breakfast in his New York apartment. Could this be Rosie's work? She's certainly up to it. God, if it is, I owe her one. I bet she's tickled pink with herself; hasn't lost her touch. The woman dotes on intrigue.

He finished the paper and called her in Miami. "Rosie!" he said. "I've just read the news."

"Quite a break, eh General?"

"Who do you think was behind the leak?"

"Beats me. The media I guess."

"Right. The media. Some reporter bucking for a raise. And the Albuquerque piece. That'll help focus attention on the blades. Really visual, a guy maybe having a drink and suddenly blown through the cabin window."

"Just lucky. You need a little luck now and then."

"How do things look for the long run? Do you think our luck will last?"

"The word is around that Schnell is preparing a class action suit with General Tech one of the parties."

"So I've heard."

"Big money's involved. I talked to legal before coming here yesterday. They told me they see an uninsured liability in the billions if we're at fault."

Great, just great, Barker thought, scowling. There's no way the underwriters can proceed with our stock offering with this hanging over our head. No way.

"Sounds pretty grim," he said, "even after our bit of luck. What do the men in the Disk Division think our odds are now?"

"Still worried shitless, Sir. The latest from the plant is that the control samples of the disk material check out—no anomalies. Reassuring, but the men tell me that doesn't mean diddly squat for the long run. Ever heard of a hard alpha defect in titanium?"

"No."

"Neither had I; still not sure what it is. Has something to do with too much nitrogen in spots in the material when it's molten."

"I believe you." Three years in the business, he thought, and I've still got a lot to learn.

"Anyhow, there's a history of such defects going undetected in disks. They can lead to stress cracks and ultimately, fracture."

"What the hell. After all our inspections?"

"Ultrasonic, the works. The company has settled a number of lawsuits over the years, but nothing vaguely approaching this."

"When will we have a better idea where we stand?"

"When they find the disk."

"That's a problem? They've found a blade."

"As of an hour ago they were still looking."

"Umm . . . Are there any crashes on record where the disk has not been found?"

"Several. Usually where water's involved. One over Hong Kong harbor some years ago."

"Ours?"

"No, a competitor's."

"What was the finding in that case?"

"We've been together too long, General," she laughed. "I asked the same question. Not enough evidence to determine a probable cause."

"I get the drift," he chuckled. "Then I guess we have to hope they don't find this one, Rosie."

"Sometimes, General, we need more than hope. We need a little luck."

Rosie, still in her room at the Miami Airport Inn on Le Jeune, called Victor Gonzales, the local specialist in "delicate ops". Craig Cook, a former officer on her staff in Vietnam, now with the CIA, had recommended him the morning of the crash.

"Mr. Gonzales?"

"Himself."

"This is Rosie Donovan, remember me, a friend of Craig Cook?"

"Sure, handled your bugs. Whatcha got now?"

"I need to deep six something—offshore if possible."

"We don't do no bodies, lady."

"Not a body, Mr. Gonzales! Metal, a big chunk of metal, maybe three hundred fifty pounds."

"Where is it?"

"Near the Miami Airport."

"Then you need a truck, three big men and a boat. I can arrange that. When?"

"That's the problem. I haven't found it yet—weeks, maybe never. So I propose a twenty five thousand retainer for standing by, another fifty if I need you."

"I'll put my money on you, lady. Forget the retainer. Make it a straight hunnert."

"It's a deal."

Rosie called Dusty at the command center.

"Rosie Donovan! I can't believe it. How are you?"

"Still a little gimpy, but otherwise okay."

"You in town? I'd love to see you. Been over twenty years, hasn't it?"

"Much too long. I'm at the Miami Airport Inn."

"How did you know where to find me?"

"You kidding? I read the papers."

"I'd ask you for dinner but I'm terribly tied up all day. How about a drink later tonight? Say ten thirty?"

"I'd love it. I've missed you, Dusty."

"Meet me at the Penthouse Lounge in the Sheraton."

"You won't recognize me in civvies."

"Don't bet on it. I'd know that bod anywhere."

CHAPTER 17

7:30 A.M. EST

"You're not going to like what you see outside," Bledsoe said to Fisk when they met in the lobby.

"What do you mean?" Fisk asked, alarmed.

"You're an instant celebrity." Bledsoe smiled obsequiously. "A reporter recognized you at breakfast."

Damn, the picture in the Times, Fisk thought. I don't need this.

"A crowd?"

"A mob scene. You'd better get used to it."

Outside, the horde swallowed them up as they pressed their way toward the car. Not quite like Dusty's arrival, Fisk thought, but almost.

A reporter with a mike elbowed his way to Fisk. "Did your blades cause the crash?" he asked.

Fisk walked on. *Fuck you brother.*

"You heard what the pilot said."

Fisk stopped and turned to face him. "Look, you can't expect me to comment on a man's last words."

"The tape's pretty incriminating. You must have something to say to the public."

"No comment."

"Hundreds of innocent dead and no comment?"

Fisk's nails dug into the flesh of his clenched fists. Don't let it get to you, he thought.

The reporter sneered at him. "It isn't the first time."

Enraged, Fisk spun around to confront the reporter. Bledsoe, a brawny man, took Fisk by the arm and rushed him toward the car.

A man in a cowboy hat and boots suddenly appeared out of the crowd and thrust a copy of the local tabloid into Fisk's hands. "Murderer!" he shouted in his face.

Fisk, startled, glanced at the cover. "**THE SPAGHETTI MAN**" the headline read. Beneath was a photo of a man's deformed body lying in the desert sand.

Fisk lunged at him with fury in his eyes. Bledsoe threw a beefy arm around Fisk's chest and restrained him as flashbulbs popped. "I'll kill you!" Fisk shouted, struggling to free himself.

"Touch me, just you touch me!" the man taunted.

Bledsoe yanked Fisk aside and hustled him into the car. "That man was a setup, a fuckin setup," Bledsoe said as they sped away. He made a quick right down a side street, two lefts, then another right. "Shit! I thought I had lost them." He looked back at the swarm of cars and motorcycles now behind them, weaving and jockeying for position. "It's going to be an interesting day."

Fisk, still trembling with rage, sat silently while Bledsoe concentrated on the rear view mirror. Maybe Cass was right, Fisk thought. The game is played in the press. Maybe I am a boy scout, thinking all I had to do was come down and try to do the right thing. Yah, tell me about it. Albuquerque was then, this is now; you had better damned well realize it. This is a different country these days.

Fisk turned to Bledsoe. "You really think that guy back there was part of a setup?"

"Wait 'till you see the coverage. Another blade story—that's where somebody wants our attention."

He's right. And that somebody? Fisk was thinking. One of the parties? . . . General Tech? Could be; could well be.

*   *   *

Bledsoe parked in front of Bon Secours, a Catholic hospital dating to the early nineteen hundreds in a working class section of North Miami and remained outside to spin the arriving media. Inside, Fisk was met by Annie Foster, the head nurse, a bustling, forthright woman with whom Fisk had arranged the visit. "What a wonderful thing to do," she greeted him. "Flying all the way from Chicago. Lordy me! I've made sure the patients know what this is all about." She hurried him down the corridor. "There's one person really needs comfort," she said. "Man named Howard. Won't ever walk again."

When they entered Howard's room Fisk saw him propped up in bed with his head swathed in bandages, his wife sitting nearby. "This is the good man from Chicago I told you about this morning," the nurse said. He ain't hustlin anything. Just wants you to know he cares."

Fisk walked to the bedside and took Howard's hand in his. Good God! Those eyes . . . The man in the elevator!

"Hello Howard. I'm Alan Fisk," he said.

Can he talk? His face is so expressionless.

Howard moved his lips. "Nurse said you're one of the airplane people."

Thank God he's not out of it. "Not really. My company makes jet . . . ah, parts for the engines."

Fisk saw Howard's eyes brighten. "My boy Hobie, he know all about that," he said proudly. "That boy is crazy about airplanes. Buildin them models all the time."

A wife and a son, Who's going to look after them? "How old's the boy?"

"Twelve . . ." Fisk watched his eyes narrow. "Them parts you make, they the problem?"

Fisk felt his censure. What was he to say to this man who sat before him, a man whose life had been changed forever; say that somebody in his company, his responsibility, might have done this to him and his family, and say that he will never rest until the truth is known to make himself feel better?

Lot of good that would do him, me worrying about my ass. "We don't know yet," he said, "but we'll find out, I promise you."

Fisk turned to Howard's wife. "I'd like to meet your son sometime, Mrs . . ."

"Elkins, Yolanda Elkins. Hobie'll be here any minute," she said eagerly. "Could you just shake his hand? He's never met an airplane man."

"More than that, Mrs. Elkins. I want to talk to him."

Hobie arrived accompanied by his grandmother and walked to the bedside. He was of medium height for his age with an extraordinarily broad forehead and narrow chin which gave an intriguing, guileless look to his face. Howard stared at him. "You remind me so much of my boy. You smile just like him."

Fisk saw the stricken look on the boy's face. "Mom . . . ?"

Howard sat quietly for a moment, then "Where do you live, boy?" he said.

"You know, Papa! Miami Springs."

"So far away? That's too bad. You'd like my boy. You're so much alike."

"But Papa, I am your boy!" Hobie broke into tears.

Howard's eyes glazed over.

Jesus, it's his mind too! Fisk felt chilled, embalmed.

"I think it's time to leave," the nurse said, shepherding them all to the door.

"But I am his boy," Hobie sobbed as he and his mother walked down the hall.

"Yes, Hobie, you are."

Fisk followed them. What to say? The boy seemed so vulnerable. But he could do something that might help cheer him up. He approached Hobie and shook his hand. "Your father tells me you like airplanes," he said.

Hobie wiped his eyes. "Yes, sir."

"Ever been up in a jet?"

"No, sir."

"Hey, we've got to change that. Ever been to Chicago?"

"No, sir."

"Then write on a piece of paper how I can reach you. Next time our company jet is here we'll pick you up and fly you to Chicago. Would you like that?"

"A jet??"

"A small jet and you can sit next to the pilot."

"Really, mister, really? And maybe touch the controls?"

"Sure, even fly the plane a little."

"Oh! mister . . ."

"And I'll take you through our jet engine plant north of Chicago. Sound good?"

"Oh, yes sir!"

"Then let's count on it."

Hobie's mother was busy writing their address. She handed it to Fisk. "You would do that for Hobie?"

"Yes, I would. I want to, very much."

It wasn't enough, Fisk knew. Nothing would be enough.

"Uh, oh," Fisk thought when he stepped out of the hospital and looked upon a clamorous gathering on the lawn. Dogs barking, children gawking at the media vans with their mysterious satellite antennas, and street vendors hawking hot dogs, cold drinks, and Michael Crichton's "Airframe" in paperback; everywhere, people, several hundred he guessed. Mostly locals, others there from a distance by the look of the lineup of cars jockeying for parking space. So people knew about his visit. The article, no doubt. How else? It revealed his intention to visit the injured, and specifically, Bon Secours.

Bledsoe joined him. "Quite a turnout!" he said with a broad sweep of his hand.

Fisk thought he detected a note of paternity in his enthusi-
asm. Could Bledsoe be the source of the article? Why hadn't he
thought of it? Only he knew the details of his visit. Fisk hesitated, ambivalent about the thought. He had not come looking
for PR, and in that sense, Bledsoe had betrayed a confidence. But
if somebody was intent on making the investigation a public
case, well, he had been handed a gift. He would make the occasion work to his advantage. He was trying to do the right thing,
wasn't he. So let it come out.

Fisk recognized Jack Schnell surrounded by TV cameras and
an intent crowd of reporters and spectators. A squat, balding
man with bulging eyes, he had the cranky look of a hungry in-
fant; the walking fetus, Cutler called him.

Fisk and Bledsoe walked toward him. Prepare yourself, Fisk
thought. He's sure to gig you with Albuquerque.

"Ah, so we meet again," Schnell greeted him. "I heard you
were in town."

"So you did, I guess," Fisk said as the TV cameras were maneuvered for the best angle.

"Would you care to state for the record why you're here?"

"Is this a deposition?"

"Just a friendly inquiry. Surely you must realize we're all interested in the source of your concern. Guilt, perhaps, over what
has happened again? The pain, the suffering, the death this time
of hundreds of people."

Fisk braced himself. Give Schnell plenty of rope, and at the
right moment . . . Pow! "Not at all. I came because I wanted to,"
he said. "I care."

"Oh, my, a caring person. A nice sentiment, but who's going
to care for the victims and their families? Who is going to make
restitution for the grievous injury they have suffered? Who is
going to pay?"

Fisk smiled. "You sound like a lawyer."

The crowd laughed and a man in a tractor-green Deere cap
shouted "Right on! You deserve better."

"This is not a laughing matter, Mr. Fisk."

The crowd's with me, Fisk thought. Now's the time. Give it to him.

"I know it's not. It's a human matter, deeply human, and as such admits of a little humor now and then, especially when you persist in acting like an, . . ."

"Asshole! Say it Alan, like an asshole!" the man in the green cap shouted.

"When I made this trip I wasn't quite sure why," Fisk continued. "But I know now. If being here has made a difference to just one person, just one, then it's all worthwhile. And another thing you should know about me, Mr. Schnell, I love airplanes. And when something happens to one of these planes, I'm sick about it far beyond any commercial considerations. I care. I want to know the cause so it can never happen again. Of course the victims are entitled to compensation. But you're not my kind of lawyer. I resent the hell out of anybody who tries to profit from tragedy."

Fisk turned abruptly and walked with Bledsoe to the car. "How did I do?"

Bledsoe laughed. "You had them cheering."

"I meant every word of it. And don't you forget it."

On the way to his six o'clock meeting with Dusty and Rick Munson, head of the structures working group, Fisk had Bledsoe drive him around the airport's perimeter before dropping him off at the command center. When they reached 36th Street, Fisk saw squads of Guardsmen searching storage areas to the right of the end of runway 27R, containing mounds of old tires, empty engine shipment containers, and piles of old engine nacelles; and a large fenced in area filled with derelict planes, impounded or being scavenged for parts. As they neared the Hialeah Freight Yards stretching a mile north perpendicular to the end of the airfield, he saw several hundred more troops arrayed in a line across the quarter mile wide corridor, walking the tracks. South toward the edge of the airport bordering the Tamiami Canal, still more men slogged their way hip deep through drainage ditches.

"Think they'll find it?" Bledsoe asked.

So he knows, Fisk thought. "Find what?"

"The disk. They seem to be having a hard time."

Was it his imagination, Fisk asked himself, or was Bledsoe pleased at the thought?

"We have to find it," he said. "And soon!"

Fisk entered the Sheraton from the side parking lot to avoid the pack of reporters hounding investigators returning from the crash site, and walked quickly to the command center where he was let in by an armed security guard. Jesus! he thought viewing the turmoil. Looks like I've wandered onto the floor of the New York Stock Exchange. Instead of the handful of investigators and support personnel at the investigation in Albuquerque, he saw a room alive with people: groups conferring; men and women at desks pouring over manuals or starring at their PC screens; a few hurrying about with a sheaf of papers, just going from here to there. And throughout, the sound of touch-tone phones and the warble of FAX machines; only the ubiquitous coffee urns seemed from an earlier time.

A guard approached, examined his pass, and escorted him to Dusty's hangout in a side room. Dusty, in shirtsleeves, was seated alone at the conference table that dominated the small room. "I needed a minute to myself," he said looking up from the pad on which he had been writing. "Two hours and I'll be facing the assholes again. Mary Joe will be running the show this time, but they'll be looking to me for results. And what do I have? Zilch!

Except for the final tally of casualties, a few odds and ends of engine parts we found today, and . . ."

No disk? How could that be? Fisk's hope faded.

"that U.S. Geological Survey map of the Hialeah Quadrangle over there." He pointed to a five foot square exhibit on an easel portraying the Miami Airport and every feature for five miles around. Handwritten red circles, individually numbered, dotted the end of the runway. A legend pasted in a corner of the map located the recovered parts :

1. First-stage fan section blade.
2. One-half of fan containment ring.
3. Starter air tube.
4. Three cowl hold-open rods.
5. Hydraulic system accumulator for number three engine-driven hydraulic pump.
6. Two pieces of insulated metal braid-covered hydraulic hose clamped together.
7. Segment of aluminum material broken out of the large structural "banjo" from the inlet duct structure.

Fisk went for a closer look at the exhibit. That's yesterday, he was thinking. And today, only odds and ends to add after a search by over two hundred Guardsmen? The disk? Dusty, the disk? He wanted to ask, but stopped short. Give him a chance to say something. He'd be sure to misinterpret my concern as an excuse for dodging blame.

Dusty motioned him over. "Sit down," he said. "We have a few minutes before Munson arrives, and there are some things you ought to know. You heard the pressure I was under during that call from Senator Bixby last night. Well, I've got to tell you, Alan, after the headlines this morning, it's been that way all day. The investigation's rapidly becoming politicized, with everybody pointing fingers: media conscious politicians, reporters, victims' groups, and the parties themselves. Like the TWA 800 circus

without the FBI. And in the absence of the disk, a lot of the
fingers are pointed at you."

Fisk's head snapped back in an involuntary expression of panic.
"You haven't found it?"

"No, but let's hold that for Rick's briefing. The good news is
that we've made a quick metallurgical examination of the broken blade and find no obvious flaw. We'll have a better idea of
where we stand when we receive your documentation for the
blades."

Documentation? Fisk's moment of elation turned to dread.
Had Dusty heard something? Why was he eyeing him so intently? To gage his reaction?

"There is no documentation," he said.

Dusty lurched forward, adrenaline pumping; Fisk could see
it in his eyes. "What do you mean, no documentation?"

He hasn't heard. I have to tell him.

"We've found no control samples for that production run;
no record of final inspection. Jesus, Dusty, it's probably my fault.
I pressed my men to consolidate the Sedalia acquisition's Q.C.
department with mine in Waukegan. Last night I learned the
blades were made at Sedalia during the transition. Somebody
must have fouled up during the confusion."

"But final inspection, Alan. Peoples' lives depend on it. I
find this hard to believe."

Things will never be the same between us, Fisk knew, suddenly
immeasurably sad. "So do I. But what more can I say."

"You know what this means," Dusty said, annoyance in his
voice. "More finger pointing that we don't need this early."

"You're right. There'll be talk, especially since Sedalia didn't
have the best of reputations when we acquired it. That's why I
would appreciate your keeping this to yourself until I have a
chance to talk to my people face to face tomorrow."

Dusty folded his arms and looked sternly at Fisk. "I can't do
that. I have to tell the members of my Go Team."

"But not the media until I'm absolutely certain of the facts."

"Well, okay, I can do that . . ."

Rick Munson entered the room.

Dusty lowered his voice. ". . . but no later than tomorrow night."

"Rick, this is Alan Fisk, Executive Vice President of Hi Tech," Dusty said. "You can speak freely in front of him. Any luck since we talked after lunch?"

"Just a few fan blade fragments besides the anti-ice pneumatic tube and the front flange of the engine's rotor shaft I told you about. The size and deformation of the blade fragments suggest they failed as the disk exited the engine. Still no trace of the disk itself. We spent the afternoon combing areas adjacent to the runway and a mile north, guided by initial trajectory analyses based on the speed, altitude, and winds aloft at the moment of ejection. Years ago I headed up a search along this same runway for the turbine disk that exploded from an Air Florida plane on takeoff roll. We finally found it a half mile south though the plane never left the runway."

"Then you're saying this disk might be even further away," Fisk suggested.

"With the failure occurring during climb out and at higher speed, a mile, sure, maybe more. You never know."

"What's the next step," Dusty asked.

"The Navy Seals arrive tomorrow to check the waterways. They're our best hope."

"Hope, hell. Find that disk!"

Find it, Fisk echoed in his mind.

After Rick had gone, Dusty sat doodling on his pad. "Are you going to attend the press briefing?" he asked .

"Can't. I'm leaving on the eight-thirty for a midnight session at my Waukegan plant."

"Then you should know I'm meeting here with the team

shortly to decide what to tell the public. The first item on the agenda is confirmation that the disk is missing. The second is based on news I received minutes ago from Pete DiBella in Cincinnati where he's stationed during tear-down and inspection of the number three engine. There's no evidence of shaft or bearing failure; everything still points to the disk or blades. The third is that we've received General Tech's documentation on the disk. Everything's in order."

Fisk stared at him, stunned by the news. The media will jump on this, he thought. General Tech's documentation in the clear, but no word from Hi Tech.

"I know the spot this puts you in, "Dusty said.

Fisk nodded dejectedly.

"So I'm going to suggest to the team that we delay any announcement on General Tech until I hear from you tomorrow."

Fisk's face relaxed. "Thank you Dusty. I'll call you first thing."

This is one day I'm glad to have behind me, Fisk thought as he left for the plane home. I'm bushed. But the day isn't over. There's still the meeting at the plant tonight. And Christ! Explaining to Cutler in the morning.

Martha, he thought his pace quickening. At least I'll be seeing Martha.

CHAPTER 18

10:30 P.M. EST

Dusty was in the Penthouse Lounge sipping a crystal yum-yum, waiting for Rosie. He glanced at his watch. She's late! As if I don't have anything better to do. If the media had their way I'd be out there tonight with a flashlight looking for that goddamned disk. All their yak-yak about TWA 800 and the job Al Dickinson did retrieving practically every piece of a 747 scattered under a hundred feet of water. And you, you idiot, can't find a three foot disk on land. Gimmie a break.

He saw Rosie walking across the room in a green form fitting Jersey dress. Well looky here he thought, she still walks like a queen, even with a cane. And the same assured look on her face as if she knows she's being watched.

"Gosh, it's good seeing you!" he said. "Smashing as ever. I love the long hair. And that dress. Wow! Let me give you a hug."

"So you approve of the civvies."

"Doesn't stop there."

He helped her to her seat.

"Aren't you going to offer a girl a drink?"

"What'll it be."

"Bourbon on the rocks."

"Three ounces," he told the waiter. "She likes a little extra."

"So you remember."

"I remember a lot."

She broke out laughing, that sensual laugh of her's that made his neck tingle. "Then you'll remember that this is the first time we've been together in an air-conditioned room," she said. "Finally, finally!"

He knew exactly what she meant. My God! she's coming on to me, he thought, remembering the wild week they spent together in the sweltering heat of Saigon when they both found themselves there for R&R after her injury behind enemy lines. Hot, hot, hot, dripping with sweat, but deliriously happy, thrashing around in bed day after day like two slippery eels.

"Whatever happened to you after you were transferred?" she asked. "You disappeared off the face of the earth."

"Oh, sorta predictable, I guess. Flew the Pacific route for United for awhile after I served my hitch. Married my stewardess. Two children, house in Bethesda, you know. How about you? Still a career girl?"

She laughed again. "You always were a male chauvinist, Dusty. To your way of thinking you're asking if I'm married. Right?"

"Are you?"

"No."

"Where are you living?"

"New York City for the past three years."

"Ah, New York. I get there a lot."

"You'll have to come see me."

God, I feel like I've fallen into a vat of warm honey, he thought, just as his beeper sounded. "Sorry, gotta take it," he said, and dialed the number on his cell phone.

"What's on your mind at this hour Pete? Did you discover something new in the engine tear-down?"

. . .

"So you saw the media circus tonight on television?"

. . .

"I know, Pete, I know, sorry you're pissed. But at our meeting before the briefing, the team decided we should hold off on announcing receipt of General Tech's disk documentation until we gave the other party a chance to verify that its documentation is missing. I guess I should have patched you in over the speaker phone. Sorry."

. . .

"It won't drag on. I've set tomorrow night as the deadline."

. . .

"Okay. I'll let you know as soon as I hear from the other party."

Dusty replaced the receiver. "Let's see, where were we? Yes, you're living in New York and still single. So what sort of work are you doing?"

"I've stayed with General Barker over the years. You remember him, don't you?"

"Barker? Oh, sure. He was the genius behind that mission where I had to helicopter you out. You were his intelligence officer."

"Right."

"And he's still in the Army?"

"His last post was the Pentagon; Deputy Chief of Staff. Three years ago he was offered CEO at General Tech and we both moved to New York."

General Tech? Good God! She's with a party to the investigation? he thought, trying to remember just what he had said to Pete DiBella.

"That Sam Barker! President of General Tech. And that's the same guy from Vietnam?"

"The same. I'm now his Vice President. Sort of administrative detail."

Dusty's pulse was racing. What have I done. I was nuts, talking in front of her like that.

"Are you involved in General Tech's investigation of the CCA crash?" he asked, unable to hide his concern.

"No," she said with a dismissive flick of her hand. "I don't get into those things."

Less said the better. If I ask her to forget what she heard, I'll just highlight it.

"We're dealing with one of your men, Bill Swanson, as a party. Very cooperative."

"He's from the division. But enough of that," she added, glancing at her watch. "I'm not here on business. When I read you were in Miami, too, I couldn't resist seeing you if only a few minutes."

Abruptly she leaned over and kissed him, a long, intimate kiss. "Remember," she said. "Let me see you sometime when you're in New York. I'm in the book. On 66th." And she hurried off.

Dusty sat toying with his drink. Watch out, my friend, he thought. One of these days this weakness for the ladies is going to get you in big trouble.

Joe Bledsoe called Cutler at home. "Sorry to disturb you, Chief," he said, "but I just saw the General Tech woman having a drink with McGinty."

"McGinty! Where?"

"Penthouse Lounge at the Sheraton where he stays. 'Bout half an hour together."

"He seem to know her?"

"Did he ever. His eyes were all over her from the moment she entered. Kissed him good-bye, she did."

Son of a bitch, Cutler was thinking. That's how the tape leaked yesterday.

"And she's been one busy lady all day," Bledsoe continued. "The private dick I hired said she met a man on the morning flight from New York. They drove the airport perimeter, getting out, looking around. Bought a U.S. Geological Survey map of the area this afternoon, then rented a helicopter for an hour."

"Any idea who the man is?"

"Looked kinda nerdy and in his forties. I thought he must be a company man, but no, the dick called this evening to say they got a read on him. He's a professor at the Polytechnic Institute of Brooklyn. Specializes in kinetics of rotating bodies."

I get it, Cutler thought, rubbing his eyes. First the leak about the blades, now her interest in the disk. He's there to help her find it. General Tech's anxious as hell about something, anxious enough to take chances.

"And guess what? The dick is convinced he's her boyfriend. Registered under the name William Glickman at the Miami Airport Inn where she's staying."

Boyfriend—someone she can trust.

"What has the 'dick' told you about their activities?" Cutler asked.

"He must be bopping her. Never spent a minute in his own room. She must like 'em young and kinetic."

"Yeah, yeah, Joe . . . but what are they up to? Any idea?"

"When she left Dusty, she returned to her room, and she and the guy drove to a spot near the end of runway 27R, where Ludlam joins 36th. Now they're on foot, kinda lookin around."

"They're working an angle," Cutler said. "Keep after her." He paused. "Good job. And thanks for the E-mail on Fisk's activities today. That 'corporate responsibility' note you struck with your friend at the paper last night set just the right tone for his visit. Now we have to concentrate on McGinty. Gotta find some way to plug that leak."

"I agree, but I gotta tell you, the slush fund is running low on cash."

"No problem, Joe, you know what to do."

"Gotcha, Chief."

But it isn't really the leaks, Cutler thought. It's the blades. He stared at ruin.

"So what do you think, Willie?" Rosie said as they stood near the end of the runway. "You've had a good look around."

"I think they've got it all wrong. Hell's bells! They'll never find the disk the way they're going at it. Those guys at the Safety Board are relying on airport radar, but it's notoriously inaccurate close in—gives false returns from reflections off the surrounding buildings. They're not getting anywhere, either, with their fancy trajectory analyses and space age technology. More old-fashioned footwork would help."

"So what is a poor girl to do under the circumstances? You know how much it means to me to find it before they do."

"They're wasting their time out there," he said with a sweep of his hand. "I'd stick closer to home, Rosie. From what I've heard of the speed and altitude when the failure occurred, the disk's probably not far off the runway."

Fisk saw Chicago's lights out the plane's window and called Mike Belmonte in Waukegan. "I'll be landing in fifteen minutes. Any progress finding the documentation since we talked this afternoon?"

"Dead-end. What happened to the blades between production and shipment is a black hole. We have to assume they weren't inspected."

Fisk sighed. What had he expected, some sort of magical discovery? "Great news, Alan! We found the production samples and paperwork in an empty desk left over from the move. Sorry about that."

"Are you sure you still want to meet here tonight?" Belmonte asked. "You must be dragging."

Dragging, hell. Out on my feet, Fisk thought. But bushed or not, he had to go, didn't he? "Final inspection, Alan," he remembered Dusty saying. "Peoples' lives depend on it. I find this hard to believe." Yes, peoples' lives did depend on it, and he had to know where his own leadership may have failed them.

"I have to be fully briefed on what may have gone wrong

before I see Cass in the morning," he said. "I'll be there in an hour, Mike," and he hung up.

He looked at his watch. *Midnight! The end to the shittiest day of my life.*

THURSDAY

CHAPTER 19

4:00 A.M. CST

Four o'clock in the morning Fisk awakened in terror to find Martha watching him.

"I didn't hear you come in last night. Are you all right?" she asked putting her hand to his forehead. "You're perspiring all over."

"It's the dream, Martha, the dream!"

"It'll be all right. Take a few deep breaths." She patted away the perspiration with a Kleenex.

"It won't be all right!" he panted, staring wild-eyed at the ceiling. "It will never be all right. I killed her."

"Her . . . ?" she asked, nonplused. "Wake up, sweetheart, you're not making any sense. The man in Albuquerque . . . you mean him!"

Fisk sat up looking dazed. Jesus! The woman in the elevator! he thought and began shaking violently. "You're right. I'm not making any sense. It's a new nightmare . . . I watched a woman die at the crash site Tuesday night." He wiped his eyes. "I shouldn't have gone there," he said. "Maybe I could have lived with the thought of fifteen hundred people—maybe. But seeing her lying there . . ." he writhed at the perception . . . "I was no longer dealing with shadowy numbers—I was looking at one person with her own mysterious life, and I might have killed her."

Martha cradled his head in her arms. "And you saw her die?"

"I couldn't sleep—went to the site around midnight. The place was a virtual day-time city, lighted by diesel-powered generators and swarming with firemen and rescue workers. And yet the scene was strangely impersonal except for the smell everywhere of burned . . . oh, my God, Pasadena . . . !" He began retching.

Martha tried to embrace him. He shoved her away. "Don't torment yourself," she said. "I shouldn't have asked. This is affecting you on so many levels of the past."

He began to sob. "I have to speak of it, I can't keep it in . . . Inside the building . . ."

"You went in . . . you were allowed in?"

"With a team of firemen and paramedics to see if anyone was trapped in a crashed elevator in the basement."

"And you found her there, alive?"

"Barely; the diagnosis was cardiac arrest. Another passenger with a serious head injury was taken to the hospital and survived. Paramedics tried to save her on the grass outside, but they couldn't. Strange the personal things that go through your head at a time like that. I thought of her fancy dress and gardenia corsage. Who was she? Why had she been in the hotel? Her honeymoon? An anniversary? Trifling thoughts in the face of death. A kind of denial, I think. It wasn't until she was taken away and I stood alone that I felt the truth of the moment. She was gone. And maybe—probably—I had killed her."

The sobbing increased. Martha ran her fingers through his hair. "I don't like the word 'probably'," she said gently. "You're tormenting yourself again. You've got to stop that." She paused. "When you called me this morning, what is the first thing you told me?"

"About the morning paper—the headline, the leaked tape." His tears stopped and he looked at her quizzically.

"And then you spoke of the article on the Albuquerque tragedy."

"The bastards! I told you. They're out to discredit me."

"And what else was in the paper?"

"For christsakes, Martha! How would I remember? I was rushing that morning."

"There was a wonderful article on you: '**Chicago Exec Flies To Miami On Mission Of Mercy**'. And you never mentioned it."

"Maybe there was. What does that have to do with anything."

"You've got to stop keying in on the negative, Alan, or you'll drive yourself wild. You tend to do that, you know. See the glass half empty."

Glass my ass, he thought. Let her try to keep a smile when she's carrying the load on my shoulders.

"I know you're trying to help me," he said. "But I don't feel like being lectured to, not when it's almost daybreak." He buried his face in the pillow abruptly before he could express his rage.

Fisk opened the front door in his shorts and picked up the morning paper. He removed the wrapper and stood dumbfounded by the headline: "**CCA 181's ENGINE BLADES ESCAPED INSPECTION**". A chill shot through his body, more from anger than the cool morning air. Shaking, he began the lead article: "Miami, May 26—Reliable sources report . . ." and abruptly stopped. Sources, shit! Somebody out there is leaking again, somebody's already spinning to a potential jury pool, the whole country. He continued to scan the page to an article on Dusty's press briefing: "**Engine Fan Disk Reported Missing.**" Dusty was true to his word, he thought, relieved. Not a word about blade inspection. Interesting, too, no mention of General Tech's disk documentation.

Martha came to the door in her nightgown, portable phone in hand. "So there you are," she said. "Dusty McGinty's on the line. Says it's urgent he speak to you. Is something wrong?"

He thrust the paper into her hand and took the receiver. "What the hell's going on, Dusty?" he said. "I just saw the paper."

"I had hoped to get to you early but you've obviously seen the news. I have to apologize. I may inadvertently have been the source of the leak."

"You . . . ?"

"Last night after I saw you I took a call regarding your lack of documentation in front of an old friend I hadn't seen for twenty years. She turned out to work for General Tech. No names were mentioned but she's smart enough to have put two and two together."

God, maybe Cutler's right about Dusty, Fisk thought. Maybe he can't be trusted.

"Who is this woman?"

"Name's Rosie Donovan. Works directly for Barker. Was his intelligence officer in Vietnam."

"Intelligence? Christ, Dusty, that's exactly what happened. And I was trying to proceed in a responsible way, making sure of the facts, none of that ah ha effect you guys dread. Now I get this."

Martha was grimacing at him, shaking her head.

Fisk hesitated. Stop the whining. Martha often warned him about self pity.

"It's put me in an impossible situation with Cutler."

"You haven't told him?"

"Not yet."

"Why?"

"I have my reasons. I planned to tell him at our meeting this morning."

"Then he's hearing about it on the morning news?"

"You've got it. I expect a call any second. He'll be apoplectic, and with good reason."

"Then you satisfied yourself when you got back that there was no documentation?"

"Unfortunately, yes. At three in the morning."

"For what it's worth, I can tell you the NTSB won't comment on the story until we receive your statement for the record. Again, I apologize."

Martha was mouthing words indicating the other phone was ringing.

"Somebody's calling on my business line," Fisk said. "Probably Cutler."

"Then I'll get off. I just want you to know I now realize the position I put you in when I mentioned documentation last night. Yes, Alan, you are the man I worked with in Albuquerque."

Fisk went inside, feeling better about himself, but still wondering about Dusty. Martha was standing at the phone. "He's right here Cass."

"You've read the news?" Cutler asked in a tone so icy the receiver felt frigid in Fisk's hand. He rolled his eyes at Martha. "Minutes ago."

"Is it true?"

"I confirmed it with Belmonte at the plant last night. They were replacement blades from Sedalia and somehow escaped inspection."

"When did you first know about it?"

"Tuesday night before I left for Miami."

"And you didn't tell me?"

"I wanted to meet with Belmonte first when I returned."

"I said, and you didn't tell me?"

"No."

"Then you'd better get your ass in here."

Cutler slammed down the receiver. What's Fisk up to? He knows better than to let me be blindsided like that. Suppose one of our directors had called an hour ago? They're already scarred shitless about some big personal liability. "The headlines, Cass. What the hell's going on?" And I'm to say, Oh, I'll check into that and call you?

The phone rang. "Sam Barker, Cass. Just keeping in touch. We're sorta in this thing together, you know, although I've gotta say it doesn't look too good for your boys after what I've just read."

Yeah. Up yours! "Why do you say that?"

"Well, you know, it looks like something kinda slipped by."

"Depends on where you stand. Let's cut the bullshit. Looks to me that somebody's awfully anxious to get that idea around—first the leak of the tape, now this." Cutler's anger welled up at the thought of General Tech's vice president meeting with McGinty. "Couldn't be you Sam, could it?"

"Is that an accusation? If it is, you'd better have something to back it up."

"Just thinking. One of my men says he saw your Vice President for Special Projects poking around the scene soon after the crash, then having a chummy drink with McGinty last night. Fascinating background, that woman; your intelligence officer in Vietnam, I hear. Be careful you don't cross the line, Sam."

Cutler could almost hear him thinking.

"I see you're living up to your reputation, Cass. Glad you warned me. I always like to get a peek at the other fellow's hand. I think we both know now where we stand."

"As you said, we're in this together. It's you or me."

Uh, oh, Fisk thought as he entered Cutler's office and saw him seated at his desk with his back to the harsh morning sun. The window blinds were up, a long-standing ploy of Cutler's to place his visitor at a disadvantage whenever it pleased him. He sat down, squinting into the sun, wishing the boss would hurry up and say something instead of just sitting there.

"When you came on board a year ago," Cutler said, "I told you the one thing I won't tolerate is not being kept informed on important matters. No surprises . . ."

He's decided to play it cool, Fisk thought.

"And yet you let over a day pass without telling me the blades weren't inspected. You didn't even mention it when you called yesterday morning after the CVR leak hit the headlines. What the hell were you thinking of?"

Fisk swallowed hard. He knew exactly what he had been thinking. And Cutler's reaction would not be pleasant.

"I wanted time to check the facts for myself and talk to you this morning."

"So tell me what happened," Cutler said.

"Sedalia was a mess when I took over, especially the Q.C. function. You know that, I reported it to you. Beauchamp hadn't paid attention to the business for years. After several near disasters I pressed my men hard, maybe too hard, to consolidate their Q.C. with mine in Waukegan. We were in the middle of the transition six months ago when the blades were shipped. I've checked and double checked. There's no record of inspection. Somebody screwed up."

"Shipped six months ago? Now you're telling me they were made at Sedalia under our ownership? While you've been running the place?"

Cass's secretary spoke on the intercom: "Mr. Courtwright on the phone. Do you want to take it?"

Fisk knew Courtwright was Chairman of United Aerospace. He watched Cutler squirm in his chair.

"Put him through . . . Yes, Giles, what's on your mind?"

. . .

Cutler listened impassively for ten minutes, expressing neither interest nor concern for what he was hearing. Presently Fisk saw his milk-white complexion reddening.

"We're not for sale," he said evenly.

. . .

"You didn't hear me Giles. We're not for sale, merger, acquisition, buy out—on any basis."

. . .

"Then you just try that and you'll find yourself in the fight of your life!" and he hung up.

"What's that all about?" Fisk asked.

"Just what you'd expect with our stock tanked with all the bad publicity." Cutler reached for the keyboard of his Market Watch computer. "Damn! Our stock's off another ten percent. Courtright sees us as a bargain. Says he wants to make us a merger proposal we can't refuse. Rattled off all that shit about a perfect fit, a historic deal, creating an international powerhouse that could give the Germans and Japs a run for their money in the global economy. We'd continue to run the business without interference. Bullshit. All he wants is our missile business. He'd sell the units he didn't want to the highest bidder."

Cutler walked to the window and gazed out at the lake front. "If Courtwright makes good on his threat of an unfriendly takeover," he said, "we'll face a tough fight with our stock where it is."

Fisk joined him. "The news from Florida isn't all bad," he said. "When I talked to Dusty . . ."

Cutler spun around and faced him. "You saw Dusty?"

Oh, Christ. I forgot I hadn't told him before I left. "Yes. He . . ."

"When?"

I'd better come clean. "The night of the crash and again yesterday. Before I left he told me they've made a quick metallurgical examination of the broken blade and find no obvious flaw."

Cutler was eyeing him suspiciously, seemingly oblivious to what he had just heard. "The question is, what did you tell him?"

Fisk's jaw was twitching in fear. "He said when they received our documentation they'd have a better idea whether the blades were in the clear."

"And?"

"I had to keep his confidence, Cass, had to if I'm to be able to help in the investigation. I told him there is no documentation."

"You what?" Cutler's face was crimson. "You told the IIC there is no documentation? Dusty? One of these days you're going to believe me that he can't be trusted. He talks too much. We're going to have to shut him up."

"He promised me that . . ."

"Oh, for christsakes, man, you act like a child. I see it all now. You planned it this way. Couldn't wait to tell McGinty—hustled off to see him after you left Joe. And you know what your friend does? He has a cozy drink with General Tech's Vice President for Special Projects, Rosie Donovan, a. k. a. Sam Barker's dirty tricks expert since their days in Vietnam."

The news made Fisk's stomach lurch. Bledsoe must have tailed her after he left me. Could he overhear their conversation and the phone call?

"You knew I would forbid you to say anything if you told me in advance," Cutler went on, his hands trembling with rage. "Stonewall 'em, delay, play for time, that's the way. Make 'em dig it out of us. Now they've got momentum. Dusty obviously passed the information along. 'The blades, it's the blades.' You still don't understand this is being fought out in the press." Cutler looked him up and down contemptuously. "I've got a mind to fire you on the spot," he said.

Fisk grasped the arms of his chair. Fuck him! he thought. What do I care? "Then you do it," he said. "But remember, I have to know what caused that crash, and inside the company or out, I'm going to pursue it. It may be your economic problem, but it's my moral problem, and don't you forget it."

A smile flitted across Cutler's face. "Got you stirred up, didn't I?"

"It's not funny, Cass."

"As a director, you're free to have your say at the board meeting tomorrow."

Yeah, with a board controlled by your cronies.

"You're already on the agenda. If you're smart, you'll be careful what you say. Play up the disk, put the best possible face on our position."

*   *   *

Fisk returned to his office blind with fury. Fire me, will he? He made light of his threat at the end; doesn't want a whistle-blower on his hands. But I'm not fooled. It's over between us. Kaput. Otto was right. I need allies.

He picked up the phone and called John Hancock. "John, can you see me in your office this afternoon?" he asked.

"Sounds important."

"It is."

"Four o'clock all right?"

"I'll be there."

Fisk put down the phone. It was a start.

CHAPTER 20

4:00 P.M. CST

When Fisk arrived, John Hancock was standing behind his antique desk toying with the Phi Beta Kappa key that hung from his vest-pocket watch chain. He looked composed and at ease, Fisk thought, for a man who had lost twenty million in a matter of days. Too at ease.

"I appreciate your seeing me," Fisk said.

"Not at all," Hancock replied, motioning him to be seated. "I rather welcome the occasion." And lowering his voice, "Maybe you can tell me some things I should know."

The way he said it made Fisk feel like a sneak. What was he doing there? He was about to snitch on the boss to a director and largest shareholder; the ultimate taboo. But he had already made that decision when he called, hadn't he? So be careful, he cautioned himself, avoid a lot of flimsy accusations.

"I'm having a problem with Cass," he said. "He's ordering me to be less than forthright in the crash investigation."

"Come now, Alan. You can do better than that. Say what you mean."

Fisk's puckered his lips. He had known all along, hadn't he, that this moment would come. It was one thing to sit with Otto and tell him of his growing doubts of Cutler's honesty and intimations of a cover-up, another to be going public with Hancock and the board.

"All right, cover-up," he said.

Hancock leaned forward. "Tell me."

Fisk took a breath. "The afternoon of the crash he forbade me to go to Miami to visit the area hospitals. I felt I owed it to the victims whether Hi Tech is responsible or not. He had a point; was worried Schnell would gull me in public. But he backed off."

"Yes, Schnell. The man's an embarrassment to the profession. I felt you handled yourself just right on TV. Got the crowd with you; made him look the fool he is."

Fisk hurried on. "Before I left, Cass told me he wanted the files clean, nothing in the records that can be used against us. I said, 'Even if it's the truth?' and he replied, 'Especially if it's the truth. There's too much at stake. We have to be in the clear.' Those are our exact words."

Hancock's body stiffened. "You're not telling me that you listened to him and destroyed the documentation records, are you?"

"Hardly. Just the opposite. When I heard they were missing, I decided not to tell Cass before I had a chance to advise the Investigator In Charge while I was in Miami. Unfortunately the word leaked and Cass first heard about it in the papers this morning. He was furious."

"I can imagine. You don't do that to the CEO."

"I had to. He would have ordered me to stonewall the investigation. I would have lost all credibility with the IIC, a good friend of mine, if we made him subpoena the information, made him 'dig it out of us' to use Cass's words to me this morning."

"Sounds like him. We've fought bitterly in the past over his tactics. It's part of his personality."

"He threatened to fire me."

"Threatened? Then he backed off?"

"For the moment, I think. But the issue isn't my job. It's the integrity of the investigation. The meeting tomorrow may turn ugly so I wanted you to know the background."

"Will you be briefing the board on the story of missing documentation. Is it true? I've been trying to get something out of Cutler, but he says wait till the meeting."

"Sorry to say, yes."

"How did it happen, Alan? Frankly I'm surprised. This mistake isn't like you. The reason we were so eager to acquire your company was your management and manufacturing skills. Quality through and through. The way we like to think of ourselves."

"I'm not proud of what happened, I assure you. But documentation is just one small piece of evidence. Still, it makes us look bad. I should have been more on top of things. I assumed the blades were from my Waukegan plant . . ."

"Assumed? You mean they weren't?"

"No, Sedalia."

Hancock grabbed the edge of his desk, a wild look in his eyes. "This is the first I've heard of it." Then, "I knew it!" he snarled in a sudden show of emotion. "I knew it would happen."

I must have pushed his hot button, Fisk thought. Why?

"Sedalia was a rotten deal from the start. And I told Cutler so in front of the board. Our due diligence turned up rumors that the company had sold blades to the airlines after they had been rejected by the airforce. And he said it was all 'hogwash.' That's the word he used, 'hogwash'. What you'd expect from a man with no background."

Fisk shrugged. "Give me a break, John! I, too, have no 'background'."

"It's not the same thing. You have class. The purchase and sale agreement was enough to throw up over. None of the seller's warranties survive the closing of the deal. We're on the hook for any past product liability costs. And Cutler agreed to it. Now Beauchamp is gone, clean out of it, chasing every woman in sight, and we're left holding a shitty company. Nobody listened to me. I received no support from the rest of the board. They're all in his pocket . . .

". . . And now you tell me Sedalia made the blades?"

Fisk shifted in his chair. Past liability costs, he thought. My god! He doesn't understand. He's assuming the blades were made by Sedalia before Hi Tech acquired them. He wants to blame Cutler. Now's the time. Tell the truth, then duck.

"Beauchamp's not in this. The blades were made six months ago under Hi Tech's ownership," he said. "On my watch."

Hancock rested his chin on his clasped hands, for an eternity it seemed to Fisk. "Watch be darned. This is not the Navy," he said. "It's Cutler's fault, not yours. You inherited a handful. He got us in this mess playing up to The Great White Father."

Fisk's body relaxed. He is my ally!

"Thanks for the confidence, John, but if we're found at fault, those deaths are on my shoulders. And I have to know. Sooner the better."

"Are you going to make your confrontation with Cutler an issue tomorrow?"

Fisk got the impression Hancock relished the prospect.

"Yes, with his encouragement to my surprise. He must feel very secure."

Hancock's secretary entered the room with his afternoon tea. "Would you prefer coffee, Mr. Fisk?" she asked.

"No," he lied.

Hancock poured, then asked abruptly, "George Trueslow. You know the man. What can you tell me about him?"

Trueslow? What does he have to do with the crash? Is this why Hancock welcomed my visit?

"Social or business?"

"As a potential board member . . ."

Fisk shifted in his chair. Board member! This is too good to be true, he thought, remembering Otto Gitner's suggestion that he consider Trueslow as an ally along with Hancock.

"He's the second largest stockholder, you know," Hancock continued. "Cutler says with our stock down he'd like to see his block of stock represented on the board where he can keep an eye on it in case somebody decides to make a run on the company. As Chairman of the Nominating Committee it's up to me to take the initiative."

Cutler must have called Hancock after his conversation with Courtwright, Fisk mused. He's obviously taking the overture seriously.

"We play golf together," he said. "I see him at parties. Quite a man about town since his divorce a year ago. We've been friends for a long time."

"You like him?"

"Everybody likes George."

"Then how does he strike you?"

"Let's put it this way. He'd do a good job. He has the time, retired you know, eased out of Trueslow Chemical after a takeover."

"I remember the battle. After his father's death."

"And he's loyal."

"To Cutler?"

What's Hancock getting at? Sounds like he too is looking for allies. "He'd fight any takeover attempt if that's what you mean, especially in light of his own experience."

"So what about Cutler?"

"Loyal? To Cass? I'm not so sure."

"Oh?" Hancock said. "Tell me."

Fisk saw him brighten at the thought. *Ah, ha! I was right.*

"Cass seems to take special delight beating up on him whenever they're together. You know, put downs about his business ability, being a rich man's son, whatever."

"And he takes it?"

Fisk chose his words carefully. "So far. He was under his father's thumb all his life—that kind of personality. But you never know."

"Then you think Cutler's wrong thinking he can dominate him?"

"Yes. People do change, you know. But it's just a guess."

"A shrewd guess, I dare say. I've been watching you since

you've been on the board, Alan. I admire your independence. You stand up to Cutler."

"You have to stand up for what you believe in."

Hancock smiled. "Shrewd and politic," he said, rising from his chair. "You've told me what I need to know. You're a welcome addition to the board."

Fisk beamed. His body seemed lighter.

"Yes, very welcome," Hancock added. Then, leading him to the door: "See you at the meeting tomorrow."

Fisk called Trueslow at his Michigan Avenue apartment.

"Hello George," he said. "This is Alan Fisk."

"The Alan Fisk? Where the hell are ya?"

"Couple blocks away. Mind if I stop by the apartment? I'd love to see you, catch up on your bachelorship."

"Better than that. Meet me in the bar downstairs. My girl-friend is here from New York; napping now and she's a bear when she just wakes up."

"You've got a deal."

CHAPTER 21

5:00 P.M. CST

Fisk saw George Trueslow waving to him from a corner table in the bar. Good God!, could this be George? he asked himself—blue jeans, matching shirt with epaulets, leather boat shoes. The last time I saw him he was wearing a blue business suit at a party shortly after he and his wife were divorced. Now he could pass for the old hippie I saw on the Avenue in the sixties shouting "power to the grays".

"I know, I know," George said as they shook hands. "I look like hell. But it's catnip with the younger set."

George you devil, Fisk thought. Enjoy

"You won't believe this," he said, "but I was thinking of you this afternoon . . . no, really."

"You don't have to butter me up old friend," George said. "It's good enough seein you. Maybe you can give me some inside information on the crash, like whether I'm still solvent. I'll bet old Cass shit in his pants when he heard the news."

"Insider information? No way, George! That's a federal offense. You want us both to land in the pokey?"

"Okay, okay! I've gottcha. Anyway, I have some information of my own that might interest you."

Information? Fisk thought. I wonder if he knows Cutler has him in his sights as a director? Maybe that's what he wants to tell me. "I'm listening," he said.

They sat down and George crossed his good right leg over his replacement limb. "My leg's killin me," he said. "But it was worth it. What a week I've had! Shirley takes my mind off the stock market. She and I have been up until three in the morning every day she's been in town!" He paused. "You don't want to hear all this."

"I do. That's why I wanted to see you." He waited patiently for the promised information. All in good time.

"Then let's have that drink first. Hey, over here young lady. My son needs a drink. What'll you have Alan?"

"Bourbon on the rocks. Make it a double . . . to celebrate seeing my friend."

"Yeh, me too, the same. Now as I was saying . . . I was having a great time until . . . hey, maybe I shouldn't be telling you this . . ."

"It's up to you."

"Well, yesterday I get a call from a guy named Giles Courtwright. Ever hear of him?"

Interesting! "Sure, he's Chairman of United Aerospace."

"He calls me and says he wants me to have dinner with him in the Pump Room. Who am I to turn down dinner at the Pump Room with the Chairman of United Aerospace, so I accept. Shirley was furious."

"I can imagine."

"He's quite a guy. Ever meet him?"

"No."

"A real pisseroo. Doesn't mess around. Course, we have to go through the usual folderol with the chef himself coming to our table to chin with the big man and let me know I'm with an important person. When we're alone again Giles comes right to the point. He wants to buy my shares in Hi Tech."

So Courtwright's proposal to Cutler was the real thing. Fisk was unsurprised. And what would that do to the investigation?

"What did you say?"

"I wasn't interested."

"And?"

"He dangled the bait, said he could make me an offer I couldn't refuse—way above the current market."

"You still weren't interested?"

"No. My father knew old man Hancock when he first went public and acquired shares in the initial offering. When he died I got his stock. My father would piss in his grave if he knew I sold it and paid a quarter to Uncle Sam in taxes. He always thought I was an idiot . . . you sure you want to hear all this?"

"Look at me. I'm fascinated."

"From the time I was a runt in knickers, my father would call me into his study whenever he had nothing better to do and tell me what a shit I was. And I took it, never stood up to him, even when I was a grown man. The truth is, he never thought I could hack it. Called me Boy until the day he died."

"He made you president of the company, didn't he?"

"Called every shot, though, right to the end. People used to praise him for being his own man. He was, but always at somebody else's expense."

"You've been retired as long as I've known you. What happened?"

"One of the barracuda on Wall Street bought the controlling block of stock from his estate and made a tender offer for the rest. When he invited me to dinner I knew it was going to be the last supper. After we discussed the financial details of my resignation the sonofabitch had the gall to pull the old Broadway bit: 'Don't call us, we'll call you'."

"You must have been in your forties when all that happened. Did you go through some soul searching?"

"You mean mid-life crisis?"

"You could call it that."

"Being Charley's son, my whole life's been a mid-life crisis. After the takeover I just settled for being ole Daddy Warbucks cryin all the way to the bank." George sat quietly for a moment. "Maybe I shouldn't have turned that guy Courtwright down so fast."

"No. You did the right thing."

"I'm fed up dancing to somebody else's tune. Maybe I should think of what I want to do for a change."

Fisk didn't respond.

"Anyway, I told Cass about the call. And you know what happened . . . ? He asked me if I'd like to come on the board. Can you imagine? You think I should?"

Do I ever! But careful now . . . "Umm, I'd certainly give it careful thought if I were you. It's an interesting board and I think you could make a real contribution."

George tossed down the rest of his drink. "I've never talked like this with anyone," he said. "I suppose it's easier with you. You've always impressed me as a sensitive person . . . say, am I boring you? You're being awfully quiet."

"I'm trying to think of something sensitive to say."

And what all this means to me, Fisk thought. Courtwright's no fool. The company's no bargain if we're going to get hit with the liability. He must know something. Or figures the disk won't be found and all the parties will contribute to the pot to settle the suit.

George laughed. "Hey, I'm getting maudlin. Why didn't you stop me old friend? Must be this poison," he said, raising his empty glass. "What do you say we have another belt and then hit the road?"

Fisk looked at his watch. Six-thirty. Dusty would be in his office by now. He flipped open his cell phone and called him.

"Any luck today with the Navy Seals?"

"Not a thing, Alan, and it's frustrating. The investigation's stymied until we find that disk and the whole country is on my back. The waters around here are filled with algae—too murky for visual inspection. Besides, an object that heavy would sink several feet into the muck. Munson has had a helluva time keeping the Seals at it. First it was the water moccasins. Then the gators. Before they'd put a foot in the water he had to round up sharpshooters to stand over every dive."

"I'm making a report to the board at our monthly meeting tomorrow. Is there any next step?"

"We're having a dozen special underwater metal detectors flown in from White's Electronics in Sweet Home, Oregon. Ever hear of them?"

"No. But do you think that can do it?"

"Their new Surfmaster model. We may have to plug a few gators along the way, but if the disk is down there, we'll find it."

"If you don't, I have an idea. You said the disk might have sunk into the muck. It'd be warm compared to its surroundings. Could it be detected from the air by its infrared 'signature'? A friend in a special arms unit once told me of an aircraft with infrared sensing equipment used to locate targets in night warfare, in much the same way a rattlesnake senses the image of a rabbit against the cool background of the desert."

"Great idea, Alan. I'll have Rick Munson look into it and give you a call. And by the way, how did you make out with Cutler this morning?"

"Oh, some fireworks, but I smoothed it over."

"Did you tell him I might have been the source?"

"Didn't have to. Joe Bledsoe saw you having that drink with your friend Rosie from General Tech."

"Ah, the gofer again. Quick eyes, quick feet. The man's everywhere."

"You can imagine Cutler's reaction."

"I'm more concerned about you. I should have kept my yap shut, but I swear to you, I had no idea she was with General Tech. Last time I saw her was in 'Nam twenty years ago. Risked my own life to rescue her lying wounded in a field with the gooks approaching to finish her off."

"I think we may find she's behind the tape leak and the Spaghetti Man caper. General Tech certainly has the motive."

"You may be right, Alan. I asked my men to be on the look-out for her today, but nobody's seen her around."

"What does she look like?"

"Over six feet, long black hair, walks with a cane, great boobs. You'd never miss her."

"Let me think about this. I may want to have a quiet talk with Sam Barker at some point."

"I'll leave it with you. But if you do, count me in."

FRIDAY

CHAPTER 22

9:00 A. M. CST

Hi Tech held regular board meetings the third Friday of each month. With summer approaching, the May meeting was traditionally a festive occasion, but today Fisk found an atmosphere of disquiet pervading the room. He was there early checking his visuals for his briefing of the board. Finished, he joined the other early arrivals and listened to their talk, trying to gauge their reaction to the crash when Cutler was not around. Like children huddled around the campfire telling ghost stories, he thought, the directors sought to break the tension of the tragedy by trotting out the scariest examples of outrageous awards in recent tort cases.

University president Stuart Brattle, the only director under sixty besides Fisk and Executive Vice President Woody Bentley, spoke of a huge award to the family of a man killed by an out of control car while making a telephone call from an outdoor phone booth. The judgment was imposed on AT&T for not providing an enclosure built to resist the impact of the careening car. "It doesn't make sense," Brattle said. "It's just not rational."

"They ought to string all those tort lawyers up by the balls!" said Ian Coxe, Chairman of Superior Equipment. "We just paid twenty million dollars to the widow of a man killed in a thirty-year-old scrap paper baler. Our safety controls had been removed over the years by five different owners. And we were the deep pocket."

Coxe paused, looking straight at Brattle: "And speaking of balls, Stuart, if the world was a rational place, men, not women, would ride side saddle."

Felix Reston, Chairman of Van Hunter & Company, Hi Tech's investment bankers, listened with sympathy. "Look," he said. "There are two issues weighing on all our minds. The company's liability, and our personal exposure as directors."

You can always count on Felix to set matters straight, Fisk thought.

"If our products are found faulty, Hi Tech stands to take a serious hit. You probably saw in the papers this week that Schnell is already at work in Florida."

"The little turd," said Coxe, pulling at a lock of the thick white hair that crowned his head.

"But the company will survive," Reston continued. "Our debt to equity ratio is one of the lowest on the big board. The real threat will be a takeover, especially if our stock remains down as the potential crash liability becomes better defined to a sophisticated observer. As for our personal exposure, you can forget about it. This board has been meticulous in following the 'duty of care' rules. The courts say we must act, one, in an informed manner; two, in good faith; three, in a manner we reasonably believe to be in the best interests of shareholders; and four, without fraud or self-dealing. None of these caveats can come into play in any of our actions conceivably related to the crash."

"I'm not so sure," said Eben Vaughn, president of the company's principal bank. "I've always been uneasy the way Cass bulled through the acquisition of Beauchamp's company. I don't think we received all the information we needed to make a sound decision. We should have demanded a full investigation of the rumor that Beauchamp had sold blades to the airlines after they were rejected by the airforce. Cass stiff-armed us when John challenged him on the issue. 'Hogwash.' Remember? And we let it go at that."

"Jesus Christ, Eben!" Tom Burke, Hi Tech's lawyer, snapped. "Don't ever say that, don't even think it, even when you're sitting on the crapper."

Fisk watched Hancock's eyes as Vaughn, then Burke, spoke. They held the same wild look he had seen in Hancock's office at the mention of Sedalia. Coxe and Reston glanced uneasily at one another.

"What does Sedalia have to do with this?" Hancock asked innocently.

He knows goddamned well, Fisk thought. He's testing Eben—realizes Cutler probably picked up the phone and informed his cronies on the board without calling him as soon as he heard about Sedalia from me the afternoon of the crash.

"You know, John," Vaughn said haltingly. "The blades were made at Sedalia, not Waukegan as we first thought."

"I see," Hancock said. "I see."

I've seen that deceptively understanding attitude before, Fisk thought. He's ticked off at being excluded, and Cutler's sure to hear about it.

Burke was still glowering at Vaughn when Cutler entered the room with Woody Bentley, a tall, spare man disposed to white shirts and charcoal gray suits. His attire and studied alertness gave him the look of a secret service agent working the rope line.

Cutler motioned to the directors to be seated and took his place in the president's chair, its back a subtle two inches higher than the others. "As you may have noticed, gentlemen, there was no agenda included with the monthly directors report you received earlier this week. Things are happening so fast around here I wanted the agenda to reflect the up-to-the-minute situation. So let's take a few seconds to glance at the sheets Tom is handing out."

Meeting of Board of Directors.
Hi Tech, Inc.
May 28, 2002

AGENDA
1. Approval of minutes of April meeting.
2. Status of crash investigation.
3. Recent developments.
4. Other business.

While his fellow directors were reading, Fisk's thoughts were on the four men at the far end of the table: Cutler flanked on his right by Burke who as secretary was already taking notes for the corporate minutes; on his left by Reston, with Vaughn next to him. They probably met earlier to discuss me, he thought, maybe for breakfast at Cutler's place instead of the usual pre-conference discussion in his office. Burke is certain to know everything, down to every last word between me and Cutler and my stance against a cover-up. Reston, I'm not sure. He's the kind to have told Cutler long ago there are certain things he'd rather not know. Same with Vaughn. He'd keep his distance from anything over the line.

"We've got a lot of ground to cover, gentlemen," Cutler continued. "Do I hear a motion to approve the minutes of the last meeting?"

"So moved," said Burke.

"I second," said Bentley.

"Any discussion . . . ? All in favor say yes . . . opposed say no . . . That's a vote."

Cutler looked around the table. "This is a watershed moment for our company," he said, "and I'm glad to see that all nine directors are present. The unprecedented loss of life and property in the crash of CCA 181 on Tuesday and the possible involvement of our product make the event a threat to the company's very existence, at least as we now know it. So I've asked Alan Fisk who heads the division in question to brief us on the crash investigation.

"You're on, Alan," Cutler said, and Fisk started for the podium at the head of the room.

"You've all read the papers," Cutler added, "so you saw the article on his flight to Miami and visit to the area hospitals. Great idea, Alan . . ."

The words took Fisk by surprise. His antennae went up.

". . . 'Era of corporate responsibility.' Gave us the only positive press the whole three days. That and his adroit handling of Schnell."

I think I get it. He's acting on advice of Burke alone—it's too dangerous to try to discredit me before the board and what might come out of it. But if I decide to make a fuss, he's setting me up for a fall. How can there be the slightest suggestion of a cover-up when he's been with me all the way.

He glanced at his notes when he reached the podium, then put them down. "Thank you Cass," he said. "I wasn't going to mention the trip. Yes, I'm glad I went.

"For those of you not totally familiar with the workings of a jet engine," he began, "I've prepared a cutaway picture to help explain the nature of our potential product liability resulting from the crash." He pressed the button on the remote projector control and the first slide appeared on the screen beside him. For the next half hour, pointer in hand, he led his audience through the basics of jet engine design.

"So much for background," Fisk said. "The investigators from the National Transportation Safety Board have determined that the engine failure began here." He pointed to the fan-section just inside the engine inlet. "No doubt about it based on their examination of the debris. And that means either our blades or the disk to which they are attached is at fault. Rotating at ten thousand rpm you can imagine what happens when either lets go. Failure is usually caused by stress induced cracks from improper design, voids or other metallurgical anomalies."

"The pilot said it was the blades," Brattle observed.

"The reporters raised that with me in Florida, Stuart, and I wasn't about to contradict the pilot in public. But the tape doesn't prove a thing. Our people searched the records and found the pilot had an aborted takeoff earlier this year involving a fan blade failure in his number three engine. Blaming the blades again may have been a knee-jerk reaction, a sort of conditioned reflex. This sort of thing happens often."

"How likely is it to be the fan disk?" Reston asked.

"We won't know for certain until they find the disk."

"Any late news? The paper said yesterday it's still missing. Surely it's not that difficult to find at the Miami Airport."

"Harder than you might imagine, Felix. There are many wetlands in the area. Two hundred guardsmen searched a wide area around and beyond the runway Wednesday with no success. Ditto yesterday when the Navy Seals searched the surrounding bodies of water. Anticipating your question, I spoke last night to Dusty McGinty, the Investigator in Charge of the investigation. He told me they're planning another search after delivery of underwater metal detection equipment. If that doesn't work, I had an idea he's going to look into."

"Absent inspection of the disk, can you give us any comfort?"

"Some. McGinty told me the NTSB lab has made a quick metallurgical examination of the broken blade and finds no obvious flaw at the point of fracture."

"Anything else positive to brighten our day?" Reston asked.

"There's been a history of disk problems."

"Many?"

"Yes. But the same is true of the blades. We have to find that disk!"

Fisk looked around the room for a moment, waiting for questions. "So in summary," he continued, "the first determination is that either our blades or the disk is at fault. The second is that the blades were made at our Sedalia plant and . . ."

"Sedalia?" Brattle interrupted.

"Let him finish," Cutler said.

"I understand your surprise. When I first learned of the crash and my blades possible involvement, I assumed they were made in Waukegan; the plant has been sole supplier for the engines for years. About noon the day of the crash, I first heard Sedalia had made replacement blades for CCA's maintenance for years."

"Was that made known to us by Beauchamp during the due diligence investigation when we acquired Sedalia?" Hancock asked.

"No, but only because the records were a shambles, I assume."

"A frightening thought," Brattle said, "for a company making jet engine blades."

"We should never have acquired the company," Hancock said.

Cutler shot him a dirty look, Fisk noticed, rejoicing.

"It wasn't until shortly before I left for Miami that I confirmed the blades were Sedalia's and were shipped from their plant six months ago. On my watch."

"Surely you knew Sedalia was shipping replacement blades to CCA," Bentley said.

"I didn't, nor did Mike Belmonte, my manager of that division. I take full responsibility, Woody. My only defense is my team had our work cut out for us getting that operation in shape when we came in."

"Yes, that was your job," Bentley said.

Smart ass, Fisk thought. Know-it-all.

"And to make matters worse I learned that evening that Sedalia couldn't find any record of inspection of the blades. We were in the process of consolidating their quality control with ours in Waukegan when the blades were shipped. Maybe I pressed my men too hard during the transition. Somebody fouled up."

Brattle looked startled. "Then the rumor in yesterday's headlines was true," he said.

"Not exactly. It's just that we can't find any records."

Fisk saw Hancock lean forward, his hands pressed against the table top. That wild look again . . .

"Mr. Cutler," Hancock snapped. "All this talk about Sedalia making the blades. This is the first I've heard about it."

He's lying, Fisk thought. I told him about it in his office. He wants to put Cutler on the defensive.

"Am I some kind of outcast?" Hancock continued. "Earlier I heard Eben say he knew. He and the rest of your little clique had to hear it from you." He turned to Brattle next to him. "You hear about it?"

"No."

"Woody?"

"No."

"Tom?"

No answer.

"I assume that means yes. Felix?"

Again no response. Fisk could feel the heat of Hancock's anger.

"That's an outrage. The whole board should have been called. Then we read about the missing documentation in the papers."

Jesus, what's John up to? Fisk thought. He's lying again. He knows I didn't tell Cutler about the missing documentation until yesterday. Cutler's going to have to defend himself with the board. This whole thing's going to unravel. Is John my friend or enemy?

"Calm down, Johnny," Cutler said. "For one thing I didn't know myself until yesterday morning . . ."

Fisk blanched. I knew it!

"Yesterday morning?" Brattle exclaimed.

Cutler ignored him. "Besides," he said, "I've been working my ass off on the Courtwright matter I called you about yesterday."

"That's no excuse," Hancock said. "Sounds like you're ashamed of the Sedalia acquisition?"

Cutler folded his arms defiantly. "Look," he said, "we're getting into item three on the agenda and I might as well cover that now for those of you who haven't heard."

Playing for time, Fisk thought. Or was it a ploy to change the subject?

Cutler gave the board the details of Courtwright's abrupt merger proposal and subsequent takeover threat.

"I've had Tom and Felix and their boys studying our defenses for a presentation to this board at a special meeting," he said. "I'll tell you then about a plan I have to bomb the son-of-a-bitch if he makes a run on us. Which seems likely. I learned yesterday morning that he met with George Trueslow Wednesday night with an offer to buy his stock at a price substantially over market. Trueslow refused, but you never know. As for open market purchases, we see nothing in our price and volume action on the exchange to indicate he's accumulating stock. Felix's people think he'll lay low, maybe accumulate less than five percent so he won't have to file a 13 D and go public. They doubt he'll make a pre-emptive bid until he has a better handle on our liabilities. At that point we'll have to be prepared for the worst. Selling under book and at less than fifteen times earnings we're a sitting duck."

"That's very disturbing news, Cass," Brattle said, "but I want to go back to something you glossed over earlier. Did I understand you to say that you didn't hear about the missing documentation until yesterday morning? Alan hadn't told you?"

For god sakes, Stuart, hadn't we gotten safely past that? Fisk thought. Leave it alone. You're going to get me fired, and I want to stay here where I can be on top of the investigation.

"No, I called him after I read about it. There's been nothing in the papers about the blades being made in Sedalia, by the way. Nobody seems to care about that except our friend Johnny."

Brattle turned to Fisk. "Forget about Sedalia. I find it hard to believe you didn't tell Cass about the documentation the moment you knew."

Very little gets by him, Fisk thought with a touch of admiration. And he's quick to let you know it. "I did give him a heads up the afternoon of the crash when Belmonte told me there was a chance they were Sedalia's blades. But no, I didn't call Cass when I heard for sure that evening they were shipped under our ownership and worse, lacked documentation."

"Was there a reason?"

"Yes."

Fisk felt like a little boy called before the principal.

"Can you tell us?"

Burke stopped taking notes.

"I felt the NTSB should know about the documentation issue as soon as possible. It's an important part of the fact gathering process and its absence will be noted in the factual report at the eventual public hearing."

"Yes, of course. So?"

Fisk squirmed. You don't cross a man like Cutler and get away free. "I was to meet that night in Miami with Dusty McGinty, the Investigator in Charge, and I wanted to be free to discuss it with him."

"And you felt you couldn't if you told Cass?"

"He and I had a confrontation that afternoon about my visiting the area hospitals . . ."

"A discussion," Cutler interrupted, drumming his fingers on the table. "I encouraged you."

Here goes, Fisk thought, his heart pounding. If he'll flat out lie like that, he'll do anything.

"Call it what you will, you forbid me to go, said 'and that's a direct order'."

"Is that true, Cass?" Coxe asked.

"Of course not. Sure I counseled him to be careful. But I was all for the idea. You heard me. And look what happened. He talked with McGinty that night and it's all over the papers in the morning. Was I right in urging caution?"

"Go on, Alan" Hancock said, ignoring Cutler.

"Before I left, he told me he wanted the files clean, nothing in the records that can be used against us. I said, 'Even if it's the truth?' and he replied, 'Especially if it's the truth. There's too much at stake. We have to be in the clear'."

"Those are the exact words between you?" Hancock asked.

John's at it again, Fisk thought. That's exactly what I told him in his office.

"Yes."

Fisk saw Burke glance at Cutler. Burke's scared shitless, he thought. He knows we're headed for a blow up.

Cutler, his face crimson, made a move to stand. Reston put his hand on his arm holding him back. "You're not saying you suspect Cass ordered the documentation destroyed, are you?" he asked Fisk.

"No, no! My immediate thought, as I said earlier, was that somebody fouled up during the transition. The point is I had the distinct impression from our several discussions after the crash that he was ordering me to stonewall anything that prejudiced our position. And the simple fact that documentation was missing for whatever reason would do just that."

"Look here, Alan," Reston said firmly. "Your 'distinct impression' isn't enough. You're making a grave charge of misconduct against the C.E.O. of this company. If the board's to take you seriously, we'll need facts, not vague allegations."

"You want more?" Fisk said. "You want it in his words? When I told him yesterday morning that I had passed the information to McGinty during my visit he said: 'I get it. You knew I'd forbid you to say anything if you told me in advance. Stonewall them, delay, play for time, that's the way. Make them dig it out of us.' Sound like him?"

"Cover-up," Hancock said.

Cutler exploded from his seat. "I've listened to enough of this shit!" he shouted, pointing his finger at Fisk. "You're fired!"

Reston looked up at him, startled. "Wait a minute Cass, this is a matter for the board to discuss. I think we should ask Alan to leave the room."

"I said he's fired!"

"Alan," Reston said. "Will you please leave for a few minutes?"

Fisk got up and walked out. Stupid son-of-a-bitch! Fire me, will he? We'll see.

*   *   *

Fisk returned to his office and plopped into his chair, slumped in agony from the searing pain shooting down his left neck muscle and into his shoulder. Desperate for relief, he took a deep breath and slowly let it out. Slowly . . . slowly . . . calmly, he murmured, and sat eyes closed for a few minutes. Relax. Don't let him throw you. Suddenly the pain was gone as fast as it had come. He sighed. I'm able to think again . . . I can see Reston and Burke trying to calm Cutler down. Maybe Martha was right. Maybe Cass is losing it. It's not like him to get himself in a box like this. Everybody in that room knows the worst move the board could make at the moment is let him fire me. I can see it: "**BLADE EXEC FIRED! HI TECH AT FAULT?**" I'd still be on the board until next April and would be a thorn in their side. Dusty would welcome my help; full time. No, they won't fire me. And I won't quit and give up my window on the day to day goings on here. No matter what, I'll stay until the investigation's concluded.

But then . . . ? Yes, what then?

Martha, he thought, remembering their talk by the pool the morning of the crash. She had made her position clear when he shared his growing concern about Cutler's integrity, hadn't she? "You're tearing yourself apart . . . Give up the business. You could lead an exciting, productive life as a sculptor . . . This is the time in your life to do what you want to do."

What I want to do . . . Suddenly his body grew as rigid as Arctic ice and he slammed his fist on the desk. One thing for sure. It won't be working for that corrupt son-of-a-bitch a second after the investigation is completed! Not a split second. His heart was pounding. I've had my fill of business—don't even know if I could continue in any business whether my blades are at fault or not.

He got up and walked to the window. Martha could be right. I may be happy as a full time sculptor. If I'm not, I could start a new company in a sector of aerospace where I could feel comfortable. Or buy a little company . . .

He paused, scowling. Stop your daydreaming, he thought. I've made the decision. I'm outa here when fault is established. So . . . His face beamed. Hey, great idea, Alan. Why not put that in writing, now.

He stretched his arms and returned to his desk. Cutler and I have been kaput ever since our set-to the morning I returned from Florida. Why not make it official. He may even cut me a little slack during the investigation.

He reached into the desk drawer for a company letterhead and began writing:

May 28, 2002

To The Board of Hi Tech:
    I hereby tender my resignation as an officer and director as of the date of the end of the NTSB Public Hearing establishing the probable cause of the crash of CCA 181.

Sincerely,
Alan Fisk

He signed the letter and put it in an envelope. It's done, he sighed, it's done, and his whole body tingled with feelings of joy.

"I want him out!" Cutler was bellowing as the door closed behind Fisk. "Out! The man's a liar."

"If anyone should be fired," Hancock shouted, "it darned well should be you."

The prissy little son-of-a-bitch, Cutler thought, I could kill him!

Hancock was now on his feet pointing at Cutler standing at the end of the table. "You're just trying to lay your mistake off on a decent man who's been doing a Herculean job cleaning up the mess you foisted on us with the acquisition of Sedalia. I want to remind you it was my father who founded this company on a policy of decency and fairness, and I'm tired of seeing you drag it's name through shit."

"Oh, for god sakes come off it, John," Coxe growled.

"You're pushing me to my limit, Mr. Cutler," Hancock continued. "I've taken a lot of abuse from you over the years out of loyalty to my father's memory, but I've about had it. If Courtwright wants stock, let him come to me. I'm in a talking mood."

"You think Courtwright will be decent and fair to the employees and customers of this company if he takes us over?" Cutler shot back. "You don't know what you're talking about."

Reston held up both hands. "Please, please, gentlemen. Dissension on this board is the last thing we need with the problem we face. None of us were prepared for this divisive turn of events so we must proceed with utmost caution . . ."

As Reston continued, Cutler was preoccupied with Hancock's threat. *Giles has wanted this company for a long time. Can't fault him. We're a perfect fit. He might even want us bad enough to offer Hancock the chairmanship of the combined companies to close out his career. Yes, dammit, he might just do that.*

". . . and so as I look around this room," Reston concluded, "I don't see many willing to risk the negative impact on Hi Tech the firing would bring. Am I right?"

No one spoke.

"I take your silence for a yes," Reston said and turned to Cutler. "Cass, if you'll allow me, I'd like to propose an informal motion aimed at reconciliation."

So I eat a little crow, Cutler thought. *I can't afford to lose Hancock's stock. And Felix is a master at smoothing things over.*

"Go on."

"I propose that it be the sense of this meeting that Alan inform Cass immediately of all significant developments on a good faith basis as the investigation proceeds. If Alan feels impeded in his work with the NTSB at any point, he will report it to a committee consisting of Tom, John, and myself. Anyone disagree? . . ."

Cutler sat silently, his mind filled with thoughts of revenge. I'll have my chance.

"No? Then let's call Alan back."

Fisk listened while Reston explained the compromise. More than I expected, he thought. At least it puts Cutler on notice to treat me with more respect. But don't be taken in. He'll suffer me, sure. But he still has his own agenda. And I have mine.

"I hope this meets with your satisfaction," Reston said.

"Yes," Fisk said agreeably, "and now we can all get on with the job of finding what caused the crash. As I said earlier, Felix, McGinty confided that lab tests have indicated our blade contained no obvious flaw. That's very good news, and I think we've lost sight of it in all the excitement. We have to hope for an early announcement that the disk has been found."

Burke whispered something in Cutler's ear. "And on that positive note," Cutler said, "I think we should adjourn, but first I have a brief proposal under agenda item four which I think you'll understand in light of Courtwright's approach to Trueslow. Our by-laws authorize a board of no more than twelve. We now have nine directors. One of our best takeover defenses is insuring that our major individual shareholders remain loyal. So I have suggested that Johnny and his nominating committee consider George Trueslow to fill one of the vacancies. George is former president of Trueslow Chemical and well qualified to join us. If the Committee acts favorably on the nomination, you'll receive his resume and we'll vote on it at a conference call board meeting—Friday June 11th okay with everybody?

"Comments . . . ?"

There were none.

"Do I hear a motion to adjourn?"

"So moved," said Coxe.

"I second," said Brattle.

"Meeting adjourned."

As they were leaving the room, Cutler motioned Fisk aside. "I guess we now know where we both stand. You embarrass me again before the board and it'll be your ass or mine. Have a look at the make-up of the board, fellah. You'll see it won't be mine."

Fisk reached into his jacket pocket and handed him the envelope. "Read this," he said, and left.

Gotta call Martha, Fisk thought back in his office. "Well, I've done it," he said when he reached her.

"Done what?"

"Resigned."

"Oh, Alan. That's wonderful! Congratulations. What happened?"

"Long story. I'll tell you about it tonight."

"No! Tell me now." Her voice grew sharp. "We've had this discussion before. You're shutting me out again. I can understand when you're in Miami and have a car waiting downstairs, but you've just finished a board meeting and you can damned well spend a few minutes on the phone with me."

Fisk smiled. Wow! At least I'm never in doubt where she stands. "Sorry about that," he said, grinning. "Things just kind of got out of hand at the board meeting. Cass fired me on the spot, but Reston, you know how he is, smoothed things over. Okay with me. But after the meeting, I handed Cass my written letter of resignation effective at the end of the investigation."

"Whatever the outcome?"

"Whatever."

"And he accepted it?"

"He didn't say. I just handed him the letter. But what choice does he have?"

"Do you think he'll tell the rest of the board?"

"Maybe, maybe not. He may want to keep his options open. But I'm determined."

"So you are going to sculpt!"

"Hey, come on, Martha. Let up. I can't decide that now. Finding the disk, that's where my mind is. Nobody seems to understand how I feel about this. I have to know what caused that crash."

She laughed. "Of all people, I should know better."

"How's that?"

"Better than to press you."

He thought for a moment. "I don't mind," he said. "It tells me that you love me." And he needed all the love he could get.

PART TWO

June

CHAPTER 23

Tuesday, June 1

Hobie's mother adjusted his tie and stood back to admire her son in the new outfit she had bought him at the local Goodwill.

"Now you be polite to the airplane man," she said.

"I will mama."

"Remember to tell him your Papa is walking a little now. And don't forget your picture."

Hobie patted his left breast to indicate it was tucked away in his inside pocket. Then he reached for his school knapsack doubling as an overnight bag, and the two walked to the front door. They kissed good-bye and the woman watched smiling as her little man left for the long journey to Waukegan.

When Fisk called to arrange the trip, he had volunteered to send a car to pick Hobie up for the drive to Miami International. But Hobie preferred his bicycle and Fisk told him there was a place to leave it at the general aviation terminal where they would meet. Hobie's house in a semi-industrial area of Miami Springs across from the Hialeah freight yards was just two miles due north of the end of the runway, and Hobie and his friend Lester often rode their bikes to the airport to play.

Now, speeding south on Ludlam Drive toward 36th Street bordering the airport, Hobie was in a joyful mood. With one hand on the handlebar, he idly rotated the other in the cool morning air streaming past, delighting in the feeling of lift as he slowly increased the angle of his flattened palm. He was making an airfoil with his hand, a concept he had grasped as a child of eight when his father took him on a brief sightseeing flight from Opalocka airport. While they were still on the ground, the pilot had explained the function of the wing, lifting him so he could touch the curved upper surface. On the way home, he had stuck his hand out of the car window and felt the airstream break away from the top of his make-believe wing.

Hobie turned left on 36th Street and peddled past the fenced-in northwest corner of the airport bordering the end of runway 27R, an area filled with derelict planes. As he passed, he turned to look at the clump of bushes off the road where he and Lester often hid their bikes and then bellied under an opening in the chain link fence to enter the deserted compound and play pilot in the planes. "Wow-ee!" he whooped. No kid stuff this time. Soon he would be sitting in a real live plane—and a jet at that.

Fisk entered the cabin of Hi Tech's Falcon Jet parked at general aviation and began reading a summary of the morning's meeting with Munson and McGinty. His idea for infrared detection of the disk with secret Army equipment had been approved by the Pentagon, and he had flown down to discuss the details. Soon he saw the captain and copilot approaching the plane with Hobie and went to meet them. He smiled at the boy. "I kinda thought you'd be early."

"Mama told me not to be late."

"Then you had no trouble finding us?"

"My friend Lester and I play here a lot."

"Here?" Fisk asked with a surprised glance at captain Sam Fouchet.

Hobie looked stricken over his admission. "You won't tell?"

"No."

"We play in the wrecks up the road."

"He must mean Cockroach Corner," Fouchet said to Fisk. "You can see some of the planes from here."

"Sam's showing his age," Hal Makie the copilot laughed. "Us youngsters know it as Cocaine Corner."

"I've never heard of it," Fisk said.

"Pilots from all over have," Makie continued. "Sort of a graveyard for defunct planes. And lately a parking lot for equipment impounded by the DEA."

"Well, let's get going," Fisk said, "and let Hobie have a go at this one."

They entered the plane. Fisk stopped at the cockpit area. "Want to try out the captain's seat?" he asked Hobie.

"Yes sir!" Without prompting the boy scrambled into the seat on the left. He looked around, wide-eyed at all the equipment. "Can I touch the wheel?" he asked.

"Move it if you want."

Hobie turned the wheel to the left and looked out the window to watch the left aileron rise. Then he pulled back on the yoke. Fouchet looked at Fisk and rolled his eyes. "The young man knows his stuff."

"Where did you learn all that?" Fisk asked.

"Playing in the wrecks," Hobie said. "I'm older than Lester, you know. I get to be captain and do the controls. He sits on the right and makes noise like the engine."

Mackie laughed. "See, Sam, now you know where the power is."

Fisk motioned Hobie toward the cabin. "Before our visit to the plant is over," he said, "you're going to know how the jet engines work too."

"Oh, I know that already," Hobie said proudly.

"You do?"

"Suck, squeeze, burn, blow."

The three men erupted in laughter. "Where did you ever hear that?" Fisk asked.

"From an airplane man. He caught us playing one day and when he saw we weren't stealing, he told us lots of things."

*   *   *

When the plane was airborne, Fisk turned to his papers while Hobie spent most of the time in the cockpit doorway, talking to the pilots. Approaching Chicago, Fisk pondered Hobie's interest in airplanes. Philosophers, he knew, would attribute it to something innate, to the boy's inner essential nature. But if his own experience at Hobie's age was any guide, the something might be less metaphysical, might simply be the kindness and interest of an older person.

Fisk asked Hobie to sit opposite him. "When did you first love airplanes?"

Hobie fished in his inside coat pocket and handed him a photograph. "When I was eight."

Fisk felt a lump in his throat. The picture was of Hobie and his father standing next to the wing of a single engine Cessna.

"Papa paid to take me up in an airplane over Opalocka. He was scared half to death, but he said he wanted me to know about modern things."

"And that's when you began making model airplanes?"

Hobie looked at him. "How you know that?"

"Your father told me about you the day I visited him at the hospital. He said you are crazy about airplanes. It made me wonder whether you know yet what you want to be when you grow up."

"Can I be anything I want?"

"Anything you want."

"An airplane man."

"And exactly what do you mean by an 'airplane man'? A pilot?"

"No!" Hobie said with a sigh of exasperation. "You know, anybody who does with airplanes."

Fisk resisted a smile. "Well, if that's the case," he said, "you're going to be spending the rest of the day mixing with a lot of people who do with airplanes."

* * *

"That's beautiful," Hobie said, admiring a gleaming titanium fan blade in final inspection at the Waukegan plant. "Can I touch it?"

"Sure," Fisk said.

Hobie ran his fingers over the blade taking obvious pleasure in the feel of its arching surface and gentle twist from root to tip. "Thas cool."

Fisk motioned to the head of quality control who had explained this phase of the operations to the boy. "Stan, do you have a reject we can give this young man as a memento of his visit?"

"Sure do. This one has a small inclusion near the root dovetail. It's headed for remelt."

"Want to take this with you?" Fisk asked, handing it to Hobie.

"Oh! Can I? Can I?"

"And I tell you what, when we get back to my office I'll give you that scale model of the 747 to take home. I could see you liked it."

Hobie began to cry.

"What's wrong?"

"You're so nice to me."

"Is that a reason to cry?"

"Mama says she's worried about you."

"About what?"

"She heard you tell Papa your blades may have caused the accident."

Oh my God! Fisk thought, remembering Howard in the hospital, and the earlier sight of his stark, pleading eyes in the crashed elevator. His eyes misted.

"Yes, that's true."

"I told Mama it couldn't be Mr. Fisk's blades, no sir, not Mr. Fisk's."

"I hope you're right, Hobie," Fisk said, putting his arm around the boy. "I hope you're right. We'll know when we find the rest of those parts we're looking for."

CHAPTER 24

Wednesday, June 2

NTSB investigator Rick Munson was seated at his desk at the Sheraton River House pondering his written report to Dusty. A week had passed since the crash with no sign of the disk. Minutes earlier, Pete DiBella had made another of his frequent calls from Cincinnati chiding Rick about his lack of progress. "All evidence still points to either the blades or the disk failure as the probable cause," Pete said, "but we're stymied until you find those parts. So don't fail us, big boy. Get your ass moving."

Just the kind of shitty remark you'd expect from Marine Air, Rick thought. What more can I do?

He reviewed the report's three sections:

Details of the land search and the first quick visual inspection by teams of navy Seals of the nearby bodies of water in which the disk might have landed—lakes, ponds, lagoons, drainage ditches, even the Tamiami Canal which ran just south of the airport perimeter. No disk.

The search by scuba divers with Surfmaster 11 metal detectors used by underwater treasure hunters around the world. Capable of operating at depths up to thirty feet, they detected hundreds of items buried in the bottom muck, from a metal back brace to a battered brass spittoon; and in the middle of one lake, an ancient double-barreled shotgun still loaded with bird shot. But no disk.

The flyover Sunday with infrared detection equipment that Fisk had proposed to Dusty. No disk.

Still chafing at DiBella's remarks, Munson called Fisk. "You saw the news, I imagine," he said, referring to the morning headlines: "**SECRET ARMY EQUIPMENT FAILS TO FIND DISK**".

"Yeh, this investigation leaks worse than the Lewinsky Grand Jury. But tell me what happened."

"The army jumped at the chance for a peacetime test of its brainchild. Sunday we dropped an identical disk from five hundred feet into the marshland. Just as we had imagined, it disappeared into the ooze. The plane then flew over the drop area, found the test disk, and recorded its infrared signature in the equipment's computer. The rest of the afternoon it flew back and forth searching for a matching image. No luck, and I'm afraid I've about shot my wad. Pete DiBella's been on my fucking back again today and I'm in a mood to try anything. Got any more ideas?"

"Maybe. What about magnetic detection?"

"For titanium? How so? It's not magnetic."

"Compared to steel, you're right. Still, it has slight magnetic properties, like aluminum or copper. Here's what I'm thinking. It's a long shot but maybe worth a try. I hear that the boys in the Pentagon—now keep this to yourself—have perfected a magnetometer that detects anomalies in the earth's magnetic field caused by a sub deep underwater. And get this—they do it from satellites monitoring the oceans. Imagine what that does for our ballistic missile defenses. Then one day the Russians put to sea a couple of experimental titanium subs with greater depth capability and virtually non-magnetic. The Pentagon goes ape and comes up with a new design."

"But this is only a two and a half foot disk, Alan, not a massive sub."

"I said it's a long shot, but what else are we going to do?"

"You think the Pentagon would make it available?"

"The project might appeal to them if we could insure security."

"How do we get started?"

"Have Dusty talk to Mary Joy" Fisk said, referring to the NTSB board member on duty. "If she signs on, she'll have to go right to the top."

"Secretary of Defense?"

"No, her friend the President."

CHAPTER 25

Thursday, June 3

Seated alone at Washington's Jockey Club, Mary Joy Lemay was not amused. Twenty after seven and still no Cutler. Bad enough that she was dining with one of the parties to a crash investigation in progress. At least he could be on time. She had come out of deference to Senator Rushmore who had called asking her to see the CEO of Hi Tech. "Mary Joy, I need your hep," he had said and you didn't refuse the Chairman of the Senate Armed Services Committee a personal favor, not when you were a political appointee in Washington.

Where the hell was he? She was becoming increasingly embarrassed sitting there alone at the power table. Known as Kissinger's table, it was the banquette on the right near the entrance so you could see and be seen by all who entered. People were staring; a congressman stopped by for an awkward hello.

Her thoughts turned to Dusty's warning about Cutler during their morning meeting to discuss the Pentagon's help in finding the missing disk. "I'd be careful if I were you," she remembered him saying. "The man uses people." And when she pressed him for details: "Nuff said, Mary Joy. Just watch your step."

Not an entirely pleasant evening to look forward to. But this? She was about to get up and leave when she saw the maitre d' approaching with the man himself.

Cutler reached across the table to shake her hand. "I've been looking forward to this all week," he said without a word of apology for his lateness. "You don't have a drink."

"I've been waiting for you," Mary Joy said tartly.

"Then what'll it be?"

"A spritzer."

"A spritzer? You'll want something stronger than that."

"A spritzer, please," she said to the maitre d'.

"I'll have my usual, Jacques. The Glenlivet." He turned to Mary Joy. "Now tell me about your interest in flying. The Senator says you're quite a pilot."

For the next twenty minutes they chatted about their wartime exploits, she as a medvac pilot in Vietnam, he as the commander of a carrier squadron in the Pacific during World War II. Presently the waiter appeared with the dinner menus.

Mary Joy welcomed the waiter's interruption. "I'm enjoying the conversation," she lied, "but I'm sure you didn't ask me here to trade war stories. What do you want of me?"

Cutler eyed her silently for a moment. "Fair enough," he said. "I appreciate directness. I'll be equally direct. I have a problem with your investigation of the Florida crash."

Dusty had it right, she thought. Watch your step.

"Shouldn't you be talking with our chairman?"

"Maybe. I wanted to give you the benefit of working it out without a lot of fuss. You were the board member on duty at the time and I assume you'll be handling the public hearing with McGinty."

"You're right. I will."

"The leak of the cockpit tape just hours after the crash has done irreparable harm to my company. It's lost billions in market value and there's the threat of a takeover. I want a statement by you or McGinty that the pilot's last words were a knee-jerk reaction to a past problem and have no bearing on the performance of our blades. I also want an investigation of the leak of confidential information given to McGinty."

"That's impossible. The tape leak was unfortunate to say the least. All incoming and outgoing calls are now over a single secure line. Your request would only compound the error. The Safety Board never speculates."

"Then I want McGinty removed as IIC. The man's a bungler."

"Out of the question! He's done nothing wrong. McGinty's the best IIC we've ever had. And for your information, Mr. Cutler, the Safety Board is well aware of the problem of leaks and goes to great lengths to see that the tapes are secure until the transcripts are released at the Public Hearing. Enormous stakes are involved . . ."

"You're telling me."

". . . in a crash like this. The media are in a frenzy and the parties, I'm sorry to say, will go to great lengths to point the finger away from themselves."

"So McGinty allows the transcript to be called in over an unsecured telephone line. He's the best?"

"Give the guy a break. He was swamped getting the investigation started. The next morning he ran an electronic sweep and found the two bugs."

"And he's seen having a cozy drink with Sam Barker's sidekick the night before the documentation leak. I said it before. The man's a bungler, or worse. He can't even find the disk"

Mary Joy paused. Would it do any good to explain the thoroughness of the search; perhaps even to hint at the pending attempt with the Pentagon's supersecret anti-submarine detection equipment. No. Cutler wouldn't be listening.

"He's done everything possible," she said.

Cutler glanced at her. "I was hoping to settle this amicably."

"Under the table you mean. So now you're going to go to our Chairman. You just do that. And I can guarantee that you'll get nowhere. We come to the accident site with no baggage, no fears, no favors, no prejudices."

"Nice speech. Right out of the manual. I want the public statement, or I want McGinty removed."

Mary Joy sat quietly for a moment, regaining her composure. " 'I want' . . ." she said softly. " 'I want' . . . Do you always get what you want, Mr. Cutler, even if it means sacrificing a man who's done nothing wrong?"

And she stalked out.

Cutler called Joe Bledsoe. "I'm beginning to think McGinty is in cahoots with General Tech," he said, "and I'm getting nowhere with the NTSB. Watch him carefully, Joe. We have to find a way to neutralize him."

CHAPTER 26

Tuesday, June 8

Dusty was back at his desk in Washington. The command center had been closed; only Jose and Rick remained in Miami. Damn! he thought and tossed the secret Pentagon report on the satellite search for the disk onto the desk top. Another dead end. We must be doing something wrong. That disk is out there and we've got to find it.

He called Rick Munson in Miami on the eve of their planned weekly meeting at the Sheraton River House. "What about a cash reward?" he asked. "If you think it makes any sense we can talk about it tomorrow at breakfast."

"You mean like we did in Iowa?"

"It worked then. To hell with the fancy technology. You get more people into the act."

Rick laughed. "I remember it well. The hayseeds were right." Then after a moment's thought: "The circumstances are different, but it's worth a try."

They were talking about the NTSB investigation of the failure of a jet engine and ejection of its fan disk at thirty seven thousand feet altitude resulting in a subsequent crash. The failure occurred on a United flight in July '89 over a rural area planted extensively in cornfields, and when the early foot-searches based on elaborate trajectory analyses using Air Traffic Control radar data failed to locate the disk, the local farmers enjoyed poking fun at the effort. "You can't just hurry it along, fella. Come harvest time, we'll find 'em for you." But the search went on, month after month. Eventually a cash reward was arranged to encourage the public, and in October a farmer and his wife harvesting their fields stumbled upon the titanium disk when it became enmeshed in the mechanism of their combine.

"Yeah, let's try it," Dusty said. "Fifty thousand. Get it in the headlines."

Before going back to Miami Dusty stopped by Mary Joy's office. "Thanks for your help with the President," he said. "You went all out for us. I'm just sorry the satellite search was a flop."

"Glad to do it. And you were right to tell me to watch my step with Cutler. But why didn't you tell me what a shit he is? You obviously don't owe him anything. He's trying to get you canned."

"My job?"

"He wants you removed as IIC; thinks you're responsible for the leak of the tape."

"And he had the balls to bring pressure through you?"

"For starters. He had the Chairman of the Senate Armed Services Committee call our chairman direct after I told him to get lost."

"Ah, the Great White Father. I'm not surprised. White and green is a wonderful color combination, now isn't it?"

"What do you mean?"

"With all of Hi Tech's business with the armed services, are you kidding? How did our leader react?"

"He refused to intervene."

God bless him, Dusty thought. He's a stranger in the Beltway.

*   *   *

Fisk slammed the phone back in its receiver, his face flushed with anger, and punched the button on his intercom. "Cass?"

"Yes?"

"Can you see me?"

"Is it important?"

"Very."

"Then come along."

Fisk strode into Cutler's office. "Dusty McGinty just called me."

Cutler assumed a stony get-on-with-it pose.

"He's outraged at the way you're out to get him."

"What's he expect? I don't cotton to being screwed by him or anybody else. I told Lemay I want him out of there."

Fisk glared at him. Son-of-a-bitch. He's proud of himself.

"So he comes crying to you. Why you? Why doesn't he have it out with me?"

"Because Dusty and I are friends, Cass, good friends."

"Do you think as CEO of this company I should sit quietly by and watch it go down the tubes because of him? You think it's wrong of me to defend our interests?"

"Cass, I'm warning you. I take this seriously. And if you continue trying to get Dusty fired, I'll go to Reston's committee. Nothing could impede my work with the NTSB more than Dusty's feeling he was being jerked around by our side. He trusts me, and whether you believe it or not, my joining with him in an all-out search for the truth will work for the benefit of the employees and stockholders of Hi Tech. That's where I'll be spending my time."

Cutler sat staring at him.

Fisk stared back. He's pissed, but what can he say? He knows he won't get anywhere with the committee on this one.

He turned to leave, then looked back. "And if the committee finds against me, you'll have my resignation before the investigation is over."

CHAPTER 27

Thursday, June 10

Allison, Fisk's secretary, announced that Dusty McGinty was calling.

"Is this line secure at your end?" Dusty asked.

He sounds excited, Fisk thought. Have they found the disk—or Jesus! evidence that the blade was defective?

"Is it that important?"

"After all the leaks?"

"You in Washington?"

"Yes."

"I'll call you from a public phone in the lobby."

Fisk rushed out of the office, and in minutes was on the line with Dusty. "You found the disk?" he asked, expectantly.

"No, no, nothing like that. It has to do with Hi Tech's acquisition of Buzz Beauchamp's company a year ago."

Sedalia! I don't like this, Fisk thought.

"A friend at the SEC told me that they're conducting a preliminary investigation of a rumor that Beauchamp had given Senator Rushmore shares in his company in return for throwing government business his way. Bad enough, but they're also investigating whether Hi Tech paid Rushmore a finder's fee from a secret slush fund for promoting the deal. Have you heard anything about this?"

Do I tell the truth and have him feel I should have confided in me? "No," he answered. But why is he telling me this? Is he that pissed at Cutler?

"Of course it's none of my business unless it impacts the investigation. And it could if it hits the papers. That's why I thought you ought to know, Alan."

"You're right, especially when reporters find out that Sedalia was such a shitty operation when we bought it."

"You have enough on your hands already with Cutler, but this has the potential to be explosive. I'm being hammered by calls from Senator Bixby: 'You heard the pilot. The blades, the blades. Why all this delay? There are families out there suffering.' I tell you it's hell. Victims groups are all over me. The President's in the act, hounding our Chairman. The people want action on what they believe to be true, not facts. It's like the early days of TWA 800 and the terrorist mongering. 'Of course it was a missile.' And today they'd jump on one more reason to point the finger at Hi Tech."

"I hear what you're telling me," Fisk said, "and I appreciate it. It shows me that you trust me. And I think I know just how to handle it."

Still smarting over what he had heard, Fisk left the building and headed for Hancock's office a few blocks away. Like it or not, he thought, I have to make a move, and John's the man to talk to.

"Alan Fisk to see Mr. Hancock," he said to the receptionist. "It's urgent."

"I can see you're all worked up," Hancock said as Fisk entered his office. "Sit down and tell me. Bad news about the crash?"

"Not exactly. The board has another problem on its hands." He told him about the call. "You're the only one I feel I can talk to."

"Sedalia again!" Hancock snarled, with the same wild look that Fisk had seen at the mention of the acquisition during his earlier visit. "You have this from someone you trust?"

"Yes, completely. And he heard it directly from a close friend in the SEC."

"Can you tell me who made the call?"

"No. But I can tell you I heard the substance of the accusation from an unimpeachable source shortly before the crash. He was told it by Beauchamp himself when Beauchamp was drunk during a flight to Paris. I was going to look for hard evidence and confront Cutler. Then the crash happened."

"You have reason to believe evidence exists?"

"Beauchamp said Cutler wouldn't acknowledge the arrangement in the contract, so Beauchamp wrote a note in his private file confirming it for his own protection. I plan to have a look around his old office when I have time."

"Make the time!" Hancock ordered, and sat drumming his fingers on the desk.

Fisk could feel Hancock's lawyerly mind working away. He was pursuing a case. He was having fun.

"We have to be smart about this," he said, turning to look directly at Fisk. "After we elect George Trueslow at tomorrow's telephone board meeting, I'll ask Cutler about the matter; keep you in the background for now. The only issue I'll raise is whether Hi Tech paid Rushmore a finder's fee in the deal. It's important to keep the issues narrow, you see."

Yes, teacher, Fisk felt like saying.

"At this point I simply want his denial before the board. For the record." Hancock sat back in his chair. "You with me?" he asked.

Fisk rested his chin on his knuckles, pondering the growing evidence of Cutler's corruption. I agree with Dusty, he thought. If all this is true, it could have a disastrous effect on the outcome of the crash investigation. I have to know the answer. "Yes," he said, "I'm with you, all the way."

CHAPTER 28

Friday, June 11

Fisk, Cutler, Bentley, and Burke were gathered around the speaker phone in Hi Tech's boardroom as the conference call operator brought the other five directors on the line. "I've promised you this'll be quick," Cutler said, "but before we get on with the election of George Trueslow, I've asked Alan to give us an update on the crash investigation."

"Unfortunately," Fisk began, "there's not much I can tell you you've not already seen or heard. All attempts to find the disk have failed. Until it's found, a cloud hangs over the blades. And of course it may remain if the disk tells us nothing. People are crying for an answer to this tragedy, and so far the blades are it to the average person."

"Is there solid evidence yet to support that?" Vaughn asked.

"Not a shred. Every test at the NTSB metallurgical lab in Washington shows that the blade that was found was flawless. The disk remains the key—it and the attached blades and blade fragments."

"The reward announced yesterday," Reston said. "Do you think it will work?"

"It has in the past. A lot of eyes will be looking in places we haven't thought of." Fisk paused— "That's about it I guess."

"Tom," Cutler said, "give us a few words from the legal standpoint."

"Schnell's class action suit in federal district court against us, General Tech, Cross Country Airlines, and Power Technology is proceeding. It's in the discovery stage but nothing much will happen until the Safety Board announces its finding. As for United Aerospace, Giles Courtwright's been buying Hi Tech stock cautiously; says he's acquiring the stock for investment but doesn't rule out merger discussions in the future . . ."

Fisk was only half listening to Burke as he spoke. He knew the moment for Hancock's confrontation with Cutler was approaching. Would Hancock be able to restrain himself, to "keep the issues narrow" as he had advised? Or would he light into Cutler as he had at the previous meeting . . . ?

Fisk chuckled to himself. Am I kidding?

"Okay," he heard Cutler say. "Let's get on with the business at hand. Can I have a motion that George Trueslow be elected to this board?"

"So moved," said Coxe.

"I second," said Reston.

"Any discussion . . . ? All in favor say yes . . . opposed say no . . . That's a vote."

Then, "Any other business?"

"John Hancock here . . ."

At the sound of his voice, Fisk snapped a look at Cutler and saw his face twitch in a spasm of annoyance.

". . . I've heard a disturbing rumor," Hancock said quietly, "that Hi Tech paid Senator Rushmore a finder's fee for his part in the Sedalia acquisition."

"Yah, I've heard it," Cutler said. "Hogwash."

Burke thrust his face at the speaker phone as if it was flesh and blood. "There was no finder in the deal," he protested. "I drafted the language in the agreement."

"Where are the rumors coming from?" Brattle asked. "Do we know?"

"Probably Beauchamp," Cutler said. "He gets a snoot full and dreams up stuff. Probably thinks it makes him look important."

"Then you're telling us flatly, Mr. Cutler," Hancock said, "that no fee was paid to the Senator?"

"Yes."

"For the record?"

"Yes, for the record."

Later, Hancock called Fisk. "He's lying. I called my own source in the SEC. Not only are they investigating, a Grand Jury is being impaneled. Apparently Beauchamp stonewalled about the rumors attributed to him, but after meeting with lawyers from the Criminal Division, says he'll testify against Cutler and Rushmore. They're now involved in plea bargaining negotiations. This is mighty serious business for the company, Alan."

And for the investigation, Fisk was thinking. Dusty was right. This could be explosive.

"Are you free Sunday afternoon?" Hancock asked.

"Well, yes."

"I'm going to try to arrange a meeting at my house with Brattle and Bentley. I'd like you to be there."

"Sure, Count me in."

"I'm comfortable with you and Brattle, but Bentley? Give me your thoughts. Can I trust him not to go running to Cutler?"

"Bentley?" Alan said. "Son of a wealthy Atlanta banker, Harvard Business School, a fine mind. But I've never really gotten to know him. I do know he considers me a rival; is determined to run the company one day. Sooner rather than later in Cutler's eyes. Which is why Cass wanted me around . . ."

Fisk was about to say he felt Cutler never cottoned to Bentley because of his "background," but caught himself in time.

". . . Yes, I think he'd be discreet about the meeting. Depends on whether he sees the investigation as a mortal threat to Cass. Then he'd want to be in your camp, especially when he sees me there."

"Good thinking. I like that. Unless you hear from me then, I'll see you my place four on Sunday."

CHAPTER 29

Saturday, June 12

Hobie and his friend Lester parked their bikes in the bushes off 36th Street and bellied under the chain link fence surrounding Cockroach Corner. Cautiously they picked their way among the derelict planes to an ancient DC-3 with the logo "GONE FISHIN" painted on its side. The cockpit and most of the cabin were intact, though a section of the fuselage near the tail had been torn wide-open during a crash landing.

Often during the summer months the planes' interiors were too hot to play in, but Hobie had picked the day with care—dull and overcast after a cooling rain. "See, I told you," he said hiking up his chino trousers with an air of authority as they entered the fuselage. "It's not too hot."

Lester gave him a broad, worshipful smile. Two years younger than Hobie and small for his age, he was looked upon as a baby by the other kids, and welcomed the opportunity to tag along with Hobie on his secret jaunts to the airport, especially after Hobie's recent flight to Waukegan had become the talk of the neighborhood.

Hobie led the way along the plane's aisle to the cockpit and slid into the left seat. Lester took the copilot's chair. "When you gonna let me be pilot, huh, Hobie?"

"One day," he reassured him, "when your legs are long enough to reach the pedals. You're doing the check list, and that's real important, you know."

"Uh, huh."

"So let's get started."

"Where we gonna go today?"

"Orlando, that's not too far." The pilot of Hi Tech's jet had pointed out the town on their flight to Waukegan.

"Shoulder harkness," Lester began.

"On," Hobie answered.

"Door warning light."

"Out."

"Wing . . . whatchmacallits?"

"Flaps, Lester, wing flaps . . . Down."

"Motor start."

Hobie placed his hand on the throttle. "Ready."

Lester emitted a short, shrill whistle, then a steady ooommm. And they were soon on their way, with Hobie working the control column and rudder pedals on their imaginary flight to Orlando.

There was not the usual resistance on the control column as he eased it back to climb, Hobie noticed. Something was wrong with the control cables. "How's about you taking over now," he said.

"Can I, Hobie, oh can I?"

"I'm going back to talk to the passengers."

"But the pedals!"

"We're flying straight, just keep the nose up."

"Oh boy!"

Hobie walked to the rear of the plane. Maybe the wire cables he had once seen exposed in the damaged section of the fuselage on an earlier sortie were the old style control cables Fisk had spoken of during their flight to Waukegan.

Just aft of the main cabin door in the rear, Hobie looked down, agog at the sight before him. A shaft of light shone through the roof and illuminated the rent flooring where Hobie had last seen the exposed cables. Protruding from the flooring like a shiny nickel stuck in a parking meter he saw the top third of a large metal disk with mangled blade stubs attached to it's rim. "Uh, oh," he mumbled, "it cut the cables." He knelt down for a look beneath the floor. There among the stubs he saw a gleaming blade, badly bent but still recognizable as a blade like the one Fisk had handed him to inspect on the production line at the Waukegan plant. His heart pounding, he glanced furtively about to see if he was still alone. Seconds later he saw the cockpit door open and Lester coming down the aisle toward him. "Get back to the controls, Lester!" he shouted. "You're gonna crash us."

"What's you doing so long, Hobie? What's you looking at?"

"Lester, the controls!"

"I'm on whatmacallit pilot."

"Auto pilot. Dummy! This plane doesn't have one."

"Oh!" Lester scrambled back to the cockpit.

Hobie followed, careful not to show his excitement. "You did a good job navigating," he said calmly. "See, there's Orlando down there," and he took over the controls for a quick trip home.

Back in Cockroach Corner, Hobie feigned airsickness. "It's been a bumpy ride back," he said rubbing his stomach. "I've gotta get home."

"Aw, Hobie. I'm having fun."

Hobie could see Lester knew something was wrong. Should he stay and keep an eye on him until he was ready to go? Could he spare the time? No, he had to tell Fisk. "You can stay, Lester, but I'm leaving before I puke."

It's spooky in here Lester thought, feeling alone and uneasy about the mysterious goings on in the rear of the plane. Gingerly he walked back to where he had seen Hobie kneeling and inspected the rent flooring. Nothing but some kinda pinwheel. Maybe Hobie was sick. Suddenly he heard a creepy tap-tap-tap on the side of the fuselage. "Ahhhh!" he screamed. Ghosts! He ran for the door and jumped down, to be met by a tall woman wearing dark glasses and walking with a cane. "Frightened you did I?" she asked, looking into his terror-filled eyes.

"I'm not stealin, Lady!"

"I didn't think you were. You play here a lot?"

"With my friend Hobie. We play pilot and copilot. We not be doing anything bad."

"I saw him leaving," the woman said.

"He got sick flying back from Orlando."

She smiled. "That's a long flight. So you spend a lot of time here?"

"When it's not too hot."

"Tell me," she said, opening her purse. "Have you ever run across anything like this in your travels?" She handed him a photograph of a fan section disk and blades.

Lester studied it carefully. Something was going on, something that felt like trouble. "No," he said avoiding her eyes.

"I can see you have," she said and reached into her purse for a hundred dollar bill. She thrust it at him. "Will this help you remember?"

"That's a hunnert dollars!" Lester exclaimed wide-eyed.

"And it can be yours."

"A hunnert dollars mine?"

"All yours."

"Well, I just seed something like it all bent up under the floor in the back of the airplane."

"This one?"

"Yah."

"Here young man. Take this. And don't tell your mama I gave it to you."

"Mama, Mama," Hobie cried out when he reached home. "Call Mr. Fisk!"

"What's that got into you, Hobie?" his mother said. "You just sush. Mama's not feeling well."

"I think I seed the parts Mr. Fisk is looking for."

"Saw, Hobie, not seed. You're hanging out too much with Lester."

"But Mama, I need to help Mr. Fisk!"

"Boy's a bad influence."

"Mama! please . . ." There were tears of frustration in his eyes.

"All right, all right, stop your crying around. What's the number?"

He reached into his pocket and handed her Fisk's card. She dialed the number and reached a recording.

"It's Saturday, Hobie. They're not open. You'll have to wait 'till Monday."

Joe Bledsoe called Cutler at home at two thirty in the morning. "Sorry Chief," he said, "but there's been big goings on down here. The dick followed Rosie to Cockroach Corner this morning—been sticking to her like flypaper, he has. And . . ."

"Wait a minute Joe. Cockroach Corner? Where are we?"

"Northwest corner of Miami International Airport. Sort of a graveyard for busted up planes. And he sees her talking to a young black kid outside a DC-3 smashed in some sort of crash. She leaves, and guess what? Comes back in the dark two hours ago with three bruisers in a truck. They cut through the chain-link fence off 36th Street, go in with a flat bed trundle, and wheel out something under a tarp. Must be the disk."

Cutler sat up in the bed. "Son-of-a-bitch!" he fumed. "Where are they now?"

"Parked at a dock at the Port of Miami."

"Rosie still with them?"

"She is but looks to be leaving. The dick just called. He's right there watching them."

"Then here's what I want you to do, Joe. Keep your phone open to him and get yourself over there as soon as you can. They obviously plan to deep six the disk. Do the men have a boat standing by?"

"He says no. The truck is parked in a deserted spot away from the water. They look to be settling in for the night."

"The two of you stay with them and let me know immediately of any developments. Take along a camera and recorder. If they make a move, you'll have to confront them."

"What if they decide not to dump it?"

Cutler felt his mouth go dry. "It'll mean they've examined the disk and it checks out. We'll have another problem to solve, won't we?" he said slyly. "We can't let them sneak it back and tip off the Feds."

"I get your thinking, Chief. We'll have to see that it stays lost."

"Or stand by and watch Hi Tech go bust. No way! Joe, no way."

Rosie returned to her room in the Miami Airport Inn. Gotta call Willie, she thought, thinking of Professor William Glickman, her boyfriend in New York who had visited her in Miami earlier in the week. Can't afford to have anyone in our General Tech lab analyze the disk before we decide what to do with it.

Rosie awakened Willie in his New York apartment. "Who's this?" he growled.

"Rosie."

"At this hour? What's happened?"

"I found the disk, Willie, thanks to you. You're a genius, hun," she cooed. "Found it 'closer to home' just as you said."

"Where? I'm intrigued."

"Cockroach Corner where they store derelict planes; buried inside the midsection of a crashed DC-3. The search teams must have walked by the spot a dozen times."

"You mean they disregarded the hole it made? Come on."

"A freak incident. The fuselage was already torn apart where it entered."

"What condition is the disk in?"

"Missing a wedge of about twenty degrees. The blades that are left are badly mangled or broken off."

"What are you doing with it?"

"It's in a truck at the docks in Miami."

"Oh?"

She paused for a moment. He's not going to like this.

"I have a favor to ask," she said. "I need your expertise. I want you to come down and give me your opinion on what failed first, the blades or the disk."

"Now wait a minute! I'm not a metallurgist and . . ."

"I know you're not but you have a good eye for this sort of thing."

"Listen to me Rosie! I don't even want to think what I suspect you have in mind."

"Then don't! I won't get you involved. Just fly down tomorrow. We'll have a good time and you can give me a little friendly advice along the way."

"Tomorrow? I can't."

"You can't or won't?"

"Leaving for a seminar in Los Angeles tomorrow through Monday noon."

"Can you change it? Do it for me, hon."

"I'm the guest speaker."

"Then take the direct flight back to Miami. You'll arrive Monday night. I'll wait for you."

"I miss you."

"Come and you won't regret it."

"Okay."

CHAPTER 30

Sunday, June 13

Fisk was standing in the bay window of his study staring out at the fern garden when Martha came in. "You're worried about the meeting this afternoon, aren't you?" she said. "I hate to see you this way. You've been dragging yourself around all weekend. You're not sleeping, not eating, drinking too much—you're a wreck!"

He turned to face her. She can be direct, he thought. But right. First the crash, now all this board stuff.

"Frustrated's the word. I'm not cut out for boardroom politics," he said. "I hate it!"

"Of course you do. That's not where your heart is."

"I hate the idea of the four of us sitting around in John's house discussing Cass's fate if we find he lied to the board. I should be working on the crash investigation. But I owe it to my men to make the effort."

"Your men? Why?"

"For what I did to them in selling my company. If what I've heard from Dusty and John is true, I sold to a cheat, to put it mildly. I owe it to Mike Belmonte and the others to set things straight before I leave."

Martha frowned. "Tell me about that."

That look. She's rattled about something, he thought.

"I couldn't leave them in the hands of a man like Cass, not after all they've done for me."

"Who'd replace him as CEO?"

"I'm sure Hancock has ideas about that. He's always seen

himself as Chairman. Not a bad idea. A few gray hairs on the premises with legal experience and good Washington connections. And CEO? Maybe Woody Bentley. He's the right age, with a solid MBA background and years of experience. He lacks the engineering expertise, but Mike Belmonte could complement him there. They'd be a great team."

Martha sat eyeing him. "What about you? Are you tempted?"

"What do you mean?"

"Maybe you'd like to run Hi Tech."

"Jesus! cut it out. I see what you're getting at. You call me a wreck, then ask me a question like that. I've told you. Come the end of the investigation, I'm out of there. Cutler has my resignation in writing, and I mean it!"

"Just making sure," Martha said.

He pulled a face and sighed. "Sitting in judgment of a man's future doesn't come easy to me. But there's compelling evidence that Hi Tech paid Rushmore a finder's fee from a secret slush fund for promoting the deal. If that's true, Cutler's got to go, no question. And I've decided to lead the effort with Hancock."

"Are you, this afternoon?"

"Yes."

"Good. I think you'll feel better about yourself now that you've made the decision."

Fisk arrived early at Hancock's house in Winnetka and was shown into the study. "I wanted a few minutes with you alone before the others come," he said as Hancock stood to greet him.

"Splendid." "It'll give us a chance to discuss strategy. You still with me on this?"

The irony of it, Fisk thought. I cozied up to him after Otto suggested I needed allies on the board. Now I'm his ally!

"If you mean the issue of Cutler's honesty, yes. I've made a decision, John. If he lied, I'll lead the charge with you to see that he's out of here."

Hancock sat staring at him. That lawyerly mind at work again, Fisk thought.

"That makes my job easier," Hancock said. "If the other two hear you're along, they're not likely to see this as my personal vendetta. Are you willing to speak out about what you've heard?"

"As long as I don't have to disclose my source."

"Of course."

"But tell me, what do you hope to achieve today?"

"If we can convince Stuart and Woody of the seriousness of the SEC investigation, we can confront Cutler with the facts at our board meeting in two weeks and force the issue."

'Force the issue' Fisk thought as he began to grasp the reasoning behind the particular makeup of today's get-together. The four of them voting together would balance off the votes of Vaughn, Reston, Burke and Coxe, all fiercely loyal to Cutler, and with Cutler having to abstain on any 'issue' involving himself, George Trueslow would cast the swing vote.

Fisk suppressed a smile. Hancock's been waiting for this opportunity for years; Cutler's given him the opening and I'm here to help him.

Stuart Brattle had arrived and was talking to Fisk and Hancock when Woody Bentley came in. He looked first at Fisk, then at Brattle, surprised at their presence. "I'm getting the idea this is not a social affair," he said.

"It isn't," Hancock said, motioning them all to be seated. "I think you'll understand my need for secrecy when you hear what I have to say. Cass Cutler flat out lied to us during our telephone board meeting when he said that no fee was paid to Senator Rushmore in the Sedalia deal."

"You're saying there was?" Brattle asked. "You know that?"

"Not only that. Over the years, Buzz Beauchamp was slipping the senator shares in his company every time an Air Force contract for jet engine blades was awarded to his plant in Sedalia—the senator's home town."

As Hancock spoke, Fisk saw Bentley staring at him like an alert shore bird in a tidal pool anticipating his next meal. The guy's desperate to know where I stand in all this, he thought. I wonder if Cutler's told him about my letter of resignation.

"Wait-a-minute," Brattle said. "This is a serious accusation against Cass. What do you base it on? You know it to be more than a rumor?"

"Tell them Alan."

His voice was firm. "What started as a rumor is now the subject of an SEC investigation. I learned this recently during a confidential call from a source in Washington I trust implicitly."

"And after Cass's denial to the board," Hancock added, "I spoke to my source at the SEC. Not only are they investigating, a Grand Jury is being impaneled. Apparently Beauchamp stonewalled about the rumors attributed to him, but now that he's met with lawyers from the Criminal Division, he says he'll testify against Mr. Cutler and Rushmore. They're involved in plea bargaining negotiations."

"It's gone that far?" Brattle asked.

"They'll be taking depositions in a few weeks."

"Out-and-out disaster!" Bentley exclaimed. "Senator Rushmore, Chairman of the Armed Services Committee! Do you know what this will do to our government business?"

"And the crash investigation," Fisk said. "That's my concern at the moment. I decided I had to be prepared with the facts in case the allegations hit the papers. So I decided to join with John to determine if the allegations are true."

"Then what should we do?" Bentley asked.

"I agree with John's position," Fisk said. "The four of us have to act together at the next board meeting. We'll confront him with the facts and see what he says."

Brattle shook his head. "Cass must know what's going on in Washington. He should have informed the board."

Hancock smiled. "True to form. Thinks he can stonewall his way out of the mess. He'll plea bargain with the government for a slap on the wrist, or at most a misdemeanor. The Senator's the man they're after. Then he'll pass it off with us as a minor transgression, a burden he assumed for the good of the company."

"Okay," Bentley said. "Let's assume he admits that he lied to us. What are you suggesting?"

"We get rid of him," Hancock snarled.

Bentley leaned forward in his chair. "Even if that's the right thing to do, and I'm not sure it is, we're just four out of ten directors."

"Wait a minute" Brattle said. "Before you start counting heads, there's a moral question involved. Won't our action prejudice his case? Is it fair for us to act before he's been found guilty in a court of law? After all, Cass has been an effective leader."

"It's our fiduciary responsibility as directors," Hancock said. "The man lied to us in answer to a direct question of utmost seriousness to the company. And don't any of you forget it."

"I'm inclined to agree with John," Bentley said. "At a minimum we stand to receive a stiff fine. At worst, we'll be blacklisted by the Pentagon in major parts of our business. The sooner we act the better our future relationship with the government. So I'm back to my question, do we have the votes? I don't know about you but my ass is at stake if we try and fail."

"Fair enough," Hancock said. "Alan, do we have your vote?"

Fisk cocked his head to one side and stared at him." Yes!" he said. "I'd like to see his ass out of here. The man's corrupt."

"And yours, Stuart?"

"If he admits to lying, yes."

"The four of us will balance off his clique. With Mr. Cutler abstaining, it will be up to George."

Brattle turned to Fisk. "You know him best. What do you think?"

"I think we have a chance."

"So do I," Hancock said. "Cutler outsmarted himself bringing George on the board."

Fisk looked around the room which was suddenly silent as the import of the moment sank in. We're all thinking the same thing, he knew.

Brattle was the first to speak. "Who would take over from Cass?"

"We'd need an ad hoc committee of the outside directors to select the new president," Hancock said. "And I'd like to formally propose you, Stuart, as its chairman if we get to that point. You're its most disinterested member."

"Well that's mighty kind of you, John. And I'd accept. You know how I feel about the company and its future. But I was thinking of the interim. We'd need a chairman to hold the place together. You're a lawyer and good businessman. Would you consider taking it on?"

Fisk couldn't believe the openness of the back scratching. Board politics at its best, he thought. Why I kept my company private for so long.

"I'd have to if the board wanted it. But only on the condition that these two able young men join me in the day to day running of the company in a three man Office of the Chairman."

What, say again? Fisk thought, startled at the suggestion. For a moment he sat speechless. Should I have told him of my plan to leave before I got so deep into this boardroom stuff?

"Anything wrong, Alan?" Hancock asked.

"Obviously Cass hasn't told the board of my letter of resignation . . ."

"Resignation?" Hancock gasped.

Bentley's eyes darted bird like over the faces of the other three men.

". . .Effective the day the NTSB establishes probable cause of the crash. I gave it to him at the end of the last board meeting."

"He's said absolutely nothing to me!" Hancock thundered, his face contorted in anger. Then, turning to Bentley and Brattle, "Say anything to you?"

They shook their heads.

Fisk could hear Hancock thinking.

"Surely, Alan, you'll change your mind if Mr. Cutler's gone," Hancock said.

"No John, I won't. I was angry at the time, but I assure you I didn't make the decision out of pique. I thought putting it in writing might ease the tension with him as I devote myself to the investigation. As for my feelings now, I've had enough of business. You'll find Mike Belmonte perfectly capable of taking over from me. He deserves the opportunity. He and Woody will make a great team."

Hancock turned to Woody. "What do you think of Mr. Belmonte?"

"Mike's terrific!" he said, beaming with goodwill. "A reflection of Alan's leadership skills. Another reason we'll all miss him."

Fisk suppressed a snicker. You, Woody Bentley, miss me? Ha! You've wanted me out of here since the day I arrived.

"Indeed, we will," Hancock said. "But we have to move on. So this is the plan: Woody, Mr. Belmonte, and I, to be the Office of the Chairman until a president is selected. And Stuart, make sure you ask Vaughn and Reston to serve on your selection committee, with Burke as counsel. They'll need reassurance their precious patronage won't be lost."

CHAPTER 31

Monday, June 14

Joe Bledsoe called Cutler in his office at nine a.m. "The truck's still sittin at the Port of Miami dock, Chief."

"Rosie, where's she?"

"Holed up at the Miami Airport Hotel ever since she left the dock early Saturday morning."

"And the men?"

"Taking turns going for take out. They slept in the truck."

"And no comings and goings by outsiders?"

"Not a soul."

"Hmm . . . they're waiting for one of their hot shots to examine the disk for flaws. Stay with it, Joe. Have your camera ready. It's about to get interesting."

"And if they make a move to dump it?"

"It means they know they're at fault. We nail 'em."

Fisk arrived at the Sears Building at nine-thirty. Two men were waiting, both tall and spare of build, carrying loaded briefcases and wearing oxford gray suits. Investment bankers? He smiled, but received no acknowledgment.

On the way up in the elevator one of the men reached for a handkerchief in his hip pocket briefly exposing an identification badge clipped to his belt. The FBI. Our floor? he thought. He followed them into the lobby, slowing down as they approached the reception desk, and heard them ask for Cutler.

Interesting. Very interesting. They must be interviewing Cutler for the Grand Jury investigation. He continued on to his office.

"A Mrs. Elkins, Yolanda Elkins calling from Florida," Fisk's secretary announced. "She put her son Hobie on. Says you know him."

"Yes, remember? The black boy who visited here with me. Put him through.

"Hobie, great to hear from you! Everything okay?"

"I think I seed the parts you're looking for!" he blurted.

Fisk pressed the phone to his ear so hard it hurt. "The blades? You found a blade like the one I gave you?"

"No, No! Not just a blade. Lots of blades. The metal wheel too."

My God, the disk! Hobie found the disk. Hallelujah! Fisk sprang to his feet ready to go.

"Where, Hobie?"

"Saturday playing in the wrecks near the airport with my friend Lester. You know, like I told you. We were flying our plane to Orlando and I saw it sticking out of the floor in the cabin."

The disk, inside a wrecked plane in Cockroach corner! Dusty's going to be livid. His men searched that area several times.

"How big a plane?"

"A DC-3 sorta busted in half."

"Have you told anybody besides your mother about it?"

"No sir, not even Lester. Mama tried to call you right away but you were closed."

Damn! Two days wasted.

"Good, then wait at home, Hobie. I'll fly down in the company jet and pick you up around three o'clock. And not a word to anybody. Not a single word. That's extremely important."

"I won't."

*   *   *

Fisk called Dusty in Washington. "I think we've found the disk."

"What, what's that? We, who's we?" His voice was extraordinarily calm.

"A young black boy, a friend of mine who lives near the airport."

"Found it where?"

"Cockroach Corner."

"To hell you say. My men walked the place."

"They obviously didn't look in the planes. He found it in the wreckage of an old DC-3 on Saturday."

"Well I'll be damned! You say the black kid called you?"

"I'm sure it's the real thing."

"I'm in awe. How the hell did you get in the loop?"

"Got connections," Fisk laughed. "Let's leave it at that. I'll tell you when I see you."

"We've got to jump on this."

"Right. I'm flying down to pick him up at his house at three. Can we rendezvous at the River House at quarter to?"

"I'll be there."

"And Dusty, please keep this to yourself until we have the disk. No one but the boy and his mother knows about it. I don't want some local muscling in on the kid's reward."

"Roger."

Fisk reached Martha at her office. "The disk, darling! I think we've finally found it," he whooped, trembling under the feeling of release. He told her about the two phone calls.

"Bless you!" she cried. "This changes everything, doesn't it? I mean, you don't have to worry anymore about the investigation dragging out like TWA 800."

"We should have a good idea what happened within a week or two, a month at the outside."

"Will you be gone long?"

"All depends. Maybe a day."

"But you will be back by Friday."

"Yes. Why do you ask?"

"It's your birthday, remember? I've planned a night on the town, just the two of us. There's an exhibit opening at your gallery that evening featuring an exciting young sculptor. We could drop by before dinner. Would you like that?"

"Would I ever!"

"I think you'll enjoy her work."

Fisk took his standby overnight bag out of the closet, told his secretary his plans, and hurried to the elevator. He stopped at Cutler's secretary's desk. "Can I have a quick word with him?"

"He's in a meeting all morning. Can't be disturbed."

"Just stick my head in? It's important."

"He said no interruptions, Mr. Fisk."

"Is he still with those two men who arrived this morning?"

That you go to hell stare of hers, he thought. Okay. They are interviewing him. It's gone that far, and still not a word to the board.

"There's the plane over there," Hobie said to Fisk and Dusty as they drove onto the tarmac at Cockroach Corner. "GONE FISHIN."

Fisk was busy surveying the scene. Would he have thought to look inside a plane that was so obviously split open by the crash, not a falling object? No he had to admit, but he could tell from the look on Dusty's face he was pissed at his team's failure.

Hobie proudly led them into the plane and through the cabin. "Uh oh," he said when they reached the rear.

"What's the matter?" Fisk asked.

"It's gone!" Hobie exclaimed.

"What's gone?"

"What's you're looking for."

Fisk experienced a stomach-hollowing feeling, like he was suddenly in free fall. "To hell you say. What are you talking about, Hobie? Gone? Gone where?"

Dusty turned to Fisk. "Gone fishin I suppose," he said sarcastically.

"It was here, I saw it here!" Hobie said tearfully.

"I am not amused," Dusty said.

"Wait-a-minute, what the hell's going on here?" Fisk said staring wide-eyed at the rent flooring. He knelt down to look into the opening. "I'll be damned! Look at this—the plane's control cables, corroded on the outside, bright as a nickel on the inside," he said, pulling at one of the wires to show Dusty the butt end. "They've been freshly severed. Something big went through the flooring and it's not here now."

"Son-of-a-bitch! I see what you mean," Dusty said, down on all fours beside him. "The disk was here and somebody beat us to it."

Hobie was sobbing. Dusty turned to him. "Could anyone else have known you saw the disk here?"

"Only my mama."

"Nobody else?"

Hobie hesitated. "Maybe my friend Lester."

"What do you mean maybe?" Dusty asked.

"He came back while I was looking at it."

"And . . . ?"

"I chased him back to the cockpit. I didn't want anybody else to know."

"After you 'flew' back, did you go home right away to call Mr. Fisk?"

"Yeh, I told Hobie I was sick at my stomach."

"And he left with you?"

"No, he said he was having fun."

Dusty stood up, deep in thought. "Did you see anyone else around when you were coming and going?"

"You mean outside?"

"Anywhere in the compound?"

"Jus this lady as I was leaving."

"A lady walking among the wrecks in the middle of the day?" Dusty said looking quizzically at Fisk. "Can you describe her?"

"A big lady with long black hair—like my mama."

"Black lady?"

"No, no, white."

"Anything unusual about her?"

"Walking with a funny cane."

"Wooden? Kinda bent?"

"I remember like the bamboo in jungle movies."

"Damn!" Dusty said turning to Fisk. "Rosie Donovan. Come on, we've got to find Lester."

They returned to Hobie's neighborhood where Hobie pointed out Lester who was riding his bicycle. Hobie stayed behind in the car.

"Are you Lester, Hobie's friend?" Dusty asked.

"Yeh."

"Then I'd like to talk to you a minute, son," He showed Lester his NTSB badge. "I understand you and Hobie were playing in the planes on Saturday."

"We not be stealin, mister."

"And you stayed behind after Hobie left?"

Fisk could see Dusty thought it best to leave him a little frightened.

"Only a little while."

"Did you see a white lady with a funny cane when you left?"
Lester looked down at the ground.

"Come on, Lester, you know something."

"She talked to me."

"What did she say?"

"She showed me a picture, something she was looking for."

"A picture of what?"

"Like the thing I seed Hobie looking at in the airplane."

"Then what?"

"The way Hobie was acting suspicious like, I thought I better not tell her. I lied."

"What did she do?"

Again looking down. "Nothing."

"Lester? . . ."

"Well she gave me some money and I telled her."

"How much money?"

"Lots."

"How much, Lester?"

"One hunnert dollars."

"Can I have a look at what she gave you?"

"You ain't going to take it away from me, are you mister?"

"No."

Lester handed him the bill. Brand new! Dusty folded it in his handkerchief and carefully tucked it into his pocket. Maybe he could get a print from it.

"Don't worry Lester, take these," Dusty said handing him five twenties. "And keep quiet about all this."

"I will, mister, I will!"

Fisk took Dusty aside. "I had the feeling all along General Tech was behind the bad publicity on Hi Tech. Now this. What's her game?"

"She handles matters like this for Barker. She'll have an expert take a look at the disk wherever she's taken it, and if the odds are good that it failed, she'll deep six it. It's as simple as that."

Fisk was stunned. "She would do that?"

"She did worse in Vietnam. Barker always gets away with it."

"Son-of-a-bitch!"

"Let's hope they're still examining it."

Dusty flipped open his cell phone and called the Miami Airport Inn. "Gotta find out if Rosie's still in town." He listened for a moment. "Do you have a Rose Donovan registered?"

"From New York City? Yes. Want me to ring?"

"No. Is she in the room?"

"I have no way of knowing, Sir!"

"Thanks."

He turned to Fisk. "We're in luck. She's here. Let me handle things by myself for a few hours. I think this may work out fine."

After dropping Fisk and Hobie off at the River House, Dusty drove to the FBI office in downtown Miami. "I need the prints on this bill checked immediately," he said, handing the officer in charge the folded handkerchief. "It's urgent."

"I'll see what I can do," he said, studying Dusty's credentials. "All depends on what the traffic's like into our central computer in Washington."

"Call me at the Miami Airport Inn. I'll leave word at the desk where I can be reached."

Dusty called Rosie's room from the hotel lobby.

"Dusty McGinty!" she exclaimed. "I've been hoping to hear from you. Where are you?"

"The lobby. Can I come up?"

"Right now?"

"This minute. It's important."

"No way, Dusty. I'm late now for a business appointment."

"I have to see you."

"You sound worked up? What have I done?"

"Cut it, Rosie! Are you going to see me or not?"

"Room 319."

She appeared at the door dressed in slacks and a matching blue shirt. Some business outfit, he thought.

"So what's the story?" she said with an "I am not amused look," and motioned him to a chair.

"You've been in Miami since at least last Friday," he said.

"And I didn't call you," she taunted him. "Is that all that's bothering you?"

"No, this is not personal."

"Then come to the point. I have work to do."

Dusty paused, drumming his finger on the arm of his chair.

"Okay," he said. "You want it this way, I'll give it to you in a few short words. I have reason to believe you've found the disk."

Rosie gave him a dismissive look. "What do you take me for?" she said. "You'd be the first to know."

"Then you're denying you know where it is?"

"Yes."

"Will you deny you were in Cockroach Corner last Friday?"

"No. What the hell are you up to Dusty?"

"Then you were there."

"I didn't say that. I could have been, wherever that is. I've been in a lot of places since I arrived. Seems to me you need all the help you can get finding the disk."

Pretty cool, Dusty thought. I can see why Barker's kept her around.

The phone rang. "For you," she said glowering, and thrust the receiver at him.

"Is this Investigator McGinty?"

"Speaking."

"FBI here. We have a match with one of the prints on the bill you left with me. Rose Donovan from our Armed Services file."

"You're sure?"

"It's never easy with an old bill. But we have equipment now that can handle multiple prints. Her's were recent and quite clear."

"Thanks."

He returned the receiver. I'll give her one more chance, he thought.

"Did you give a young black boy a hundred dollars for information about the disk."

"I've talked to a lot of people. But a hundred dollars! No way."

Dusty bit at a hangnail in frustration. I'm not going to get anywhere. She'll spend all night denying it. He opened his cell phone and began dialing.

"Who are you calling?"

"Barker. I want you to hear this."

"Do what you have to."

He reached him at home. "This is Dustin McGinty, IIC of the CCA 181 crash investigation. I'm here in Miami with your Vice President Donovan."

"McGinty, yes. I remember you from Vietnam. You and Rosie are friends." Were, Dusty thought. "What can I do for you?"

"Are you aware, sir, of the Federal law enacted in 1996 after a truck driver in Florida was accused of taking a piece of the wreckage of the Valujet crash as a souvenir?"

"I don't believe so, no. But what are you getting at Mr. McGinty?"

"The law makes it illegal to remove, conceal or remove parts of a civil aircraft involved in an accident. After the TWA crash, several people were charged with illegal possession of parts from the reassembled wreckage and withholding them from authorities. Conviction can bring up to ten years in jail."

"You're sounding like a lawyer. Get on with it, McGinty."

"I've told Ms. Donovan I have reason to believe she is in possession of the disk from the crash. She denies it."

"Then if I were you, I'd listen to her and get on with your

work. Somebody's feeding you bad information. If she'd found the disk I'd be the first to know about it."

"Then I take it you don't."

"No, and I'd trust her to tell me."

"Would you like to speak to her?"

"What is there to talk about?"

Enough of this tip toeing around the grave, Dusty thought. There's only one language he'll understand.

"Okay, General, listen to this. If the disk is not back to where it was found by nine tonight, I'll see to it that Ms. Donovan is served with a subpoena by morning to testify under oath. You and she should know that I have witnesses standing by who will place her at the scene shortly after the disk was discovered. She gave one of them a hundred dollar bill for disclosing its location and the FBI informed me minutes ago that her prints are on it. By the time I arrived on location, the disk was gone."

Dusty studied Rosie's face and saw panic in her eyes. She's cool all right, but not that cool. She knows I've got her.

He heard Barker clear his throat. "There must be a way to clear up this misunderstanding. What if Rosie was intending to turn it over all along?"

"If you're asking me if I want the disk bad enough to make a deal, the answer is yes."

"No charges, nothing in the press?"

"It'll be between us."

"Let me talk to Rosie."

. . .

"Yes, General."

. . .

"I can do that, yes, as soon as it's dark."

She returned the phone to Dusty. "By nine, General," he said, and hung up.

Rosie brushed by him and stood at the door. "Good-bye McGinty." You son-of-a-bitch.

* * *

"You won't believe this," Bledsoe said to Cutler. "Soon as it got dark, the truck leaves the dock with the three guys in it and heads toward town. We follow them, thinking this is it, they're going to dump it, and where do they go? Back to Cockroach Corner and sneak the disk back in."

Damn! Cutler thought. Somehow they learned the disk was not at fault. Maybe it was that obvious when Rosie described its condition to the experts. "You're sure? They didn't go in looking for a missing part?"

"The trundle with the tarp went in full and came out empty. I swear to it."

"Was Donovan along?"

"She met them on 36th at the fence and directed the show. Then they all left. What do we do?"

"We're in trouble, Joe."

"Think we should have a go at it? It's sittin there."

"Let me think about it."

Fisk was standing in the dark just inside the fence at Cockroach Corner, impatient for Dusty to arrive. Damn him, he thought. He said he'd be here at nine. If he doesn't come soon, I'm going to go have a look for myself. What's to say Barker lived up to the deal? Rosie may have called him back when she was alone to say the disk looked flawed. And he said to hell with it, get rid of it. Then where would the investigation be? Tangled in litigation for months based on the testimony of two kids fantasizing a flight to Orlando and "finding" the disk in "their" busted-up plane. Shit! Dusty would end up looking like an idiot.

"Sorry to be late," Dusty said, approaching. "I had to track down Munson. I want that disk out of here and on its way to the engine builder before the media hear about it. We don't need another news blitz. It'll be bad enough as is. Imagine the head-lines: 'YOUNG SON OF CCA 181 CRASH VICTIM FINDS MISSING DISK IN COCKROACH CORNER.' And hey, they'll be ecstatic over the irony of your part in it."

"You really think it's here?"

"We're going to find out, aren't we?"

"You're some operator. Did Donovan give you any trouble?"

"No questions, okay?"

He's made a deal with General Tech not to pursue charges, Fisk thought.

They walked to the plane and entered. Flashlight in hand, Dusty led the way to the rear of the cabin. "Thank God it's here all right!" he exclaimed when he saw the beam flash off the mangled blade stubs, then the disk itself.

"Yes, I see it!" Fisk whooped. "Hallelujah, it's here!" He felt an ocean of anxiety flood from his soul. The experts at the met-allurgical lab in Washington would inspect the disk. Within a week or two he would have his answer: was it his blades, or the disk?

He scrambled to one side and knelt down for a close inspec-tion. "There's a piece missing," he said, breathless at the thought it could mean the disk failed. "The fracture area extends radially to the bore and then horizontally, resulting in a chunk of the rim separating from the remainder of the disk."

"Careful now," Dusty cautioned, "No snap judgments. That's why I don't want a lot of pictures of the disk flying around be-fore the metallurgists have a chance to give us a professional opin-ion."

But there's hope, Fisk thought. You're my friend, Dusty. Say something—give me something!

Dusty took his place and knelt down beside him for a better look. "Interesting."

Interesting? That's all? I know you're as excited as I am.

"Munson should be here shortly with Jose and a few of his men. What are your plans?"

He's all business tonight.

"I'll pick up Hobie at the River House and take him home. Then I'll fly out. But not before I stop at the bar and have myself a good belt of bourbon. God, Dusty! I'm still shaking all over."

"Ah, yes, Hobie. He has to be careful what he says," Dusty cautioned. "The media will be all over him when they learn his part in the discovery. Make sure he forgets the dry run this afternoon."

"I understand. Can I tell him about the reward?"

"He doesn't know?"

"I don't think so. He's never mentioned it."

"Okay, it should come from you. But he can't tell anyone until he hears from me."

"Of course."

As he was leaving, Fisk turned to Dusty. "Tell me," he said. "The failure could have started with a stress crack, couldn't it."

"Could have, yes." Dusty smiled. "And just between us, I hope for your sake it did. You've been terrific, Alan. You deserve a break."

Hobie was still at the table when Fisk returned. "That call you heard was Mr. McGinty," he said. "You see, he trusted you and went back to your airplane tonight for a better look. The parts were where you said they were. They had just slipped down under the floor."

Hobie nodded, a look of self-congratulation on his face.

"So we won't talk about the visit this afternoon, right? It would just confuse people."

"Okay."

"There's a reward, you know."

"Reward?"

"You don't know? For finding the disk. Fifty thousand dollars. But you can't talk abut any of this until you hear it from Mr. McGinty."

Hobie's mouth dropped open. "Fifty thousand dollars! How much is that?" he asked quickly. "Is it a car?"

Fisk laughed. "That and more unless you get fancy."

"Wowee! I can buy my mama a new car now that she has to get around herself. And my Papa, can the money help him get well?"

"Maybe it can, Hobie, maybe it can," Fisk said, his thoughts turning to the day he saw Howard in the hospital and listened to him talk about his son. "Especially when he knows the money comes from you. Your daddy is very proud of you."

"You're crying, Mr. Fisk."

So I am.

"It's not bad to cry when you feel good about somebody," he said. "You're quite a young man, Hobie. Thank you for what you did for me."

CHAPTER 32

Friday, June 18

"How's the birthday boy?" Martha asked, joining Fisk in his office at the end of the day. "Any good news?"

"Nothing dramatic," he said, "but encouraging. The last two days the lab in Washington has been examining a slice from the bore of the disk with its scanning electron microscope. Going at it hot and heavy this afternoon, I hear. And that tells me they may have found a flaw. They're often no larger than a grain of sand."

"That could have caused the crash?"

"Could, and has, in other instances."

"I want to hear more. What sort of flaw?"

"It would take too long to tell you."

"Don't you talk down to me, Alan!" Her eyes flashed. "Just give me the five minute version."

If that's what you want, he thought, and reached for the NTSB Air Accident Report he had been studying.

"Tell you what. I'll read you something from this analysis of the disk failure in the United Sioux City crash; it may parallel our situation."

He opened the report. "Sure you want to hear this?"

She nodded.

"Metallurgical examination," he began, "revealed that the fatigue crack initiated near a small cavity on the surface of the disk bore, about 0.86 inch aft of the forward face of the bore . . . Fractographic, metallurgic, and chemical analysis examinations of the fatigue region revealed the presence of a nitrogen-stabilized hard alpha inclusion around the cavity . . ."

"Okay, you've made your point!"

". . . The total number of major striations along a radially outward direction from the origin area was estimated by graphically integrating . . ."

"I said enough already!"

"I'm just beginning," he teased.

She sat staring at him angrily for a moment, then broke out laughing.

"Hey, it's my birthday," he said, rising to kiss her on her cheek. "I'm looking forward to my night on the town. Come on, let's blow this place."

Their cab dropped them in front of the Renee Bullock Gallery in a converted warehouse in the River North section of Chicago.

Entering, he pulled her aside. "Quick, the name of the sculptor? Pam what?"

"For god sakes, Alan, don't call her Pam. She insists on Pamela, Pamela Spitz."

Why that Cheshire cat grin? he thought.

"You say she's good?"

"Wonderful. Wait 'till you see."

At the gallery entrance, they heard the hubbub of a crowded room. "Damn, a mob scene," Fisk muttered. "I hate this."

"Sush! You should be happy for her."

They turned into the room. Stunned, Fisk stood frozen in the doorway. "The room's filled with my sculpture!" he gasped, wide-eyed.

"Happy birthday, sweetheart," Martha said. "Your one man show."

"There's ARTIFACTS," he exclaimed, spellbound by the scene. "And Otto Gitner over there raiding the cheese table." He turned to face her. "Pamela Spitz, eh! You little scoundrel. Wait 'till I get you home."

"Promise?"

Fisk continued to look around the room. "I can't get over this, sweetheart. Look, there's QUEST, and over there the sculpture I sold Otto years ago. When did you first think of doing the show?"

"The morning of the crash. We were talking about your future, remember?"

Fisk reached for the show's brochure on a side table near the entrance. A blurb on the cover written by the art critic Jason Hartley caught his eye.

"Mr. Fisk's works offer an important insight into modern man's esthetic and philosophical relationship to technology. His work is art of the highest order."

"Wow!" he exclaimed.

"Are you pleased?" Martha asked.

"Are you kidding? Look at me. I'm ecstatic. That, from Jason Hartley!"

She shrugged. "He seems to understand what you're trying to express."

Renee Bullock approached out of the crowd with a jovial looking man in a dark blue suit, sporting a pencil-thin mustache and a red carnation in his lapel. Fisk had spotted him lingering over ARTIFACTS and took him to be a serious collector. "Break it up the two of you," Renee said laughing. "It may be your birthday, Alan, but there's serious work to be done. Mr. Gilpatrick here is one of my best clients. He's taken with your work— dying to buy ARTIFACTS, but I told him it's not for sale."

The man smiled roguishly. "Tell them I'm also your lover, Renee."

"Don't embarrass me, Warren. I'll never have a lover. I couldn't hold my stomach in that long." She started off across the room with Martha.

"Some woman! The best," Gilpatrick remarked when they were alone. "Now tell me, Mr. Fisk, the obsidian base of ARTI-FACTS—an Indian spear point I take it. Is it a found object?"

Fisk brightened. "No. I made it."

"Then you're a flint knapper as well as a sculptor."

"Is there a difference? A knapper's a sculptor, too."

Warren smiled. "You're right, there isn't. But you have to admit it's a special skill. Where did you learn it?"

"Bruce Bradley. Spent some time with him in Durango several years ago. The art has fascinated me since I was a kid."

"I know Bruce."

"Small world department. You have an interest?"

"Got this to show for it," Warren said, displaying a two inch scar in the palm of his left hand. "Now I believe it when they say obsidian produces some of the sharpest edges known—sharper than stainless."

"Then you're a knapper too."

"Learned it from D.C. Waldorf."

I like this man, Fisk thought.

"Do you buy your minerals or look for them yourself?" Warren asked.

"Looking is half the fun," Fisk lowered his voice. "I've found a neat source for obsidian on the eastern side of the Sierras north of Bishop. But don't tell anybody."

"Through Deadman's Pass, not far from Mono Lake?"

"Exactly. Several miles from the ancient Indian mine."

"My God, we are soul-mates!" Warren said. "I work the same spot."

For the next fifteen minutes they were two veteran knappers deep in conversation about mineral sources, hammer stones, deer antler tines for pressure flaking, Indian techniques for heat treating . . .

"The name of your piece," Warren said. "I'm fascinated. You

mean to link two objects from very different eras. I wouldn't have thought of a jet engine blade as an artifact."

"I see them both as tools, products of the human intellect. You start with the one at the dawn of history, and before too long you arrive at the other helping propel you across the continent at near the speed of sound."

"My, my," Warren said admiringly. "I usually find with my artists there's a moment of inspiration if I can wheedle it out of them, a special feeling that has to be expressed. Is there one here?"

Fisk hesitated, unsure whether to speak with a relative stranger about a cherished moment he had confided only to Martha. "I don't know whether I can tease the feeling into words," he said, "but I can tell you the circumstance. It's never far from my mind.

"I was walking the dry lake beds in the Stillwater Reservation outside Fallon, Nevada, in late April when I spotted a glint in the sand off in the distance. You know the feeling. The sun angle was just right and the winter winds had stripped away the loose surface. And there it was, a beautiful specimen lying exposed in the sand. I had only to bend over and pick it up."

"Unbroken?"

"The point still so sharp it would prick your finger. They say the ancient lakes were teeming with duck and desert pelican. The arrow had obviously missed its target and landed in the water; probably floated until the shaft rotted, then sank into the muck where it lay protected for centuries. Except for flecks of black, the obsidian was clear as crystal."

"Really? Clear obsidian?"

"I agree, it was unusual. So I held it against the sky to find whether I could see through it, and imagine! I found that by chance I had superimposed it on a widebody jet at forty thousand feet trailing contrails. I tell you, for me it was a spiritual moment. I saw in my mind's eye the engines' fan blades—blades are my business, you know—sucking in the air and I felt a kind of kinship between them and the arrowhead in my hand."

"Thus your inspiration for ARTIFACTS!" Warren exclaimed.

"You're reminding us that modern man is, in the anthropological sense, still a tool maker."

"Precisely," Fisk said, "but oh, what tools! And you know . . ." He looked down at the floor. Oh what the hell. I've gone this far, he thought. "I think it's all part of a natural progression from the simplicity of an arrowhead to the complexity of modern artifacts such as Apollo."

"In what sense?"

"Genes' quest for survival. Life has insinuated itself into every nook and cranny of the earth. What other way is there to spread the seed to the planets and the universe beyond?"

"You mean space travel?"

"Just a thought."

"So you see the development of the human intellect preceding toward designing rockets for the trip in the vacuum of space?"

"A good way to put it."

"Well, well. Maybe you'll show us one day."

"You've got it, Alan! You've really got it. This is your real life—or it could be if you open yourself up to it," Martha said on the way to the Drake for dinner. "Renee's ecstatic over the sales, and that man Gilpatrick, know what I heard him say to her? 'I'd give anything to be able to get into that man's mind.' "

"He said that? The son of a gun. He really got me talking. I haven't had that much fun in a long time."

"You must be flattered. He appreciates the way you look at things; bought two of your pieces. Seriously, I hope after tonight you'll give more thought to what you're going to do after you resign from Hi Tech."

"In time. Right now, I'm going to stay with my feelings at the moment. I'm on a high, Martha! I can say it to myself now. I am a sculptor."

Martha laughed. "You are ecstatic, aren't you?"

"I feel giddy—young, everything ahead of me."

"Who said you weren't young? And it's not as though you just began sculpting. You've been at it for twenty-two years."

"Thanks, darling. At fifty-five, not all that young. But what the hell, I've gotten over that attitude. Gilpatrick spoke of an artist pursuing a 'special feeling that needs to be expressed.' And I have that 'special feeling'; have had it all along, he made me realize. And I have you to thank. You knew the show would give me that extra bit of confidence to see myself as a sculptor . . ."

He looked at her in surprise. "The tears, Martha? What's wrong?"

"She wiped her eyes. "Do I need to say?"

He kissed her, his heart full of yearnings. "Strange how you meet somebody and they immediately make a difference," he said. "I hadn't known Gilpatrick half an hour, and shared with him my thoughts that only you have heard; told him about a vision I have wanted to express for some time. And you know what he said? 'Maybe you'll show us one day.'

"And maybe I will."

CHAPTER 33

Monday, June 21

Fisk arrived at the Sedalia plant at six a.m., two hours before the opening of the offices.

"Good morning, Mr. Fisk," the guard greeted him. "See you're get'n an early start this trip."

"Paperwork, Jeb," Fisk said giving him a thumbs up. "You know the way it is with these big companies."

God, how I hate this! he thought. Sneaking around in my own plant.

He walked through the empty offices to a room off the cafeteria where Beauchamp's personal files were in storage. Damned waste of time, he grumbled after digging through the first cabinet. Beauchamp was a saphead, but not the kind of idiot who would leave incriminating papers behind. A half hour later he finished the second. Nothing. He was about to leave when he spied a seventy-five millimeter artillery shell standing in the corner, a relic from the company's World War II production that Beauchamp had kept next to his desk.

Fisk went to have a look, uneasy at the thought of a shell sitting in his plant. Knowing Beauchamp, it might be live. He saw the warhead's fuse was missing, but still wary, stuck his finger in the hole. Empty! And the brass propellant casing below? he thought. Empty too I hope. He lifted the heavy steel head off and inside saw a rolled up sheaf of pages. His fingers trembled. Jesus! Beauchamp's secret file cabinet? It was zany enough. And he had left them behind. Otto was right. Beauchamp was a hit or miss kind of guy.

He unrolled the first page. Odd, he thought when he read the heading: "Small Tool Account," a designation often used by accountants for expendable shop items to be written off in one year. What was it doing here? Below written in longhand was a column of names followed by entries under the headings: Company, Date, Place, Expense, Escort, Comments. Fisk grunted. Sexual payoffs for influence, taken as business deductions for "small tools." Some sense of humor.

The third entry got his attention : "Great White Father—U S Senate—1/17/97—Fairmont, S.F.—$1,500—Latasha—She likes older men, very inventive, yum yum!"

Great White Father! Isn't that what the lobbyists call Rushmore behind his back?

He unrolled the second page and looked at a single sheet of ledger paper with the heading "GWF ACCOUNT." The document consisted of three column headings: "Date, Airforce Contract, and Number of Shares Registered to Grand Cayman Trust," with entries over a period of years.

Just what Otto said Beauchamp told him that day on the plane!

Flushed with anticipation, Fisk read the last page. Written in longhand on company stationary, it said:

> February 23, 2001
>
> Memo To The File:
> Hi Tech Deal—cash finder's fee of one million dollars payable to GWF upon closing assumed by the buyer per Cass Cutler, President.
>
> Buford Beauchamp

Fisk read it again. Concise, to the point, and probably admissible in a court of law. The hard evidence I was after. But now what?

He put the papers into his briefcase. This thing has ramifications, he thought. Does it ever. I'd better talk to somebody I can trust. I'll have a drink with Otto.

CHAPTER 34

Tuesday, June 22

Otto Gitner, at his usual Berghoff table, looked wan and older than his seventy-eight years. I've never seen him pasty-faced like this, Fisk thought.

"You all right?" he asked.

"It's that obvious, is it?"

"You're my friend, Otto, we understand each other."

Otto waved his comment aside. "Save that for later. I came here to hear about your problem."

"It can wait."

"No, no. Now! You were worked up when you called."

"All right, but I still want to hear about you. It's Buzz Beauchamp. You were dead right. He did leave behind hard evidence of the shenanigans involving Rushmore and Cutler. I found it yesterday during a visit to Sedalia."

"What's so bad about that?"

"The tactical questions it presents. A lot has happened over the last week and a half." He told Gitner about the events touched off by Dusty's call to him about the SEC investigation, and finally, the secret meeting at Hancock's house.

Fisk sighed with exasperation. "I'm not used to this high powered boardroom stuff," he concluded.

"You think I am?"

"Come on, Otto. You've been around."

"I'll do what I can."

"The timing worries me. I may be in a position to topple

Cutler with the evidence at Friday's board meeting. What effect would that have on the investigation when it hits the papers? After all, that was the concern Dusty expressed in his call that sent me to Hancock."

Otto rubbed at his face. "What effect on the investigation? I don't think that carries much weight now. From what you tell me the feds are already hot after him. News could hit the media any moment. This way your actions will show the public Hi Tech's trying to act honorably. Besides, what choice do you have? You possess the evidence. You're surely not thinking of witholding it."

"No, of course not. You're right, Otto. I'm not being very clearheaded about this." He paused. "Then the question is, do I take the evidence to Hancock now? At the moment, I plan to keep it to myself and present it at the board meeting. But is that the right thing to do?"

Otto pounded the table with his fist. "Yes, yes! Act independently. You'll be more effective. You don't want to appear part of a conspiracy; to seem in cahoots with the other three to get Cutler. Besides, you don't know what a man like Hancock would do with the evidence. He might go right to his friend at the SEC."

"Should I?"

"Do what?"

"Take the evidence to the SEC? Am I in jeopardy if I don't?"

Otto eyed him intently. "You should consult your lawyer for a definitive answer. The meeting is only three days off, though. I don't think you're taking much of a chance."

Fisk nodded. "I knew you were the man to speak to. Thank you."

Otto beamed. "I think the larger question is what you plan to do with the rest of your life. Didn't you tell me after the May meeting that you had submitted your resignation to Cutler effective when probable cause was determined? What if you heard tomorrow the disk was at fault. Do you think that would influence your decision? . . . Honest injun?"

"Let's turn that around. If my blades are found at fault, I could never be part of a manufacturing operation again."

"Of any kind?"

"Of any kind. I don't know what I would do. I might go for a full-time career as a sculptor. I know Martha thinks it would make me happy."

"Would it?"

"I thought seriously of that before I sold to Hi Tech. There are thoughts I want to explore before I die, Otto, little whispering thoughts, far removed from the give and take of business. But would sculpting be enough to occupy me for the rest of my life? I feed off of my daily contact with the aerospace world. When Cutler came along with his blarney, I thought I could have it both ways. It was a mistake, aside from the tragedy of the crash. I hate boardroom politics, hate the bureaucracy of a big company."

Otto leaned forward, an earnest look on his face. "Then I may have something to offer beyond questionable advice from an old fart. I want to sell the small company in Evanston I kept out of the deal when I sold my original business three years ago."

Wow, that neat little company, Fisk thought. When we met at Berghof's the night of the crash he said he wanted me to meet with the new manager. Thought the two of us would hit it off.

"I remember it well. Makes a line of custom-made titanium surgical implants. You want to sell it!"

"It's Ben, Ben Levine. You've heard me speak of him. We were very close."

Fisk remembered stories about how the man had befriended Gitner when he arrived from Germany. What does Levine have to do with it? he asked himself. He's not involved in the company.

"He died Friday while we were having lunch at the Chicago Club. Just fell off his chair onto the floor."

Poor Otto, Fisk thought. That's why he looks so terrible.

"I'm so sorry . . ."

"All our lives we heard, death, where is thy sting? I tell you, Alan, I felt the sting seeing him stretched out on the floor. Felt it for both of us."

Fisk saw Otto was close to tears and reached for his hand.

"His death has affected me terribly. Ben wanted two things. To be the richest man in the world and to live forever. So where is he now? What does it all amount to? I tell you, it's gotten under my skin. I've decided to close up shop and move to Florida."

"You loved the man, I know, but don't jump. Give yourself some time."

"I have."

"And you've made up your mind? You definitely want to sell?"

"As soon as I can find a buyer."

"Are you talking to anybody?"

"I'm offering it to you first. But you. Not Hi Tech."

Oh, God. Don't tempt me!

"The future of the company is in an entirely new area—tissue engineering. And there's no bureaucracy. You'd have a ball. We have licenses from several major universities to develop commercial products based on their research. Regenerated or lab-grown bone, cartilage, blood vessels and skin are all being tested in humans, today. Livers, breasts, hearts, in ten years."

Fisk tingled all over with excitement. "I've read about that. The kid at Boston's Children's Hospital who received an implant of new cartilage in an area protecting his heart. Unbelievable!"

"Exactly! The doctors made a scaffold of biodegradable polymer in the shape of his chest and seeded it with his cartilage cells. That's the kind of technology we're dealing with. Damnedest thing I've ever seen. They bathed the scaffold in growth factors, the cells multiplied, and when implanted, the cells were smart enough to recreate their proper tissue functions. The scaffold gradually degraded and normal cartilage remained."

Fantastic! A new vein for my sculpting, Fisk thought. Inner space. Body parts engineered from a person's own cells. Right down my alley. The genius of thousands of men and women living on in human tissue! I can even see it. Jesus!

"I have a crackerjack young man running the business," Otto added. "Sam Elkington. He has an equity interest and a load of options; wouldn't feel threatened. He'd welcome your ownership and guidance."

Mike Belmonte all over, Fisk thought. The fun of seeing him develop into a well rounded businessman capable of running his own show. Wasn't that one of the joys of building up my company?

"You could have it both ways; more time to sculpt. You have the talent and energy to do two things well. Many do. There are a lot of hyphenated people around."

"Hyphenated?"

"Businessman-philosopher, businessman-politician."

Yes, a hyphenated man, Fisk thought, all my life. And I tried that again last time and look what happened.

"Are you in a hurry?" he asked.

"You have the right of first refusal for a month."

A month, he thought. Four weeks, almost tomorrow as the world goes. By then I'll be packed up and out of Hi Tech. And I still can't make up my mind. All this backing and filling. Shit! I feel like ambivalence personified. Last week after the sculpture show I was at peace at the thought of walking away from the work of half a lifetime. Now my dear friend is offering me a deal and I'm tempted. God! how I'm tempted. A chance to truly have it both ways. Hi Tech Lite.

"Thank you, Otto," he said. "I'll be back to you as soon as I can."

CHAPTER 35

Thursday, June 24

Fisk's secretary called on the intercom. "Mr. McGinty from Washington on line one. I told him you're preparing for tomorrow's board meeting, but he's insisting. Says it's important. He's scheduled a news release."

Oh my god! Fisk thought. This is it. "Put him on . . . Hello, Dusty. You're about to make an announcement?"

"Shortly. I owe you this call for your part in finding the disk . . ."

Fisk's stomach muscles tightened. Please, please he prayed, trying to hear good news in his tone of voice.

"Something you'd like to hear, my friend . . ."

Like to hear! It is good news.

"The engine working group has completed preliminary work on its factual report for the Public Hearing. The disk failed!"

Disk . . . failed . . . *The disk failed!*

"You're home free, pal! Do you hear me? Home free."

Fisk fought back tears. This changes everything, he thought. For me, for the company.

"You still there?"

"They're sure? No imbalance caused by blade failure?"

"Our ETEC scanning electron microscope can do marvelous things. They've concluded the failure was caused by a near-radial bore-to-rim fracture initiated in a fatigue region on the inside diameter of the bore."

Just what I thought it was when I first saw it! "Was it an imperfection in the disk?"

"A hard alpha defect on the surface caused by excessive amounts of nitrogen absorbed by the titanium when it was in its molten state. The engine manufacturer maintains computerized listings of all critical rotating parts by serial number and General Tech's heat number for traceability. We've tracked down the other seven disks from the same titanium ingot, six of them still in service. The first we've had time to examine had a similar hard alpha inclusion."

"I can't believe it! Contamination during the vacuum melt in General Tech's new plasma furnace? And the finished disk got by all the inspections?"

"We're still trying to determine how. Everybody has a lot of explaining to do. Anyhow, I thought you'd like to know your blades were not at fault."

You thought . . . ? Are you kidding. This day is every Christmas I'll ever know rolled into one! "You're a real friend, Dusty."

"I wanted to be the first to tell you. You deserve to be out from under."

"Thank you."

"No, really. I like your style. You should be running the company, not that shit Cutler."

"He just walked past my door."

"I can't imagine he's a very happy camper these days. My friend in the SEC tells me they've discovered a secret offshore slush fund fed by illegal kickbacks from Hi Tech's international sales."

Jesus, it could involve Joe Bledsoe, he thought. He's Hi Tech's largest independent rep handling foreign sales. As sole owner of the distributorship, he would have ample opportunity to establish such a fund by cooking his books. "Do they have any idea who manages the fund?" he asked.

"Not yet, but sounds like they're on his trail. They're finding payments to foreign governments, political campaigns, and others over the years. Anyhow, I think you should give serious thought to what I said about running the company. I don't think Cutler will be walking the corridors much longer."

Fisk reached Martha in the office.

"Dusty called . . . my blades . . ." he said haltingly, and as the words he was about to utter formed in his mind, the professional reserve he had managed minutes ago dissolved in a flood of tears.

"Go on, tell me," Martha said gently.

"Are . . . not . . . at . . . fault!"

"Oh, Alan! Why can't I be with you to hear this? Sweetheart, sweetheart . . . I'm so happy for you."

"It won't help the victims, but I can face myself again. Face myself,! You know what that means to me."

"Yes I do. I've watched you being consumed by the investigation . . . I'm so happy I could dance!"

Fisk wiped his eyes and smiled. More than once when she thought she was alone he found her waltzing around the room humming a tune.

"I'm so happy I could dance with you," he said. "I can hardly believe it's over. The low point was the morning after I returned from Miami and had that dream."

"The woman in the elevator."

"Yes. I thought the nightmare might plague me the rest of my life. It's one thing to read the body count over a thousand in the paper, see the stretchers on television, even climb through the ruins, smell those god awful smells and witness body outlines on the sooty floors. Another to see one individual lying there, vulnerable and exposed in death, and to think, as I did that night, maybe—probably—I had killed her."

Fisk was silent for a moment. "I'm shaking all over at the thought."

"Enough," she said. "The important thing is that the nightmare is over."

"You really think so, I mean the dream?"

"I do."

Fisk sighed.

"You mean I've got my happy husband back again?"

"He'll be even happier after tomorrow's board meeting. We have a lot to talk over."

"Yes, we do. I can't wait."

Cutler watched a flashing cursor on High-Tech's symbol programmed in his computer along with a number of stocks of interest.

Uh, oh, he thought, and clicked on it for a quote. Off three points on high volume. Why high volume. The volatility increased. The stock was now up a half; soon down again. Something's out there. He called his broker.

"What the hell's happening with our stock?"

"There's a rumor around that the NTSB is about to make an important announcement. The market assumes it's about the CCA 181 crash investigation."

The disk, that's it, Cutler thought. They've been studying it for over a week. Christ! Everything's in the balance now. "What are they going to say?"

"Nobody knows. Unusual for Washington. They've been leak-proof so far."

Cutler hung up. GTH began flashing and he watched in alarm. Suddenly an asterisk appeared next to each symbol. News! He double clicked on HTH. A window popped up on the screen.

NEWS SCREEN

ID LXTNSP Src:DJ TM 12:noon 24 June NYC Page 1 0f 1
us:HTH   High Tech   59 1/2   Up 4 3/4
Hi Tech, Inc. A Party In Investigation of CCA 181 Crash Investigation.

> WASHINGTON (Dow Jones)—The National Transportation Safety Board has announced that after intensive metallurgical examination of the recently recovered number three engine's fan disk manufactured by General Tech, the board has concluded the disk failed catastrophically during the takeoff of CCA flight 181 from Miami International airport on May 25. While the NTSB's official determination of the probable cause must await the mandated Public Hearing and subsequent final report, it appears that the fan blades supplied by Hi Tech, previously the subject of much public speculation, are no longer under suspicion.

(END) DOW JONES NEWS   12:00 EDT   06 24 02

"Hot damn!" Cutler hooted and sank his fist into the palm of his hand with a loud clap. We beat 'em! Now I can concentrate on my troubles in Washington.

He picked up the phone. "Get me Tom Burke."

The lawyer came on the line. "Our stock's soaring, Tom. Have you heard the news?"

"No."

"Check your office's Market Watch. The NTSB announced at noon that the failure of GT's disk caused the CCA crash.

"Mother of God! No caveats?"

"Routine. The public hearing and the final report."

"That is good news!"

"So I'd like your opinion at the board meeting tomorrow whether this allows us to ask the court in Schnell's class action suit to be removed as a defendant. And Tom, I find you a little

distant since Hancock brought up the rumor about a finder's fee
in the Sedalia acquisition. Do you have a problem?"

"Only that you've got a problem."

Cutler paused. Watch the high horse buster.

"A problem you're keeping from me and the board, Cass."

Cutler continued his silence. What the hell's going on? I've
never heard him like this.

"I know you're involved in an SEC investigation. For god
sakes, Cass, if you've participated in an illegal act, I should be the
first to know, not hear about it through the legal grapevine! I'm
your lawyer and I deserve better."

Cutler seethed. He deserves better, eh? "I want you in my
office on the double quick. Now!"

Cutler slammed down the receiver and reached for a confidential file titled Burke Smythe & Trumbull, containing a list of
the law firm's billings for each of the past five years. Eight million dollars already this year he grumbled. Stick it to me with
that holier than thou shit, will he? We'll see.

Burke arrived in the doorway looking like he was entering
the chamber of horrors. "You still got problems?" Cutler asked.

"Yes."

"If you know so much about the goings on in Washington,
why didn't you come to me?"

"Because I was waiting to hear the truth from you."

"I'm worried about you," Cutler said, glowering. "I have
enough boy scouts around here. Whatdaya think this is, summer
camp?"

"Then what I've been hearing is true?"

"Yes."

"And you still intend to keep your SEC problem from the
board?"

"Until I'm ready, and I expect your cooperation. With our
resident prig Hancock snipping at my heels, I don't need my
lawyer questioning my actions."

"You're putting me in an impossible position."

"You're right. I am. You have a problem with that?"

"Don't play with me, Cass. As company counsel, I have responsibility to the company and its directors."

Cutler gave him a scathing look and reached for the file folder on his desk containing the record of his law firm's billings. "Read this!" he snapped, and watched impassively as Burke examined it. The lawyer's face turned ashen and the paper rattled in his trembling hands.

"Uh, don't get me wrong," he said, struggling to sound conciliatory. "I'm on your side, but what do you gain? As soon as the Grand Jury takes testimony the board will know the facts."

"I gain time. Our board leaks like a sinking ship. If I can strike a deal quietly in Washington before word gets out publicly and the whole thing becomes a big brouhaha, I'll get off easy. And so will the company. Those guys down there don't give a shit about me. They're after the Great White Father to embarrass the Republicans."

"The board won't take lightly to being lied to, regardless."

"So what can they do?"

"Fire you."

"They wouldn't dare."

"Don't be so sure. Remember, I wasn't in favor of your increasing the board. In the past you've had a safe majority."

"George? You're thinking of George?" Cutler guffawed.

"I've seen you pretty rough on him at times; you seem to get a kick out of humiliating him."

"Don't worry yourself," Cutler said, still smiling. "I know him well. He's one of us."

He glanced at his watch. "See you at the meeting tomorrow."

Cutler turned to the computer screen. That's what I want to see! Up another twenty points. And what about Barker, he thought. Put me down will he? I'll bet the market is burning his ass right about now. He clicked on GTH and watched gleefully as General Tech's stock plunged. Gotta call the son-of-a-bitch.

"Cass Cutler, Sam. Just keeping in touch," he said. "The NTSB announcement must have been hard to take after all the assurances you had from your people when we first spoke."

"Get on with it Cass," Baker snapped. "I'm too busy for games."

"I bet you are."

"If you have something to say, say it."

"As a friend, I just wanted you to know your sidekick Rosie is losing her edge. A little too obvious for someone with her experience. We were on top of your op every step of the way— gave me a scare when she returned the disk . . ."

"I don't know what you're talking about."

"I thought you had examined it and found it sound. Then where would I have been?"

"Are you finished?"

"Slow up. I wouldn't make me angry if I were you. One thing I didn't understand is why did you return it? You wanna know my theory? A little fast footwork at the crossroads to keep you and Rosie out of the can. Sound about right? And, oh. I just noticed on the screen. Your stock has dropped another fourteen points since we've been talking."

Fisk was about to call Cutler when his voice boomed over the intercom. "You hear the good news?"

How did he know the news so soon? "Yes, Mike Belmonte called me," he lied.

"Come on in. I want to congratulate you for a successful campaign. You really stuck to your guns."

Yeah, yeah, now you tell me. Cut the bullshit, Cass. Show some respect for my intelligence.

When he entered Cutler's office, he noticed the blinds were down. No squinting into the sun today, he thought.

Cutler came from behind his desk and shook his hand. "Great job!" he said. "Sit down, sit down."

Fisk managed a wry smile. The two of them had largely avoided one another since their donnybrook at the May board meeting, and here they were, he mused, making nice. Hypocrisy! Makes me sick. If only Cutler knew what was in store for him in the morning.

"You were right to go at the investigation the way you did," Cutler said. "I admire that tenacity of yours. We need that kind of leadership here."

Fisk shrugged.

Cutler reached for a paper on the desk and tore it up. "You can't resign," he said. "I want you on board."

Fisk looked him in the eye without replying.

Cutler's look of cheerful camaraderie faded.

I can't hide it, Fisk thought. He sees how I feel.

"I know, I know," Cutler said after an awkward silence. "I misjudged the situation from the beginning. I was wrong."

Mea culpa, he thought. Well, there's progress.

Cutler sat scanning his face. "Think about it. There's no hurry. But in my defense I have to tell you that this could have gone the other way. There were things going on out there that I don't want to say too much about. Real hardball, and I think your friend McGinty was involved in it . . ."

My God, sounds like he knows what General Tech was up to. "Hardball? What are you getting at, Cass?"

"I have good reason to believe he was in cahoots with Barker."

He must have had Bledsoe put a tail on Rosie, watched the whole thing unfold, even the return of the disk. But why didn't he intervene then? "Cahoots? I still don't know what you're talking about."

Cutler's eyes narrowed. "Yeah, in cahoots," he said angrily. "When the final report is issued I'm going to talk to the chair-

man of the Safety Board and see that Barker gets what's coming
to him. McGinty too!"

"For what? What did McGinty do?"

"Let's just leave it at that for now."

*He must be pissed that Dusty hasn't hustled Rosie and Barker
into court.* "The man is as square-dealing as they come," Fisk
said. "You're wrong about him, totally wrong. I don't know what
you think he did, but whatever, everything he did was directed at
getting at the truth as soon as possible."

"One of these days you'll rid yourself of some of the boy
scout in you. When you're running a big public company . . ."

Oh, Christ, not that again!

". . . there are others to consider: shareholders, employees,
suppliers and community."

Get off it Cass.

"I didn't get anywhere when I tried to have McGinty removed for leaking the tapes, but I'm going to have his ass this
time."

Fisk felt like walking out. "He didn't leak the tapes! Get that
through your head."

"You'll understand," Cutler said with a dismissive flick of his
hand. "Forget about Dusty and spend the time deciding what
you want to do. Let me know."

Fisk plopped into his office chair, muttering to himself. I'll let
you know all right. You're willing to destroy Dusty. Why should
I worry about destroying you? Thanks for making it easy.

CHAPTER 36

Friday, June 25

Fisk entered the boardroom early to find George Trueslow there, the first to arrive. He was walking around the table, studying the ten chairs with uncommon intensity it seemed to Fisk.

"Something's fishy here," George said. "They're not identical. That chair's back is two inches higher than the rest."

"That's Cass's chair," Fisk said.

George snickered. "It follows. So he can lord it over the rest of us peons."

The other directors began arriving and one by one, stopped to welcome Trueslow to the board. "I knew your father," Trueslow said to John Hancock. "Served on a bank board in town together. Good man. I remember . . ."

New best friends, Fisk thought and wandered off, taking in the bonhomie now pervading the room.

Stuart Brattle approached him, all smiles, and gave his hand a vigorous shake. "What a wonderful thing for you to do for that young boy," he said. "I read the article in Sunday's magazine section on your relationship. Just shows you give and you get. Was it actually the fan blade you gave him at the plant that led to the discovery of the disk?"

How can Stuart be so cheerful? Fisk thought. He knows what's ahead.

"Makes a good story, Stuart, but no. Hobie already knew what the working parts of a jet engine look like. He deserves all the credit."

"You're being too modest," Felix Reston said, joining them.

Fisk felt uncomfortable at the praise and the prospect of the accolades he could see waiting on the faces of the directors now gathering around him. After the NTSB announcement, he had received hundreds of admiring calls from all walks. *Enough's enough! Get him talking.*

"I've been wanting to ask you, Felix," he said, shrugging off his comment. "As our investment banker, you're in the best position to express an opinion about United Aerospace. What are they going to do ? Still pursue the takeover?"

Reston frowned. "Good question. With our stock back to its high we're no longer a bargain. The word's around that Courtwright may want to cut and run with his profit. I'm going to recommend that we consider a buyback of his block of stock for our Employees Stock Option plan . . ."

"That's great news," Cutler interrupted, entering the room with Burke at his side. "But save the rest for later when we're into the agenda." He turned to Trueslow, "Glad to have you aboard, George. You'll be a great addition."

Trueslow shook his hand. "I'll try hard to be a good team member."

Fisk watched as Cutler all but patted him on the head. *Hypocrite!*

"You've got it George," Cutler said, his arm still around him. "Got the spirit right from the start. A quick mind, yes, very quick."

He's overdone it Fisk thought noting Truselow's wounded look. The man's not an idiot.

Cutler motioned to the directors to be seated. "A month ago," he said, "I opened the meeting saying it was a watershed moment for our company. The unprecedented loss of life and property in the crash of CCA 181 made the event a threat to the company's very existence. Today, I'm happy to say that threat no longer exists. As all of you know from the media, the NTSB has determined that the disk, not our blades, failed. Shortly we will ask the court to remove us from the lawsuits."

The room erupted in applause.

Cutler turned to Burke. "Do you want to talk to us about the status of the lawsuit?"

"Not much to say except we'll move for summary judgment the moment the NTSB accident report is issued."

"Summary judgment?" Brattle asked.

"Judgment given without formal trial when it can be shown to the court there's no issue of fact and that the defendant is entitled to judgment as a matter of law."

"What he means, Stuart," Cutler interjected, "is that we're out from under Schnell's class action suit without paying Tom's firm a pot full to prove we're innocent."

"What's the time frame Tom?" Vaughn asked.

"I'd say two months, give or take."

"What do you think, Alan?" Cutler said. "You've been through this before. That about right?"

"Yes."

But why worry yourself. By then you'll be long gone, Fisk thought, and sat horrified that he could be so blithe at the prospect of a man's fall. Jesus! Was he becoming—ruthless—like Cutler? He closed his eyes.

Cutler glanced at the papers before him. "One last thing before we get into the agenda. While Alan has the floor, I want him to stand and receive our thanks and admiration for his inspired efforts in finding the disk."

Fisk rose slowly. *I can't believe he'd say this. To me, yes, but the whole board?*

Shouts of hear, hear erupted.

Cutler shook his hand. "This company will continue to prosper as long as we have men of your ability and dedication among us."

Sad. Still dishing out the soft soap. He has no idea what's in store for him.

"Well thanks," Fisk said returning Cutler's genial smile. "But investigator McGinty and his men deserve the credit. And that wonderful young man Hobie."

Cutler returned to the head of the table. "The first agenda item is approval of the minutes of our telephone board meeting. Do I hear a motion?"

"So moved."

"Second."

"I second."

"Any discussion? All in fav . . ."

Hancock picked up his minutes then dropped them on the table in a gesture of disgust. "They contain absolutely nothing about our discussion of the SEC investigation and Mr. Cutler's denial of involvement."

"Tom," Cutler said turning to Burke at his side. "Johnny here has a question."

"The discussion was off the record, John, on a matter involving hearsay," Burke said. "As a lawyer yourself you know it's a sensitive issue. Do you really want to pursue your objection?"

Hancock shook his head. "Let's get on with the meeting. We have more important matters to consider." His voice, Fisk felt, held menace.

"Then the minutes stand as written," Cutler said. "The question has been moved and seconded. All in favor say yes . . . opposed say no . . . That's a vote.

"The second agenda item is our chief financial officer's report for the month of July and the new estimate for the quarter to end September 30th."

As he listened to CFO Henry Hiller's presentation, Fisk grew edgy watching Hancock alternately fidgeting with his tie and drumming his finger on the table. Soon, he knew, Hancock would be confronting Cutler. If the CEO continued to stonewall as surely he would, Jesus! Fisk thought, he would have to take over and spring the Sedalia evidence on his unsuspecting boss. Is this what all his anger, all his disappointment in the man had come to? He was looking at a man like himself, wasn't he, a man with his own mysterious life and dreams, a man who had worked so hard, done so much, come so far. And he, Alan Fisk was going to be, had to be, a party to his downfall.

Hiller finished and Cutler was reaching for his agenda when Hancock interrupted: "Just a minute Mr. Cutler. I've been waiting patiently wondering whether you are going to continue this charade of business as usual. It's high time we hear what you have to say about the latest SEC investigation."

He's smooth, Fisk thought, watching Cutler's face. Not a flicker at the mention of the SEC. He's going to try to tough it through.

"You have the agenda in front of you, Johnny. Felix is next with his report of the Audit Committee. If you have something on your mind, save it for 'Other Business'."

"When we're rushing off to lunch, eh?"

"You're some piece of work, Johnny. Always assuming wicked motives."

"If you won't come out with it then I will," Hancock said. "And since it involves you I ask that you step out of the room."

Cutler leaned forward in his chair, coiled and wary. "I remind you, Johnny. As CEO I'm running this meeting. If you have something to say about me, say it to my face."

"The board has an important decision to make. They should not be intimidated by your presence."

"Would you like to call someone in to carry me out, or try it yourself?" Cutler said, his head lowered like a bull about to charge.

"Stay if you wish," Hancock said with a dismissive flick of his hand. "During our telephone board meeting Mr. Cutler flatly denied for the record any knowledge of illegal payments. He lied to us. Flat out lied."

"Is that true, Cass?" Brattle asked.

Fisk thought he saw the slightest shadow of fear in Cutler's eyes. "Let's hear what Johnny has to say," he snorted.

"Since our meeting my source at the SEC has told me that lawyers from their Criminal Division have met with Buzz Beauchamp and after initial denials, he's caved in to try to save his own skin. He's now plea bargaining his willingness to testify that Mr. Cutler paid the Senator a finder's fee under the table."

"For christsakes, Johnny, come to your senses," Cutler growled. "Everybody knows the guy's a lush and a womanizer. The Democrats are pursuing this to embarrass the Senator. It's Beauchamp's word against mine."

Hancock, fury in his eyes, was about to speak when Fisk waved him off with the flat of his hand and stood up. Continue to play with us, he thought, his chest heaving. I'll show him!

He strode around the table and stood over Cutler, Beauchamp's papers in hand.

Cutler turned to look at him, his throat pulsating in anger. "What the hell do you think you're doing? Sit down!"

Fisk ignored him and slapped Beauchamp's memo onto the table. "Your word against his, eh? Read this, Cass!"

Cutler jumped to his feet and faced him down. "I don't take orders from subordinates," he raged. "I said sit down!"

"Suit yourself," Fisk snapped and picked up the memos. Still standing, he turned to the board members sitting in awed silence. "I have here a contemporaneous writing confirming Cutler's verbal agreement to pay GWF a fee of one million dollars dated and signed by Beauchamp. As you know, Senator Rushmore is also known as The Great White Father around Washington."

Cutler was breathing heavily, face brick red. "Rubbish!" he bellowed, and snatched the paper from Fisk's hand.

"You'll want these, too," Fisk said, and handed him the "Small Tool Account" and "GWF Account" memos he was holding. "If there's any doubt about Beauchamp's relationship with Rushmore over the years, have a look at these."

Cutler, his face frozen in agony, slumped into his chair and glanced through the papers.

"By the way, I have the originals," Fisk said. "They'll be sent to the SEC after the meeting."

"Where did you find these?" Cutler whispered.

"Hidden away in Beauchamp's old office in Sedalia."

Cutler shook his head. "The idiot!"

Hancock had gotten up and was now standing over him. "Let me see those!" he demanded.

Cutler handed them over with the disconsolate look of a man defeated.

He's broken, Fisk thought, more in pity than triumph.

Hancock finished reading and slipped the memos to Bentley. "Have a look," he said.

Brattle spoke up. "A big public company like this? How could a million dollars pass unnoticed? Our internal auditors would have picked it up. And if not, then the year end audit."

"Difficult but not impossible," Fisk answered him. "And that brings me to an even more serious matter. Yesterday I learned that the SEC's investigation into the source of the cash for the payoff has led them to a secret offshore slush fund fed by illegal kickbacks from Hi Tech's international sales. They're finding that payments were made not only to the Senator but to political campaigns, and foreign governments, over a period of years."

A murmur of disbelief arose around the table. "But how?" Brattle persisted.

Fisk turned to Cutler. "Sounds like Joe Bledsoe's independent distributorship out of Miami, Cass."

Cutler remained silent. He won't admit it, Fisk thought, but I can see the answer on his face.

Hancock glared at Cutler. "If the two of them were clever enough to create a secret cash fund under the nose of our auditors, what else, I ask you, what else is happening behind our backs?"

"You sanctimonious bastard!" Cutler exploded.

Out with it, Cass, Fisk thought, fighting to control his anger. "Name calling will get us nowhere," he said. "I'll ask you: Is all this true? In past weeks, all we've had is rumor. But I find the evidence I've given you convincing."

"I'm sure we all do," Reston said, "but let's hear Cass's side of it."

Cutler leaned back in his chair with an exasperated sigh. "Look," he said. "You're all acting like a bunch of boy scouts. Do you think I or anyone else around this country in my place enjoys taking this kind of responsibility on himself? I did your dirty work to help make this the great company it is and I shielded you from any embarrassment. Would you rather have known?"

"You think we would have allowed it?" Hancock asked in disbelief.

"You'd have been against it, huh? It's just the kind of skullduggery that should appeal to a blue-blood, pious Descendent of the Founders like you."

Against what? Fisk thought, fed up. Say it! "Then you did lie to us."

"I had to."

"You really believe that, don't you?"

"Look, Alan. You know as well as I do how this board leaks. I thought if I could quietly strike a deal with the SEC in Washington before the word got out in the media with the crash investigation going on, we'd all be better off. And I'll say just one more thing and we can conclude this discussion. I never profited one penny in any of the transactions. Neither did Joe. Everything was in the best interests of the company and its stockholders as I saw it at the time. Now can we continue with the agenda?"

"Mr. Cutler," Hancock interrupted. "You don't seem to understand. A number of us consider this a matter of utmost seriousness and have a formal proposal to put before this board. If you insist on following the agenda, I'll call for a vote that you be asked to leave the room and that as the senior director present I act as chairman in your absence."

"I told you once, Johnny, and I'll say it one more time," Cutler answered through clenched teeth. "As CEO, I'm running this meeting. If you have a proposal and it's brief, make your motion so we can get on."

Fisk noted Cutler's defiant tone. A study in confidence, he thought. By now he must have written me off. But he has no idea that Bentley and Brattle might go against him. And he's obviously taking Trueslow for granted.

Hancock glared at Cutler. "I move that Mr. Cutler be removed from the office of President and Chief Executive Officer, for cause, effective immediately."

Burke abruptly leaned toward Cutler and with his hand cupped to his mouth, whispered urgently in his ear.

"Jesus Christ, John!" Coxe yelled across the table. "Are you out of your fucking mind?"

Fisk winced. And I once thought big company boardrooms were civil.

Cutler angrily waved Burke off. "Do I hear a second?" he said without a trace of emotion.

"I second the motion," Brattle said.

Brattle? Fisk saw the surprise on Cutler's face. He expected it from me.

"Discussion?" Cutler asked, shooting a glance at Reston as if to say help me.

"Just a minute!" Reston said firmly, making eye contact around the table. "Let's slow down."

Coxe pounded the table with his fist. "Slow down, you say? Balls! This whole thing is starting to smell like a conspiracy to get rid of Cass. First John; been stalking him for years. Then our employee Alan. Now our academic. Who else is part of this cabal?"

Fisk saw Bentley fidgeting with his watch band as if it needed his immediate attention.

"I've known Cass since he was a kid," Coxe continued. "Went to school with him in Akron. He's a fine man, strong, decisive.

Made this great company what it is. I think he's right in what he just said. We'll all be better off if we let him work this out with Washington. Hell, this slush fund business is nothing new. Everybody does it. It's a tough world out there."

"There's a motion before us, duly made and seconded," Hancock reminded him.

"I agree with Ian," Reston said. "It's unfair to Cass to take action now."

"Me too," said Vaughn.

Fisk had watched Cutler's body language as his friends spoke up. I can see it now, he thought. He thinks he'll win. He's going to bring it to a vote.

Cutler squared his shoulders and folded his hands on the table. "Let the record show that I abstain," he said. Then, in a ploy Fisk had seen him use in tight situations: "All in favor, please stand up!" There would be no hiding behind a mumbled yes or no. Hancock quickly rose to his feet followed by Fisk and Brattle; then Bentley, slowly.

Fisk saw the oh my God! look on Cutler's face. Burke bit at the cuticle of his thumbnail.

Cutler smiled broadly, approvingly, at George Trueslow still seated.

Trueslow sat glaring at Cutler for what seemed an eternity. "So that's it, Cass," he said. "Give the little runt in knickers a big smile and a pat on the head. I'm a slow learner but I finally got the point. That's all I'm good for, to be here when you need me. Well, I gotta tell you. I'm sick to death of being somebody's boy!" He stood.

Cutler showed no emotion as the group sat down. "Opposed, please stand," he said. The remaining four directors rose. That's a vote," Cutler said crisply. "The motion is carried."

"Shall we make it unanimous?" Fisk asked. "Word of a split board won't help any of us."

Cutler's four loyal supporters looked at him for guidance. Without hesitation he nodded his assent.

That's the good side of him, Fisk thought. Loyalty was a two-way street. He wouldn't jeopardize their futures.

Cutler got up to leave, but Hancock motioned him to wait. "I'm sure Ian and his Compensation Committee will be generous in the severance package they recommend to this board," Hancock said. Then, as Cutler passed his chair on the way out: "Nothing personal, Mr. Cutler."

Fisk heard the words and recoiled. "Nothing personal," he thought watching Cutler leave, his shoulders slumped in defeat. You destroy a man, and it's "nothing personal". Then what is it, all in a day's work? Part of the job that he himself had found all too congenial? Time to get out.

On the way back to his office, Fisk stopped in the men's room. Cutler was standing at one of the two urinals, and after a moment's awkward hesitation, Fisk joined him. Jesus! he thought. How did this happen? The two stood silently side by side, the kind of painful silence Fisk had experienced after firing an employee of Cast Profiles years ago, and found himself alone in the company elevator with the man and his boxes of personal possessions.

"So you did what you had to do," Cutler said. "Is that what you're thinking?"

You bet your ass! "I suppose that's a fair way to put it, Cass. Yes."

"In the best interests of the shareholders and the company," Cutler said, sarcastically.

"That wasn't the issue. I did it for myself. What you don't seem to understand is that we have different ways of looking at business. I heard about the accusations against you the last week in May, and if it hadn't been for the crash several days later and my responsibility to the victims, I'd have left the company quietly before the graft ever became an issue before the board. That's why I signed a letter of resignation. I just don't like your way of doing business. And your treatment of Dusty didn't help."

Fisk left the urinal and was now standing behind Cutler, talking to his back. "Early on I was hoping you were telling the truth, trying to believe that—well, how else to put it, that you wouldn't do something this sleazy."

Cutler zipped up his fly and turned. "At least you're honest," he said. "You did it for yourself. What did Johnny promise you?"

Always on the attack. "He didn't have to promise anything."

"Don't give me that bullshit! You're lying."

"Watch you language," Fisk said, his face scarlet. "John said he would serve as Chairman only if Woody and I would join him in the running of the company in a three man Office of the Chairman."

"Chairman, eh? That's what he always wanted. And he bought you guys off to achieve it. I'd have been smart to throw him that bone, the turd."

Bought off—The words blasted his ears like a shot at close range. "You can't stop being a shit, can you?" Fisk said. "You've got me wrong, dead wrong. I turned him down. Two months and I'm outta here. I've had it with the corporate world."

"I don't want to hear about it. That's your business."

They had finished washing up and were headed for the door when Cutler stopped. "One last thing, Alan. The big mistake I made was in not sizing you up correctly and it worries me because it's always been my strong point. You're a helluva lot tougher than I ever imagined."

Maybe it's because you're over the hill, Fisk felt like saying.

"And you're a clever son-of-a-bitch, sneaking around in Sedalia looking for Beauchamp's documents. Give Johnny's come-on some thought. You'd fit in well with that scheming crowd."

Fisk opened his mouth to speak, but Cutler turned and left.

Good riddance! Fisk thought. No way will I ever find myself in this situation again.

*   *   *

Back in the office Fisk sat quietly in his chair, drained of all the feelings of fear, of anger, the twinges of momentary triumph and compassion, he had experienced during the past hours. Only the sad image of Cutler, walking slowly down the corridor ahead of him, remained; this man who had worked so hard, done so much, come so far. He took a deep breath and exhaled. Yes, Cutler was right. I did what I had to do. But why, dear God, did it have to be me?

CHAPTER 37

Friday Evening, June 25

Martha was chopping a garlic clove for the linguine dinner she was preparing in the tiny pool cabana kitchen when Fisk arrived. "You look excited about something. Get comfortable and come join me," she said. "You do realize, don't you?"

"Realize what?"

"We haven't had a minute's conversation together since you got home. One of the most important moments in your life and all I know is that Cass is out. From what you told me over the phone, he was a shit to the end."

"As always." He nestled into one of the cushy vinyl bean bags that served as chairs in the main room and motioned her to join him. "I put all that behind me. I had some serious thinking to do now that he's off my mind."

She plopped into the one next to him and reached over and kissed him. "Tell me."

"Last Tuesday Otto made me an interesting proposal. He wants to sell his company and move to Florida . . ."

"Oh? You didn't say anything about . . ."

". . . and he gave me what amounts to an option to buy it."

Her features hardened in alarm. "I thought he sold his business three years ago."

"The main operations, yes. This is the small company in Evanston he kept out of the deal. It's a neat little company that makes a line of custom-made titanium surgical implants. And best of all, according to Otto, it has excellent management. A young man I would have fun working with; like Mike Belmonte."

"Then you've decided to take Otto up on it," she said.

Fisk saw the questioning in her eyes. He leaned over and whispered in her ear. "Come on. When have I ever made an important decision without talking with you?"

"But you're leaning toward it, I can tell it in your voice."

"I wish it were that easy. I've been stewing about it since Tuesday to the point that my stomach is bound up in knots. Please understand! I'm wrestling with giving up half my life. Help me."

Her voice was tranquil. "There are endings, Alan. Life's a series of endings. Isn't that why the world's so fascinated with time? If we're lucky we're free to mourn the loss and move on. Meantime it's painful; it's frightening. And that is where you are now. You told me that as Cutler left you the one thought in your mind was that you're determined not to find yourself in that situation again."

"Exactly. But I keep thinking I'll miss the phone calls, the meetings, decisions to be made, people to be inspired, the thrill of seeing an idea in your head become a piece of useful hardware. I might even miss the thing I complained about most, the feeling of going to the office and being cycled day long by the demands of all the goings on. I've led an active life in business for the past thirty two years." He paused, his head in his hands. "So I don't know. I really don't know. Do I see myself retiring to my studio, leaving behind the work of half a lifetime? This is what I have been asking myself."

"Do you?"

"I tested myself when I got home and went to the sculpture garden to meditate. I stood for the longest while thinking about all this, especially whether Otto's company would be the untroubled opportunity I want to believe it to be. Small technology companies run by an aggressive young man can be a pain in the ass these days. Finally, I asked myself a simple question: Where did I see myself happiest the rest of my years? Sculpting won hands down."

Now there was joy in her tone. "You're sure? You're not being carried away by the success of your show?"

"I'll miss the hurly-burly. That'll be the hardest part."

"I don't know. The art world can have it's own fume at times."

Fisk laughed. "I guess I've made my decision without realizing it. Wow! I can breathe again. I'll call Otto in the morning and tell him I'm not a buyer for his company. Maybe I'll find that I have little to say beyond the vein I've been working. So what. At least I'll know before I go to my grave."

"Are most people that casual?" Martha asked. "I mean speaking of their own death."

"Probably not," Fisk said. "And I'm not either. Notice that I didn't say before I die. Going to my grave sounds a little less definite."

"It sounded pretty graphic to me."

Fisk began massaging the nape of her neck. She looked up at him. "From the time my father died I've had a fear of death," she said. "I'm sure it lay behind my choice of profession and I thought through the years of my training analysis I'd come to terms with it. One day I'll no longer have you. You'll leave, or I'll leave—for good. That's reality. And accepting that reality gave me a feeling of great release. Now I'm not sure . . . Do you think we'll ever see one another again—in the afterlife?"

"Who knows?"

"You're not answering."

"I think you know my answer."

"No, I'm not sure ."

"I think this moment on earth is all we have and we'd better make the best of it. Time isn't ours forever; last month taught me that. That's why I decided tonight it was time to move on, time for me to declare myself."

Martha cuddled closer. "You're my happy man again," she

said. "Tell me something. How do you think of yourself at this moment?"

Fisk smiled.

"Come on, tell me!"

"As a young man with possibilities."